THE QUEEN OF OCTOBER

THE QUEEN

OF

OCTOBER

—— *a novel by* ——

SHELLEY FRASER MICKLE

Algonquin Books of Chapel Hill

1989

Published by
Algonquin Books of Chapel Hill
Post Office Box 2225
Chapel Hill, North Carolina 27515-2225
a division of
Workman Publishing Company, Inc.
708 Broadway
New York, New York 10003

Design by Molly Renda

Parts of this novel were published as "The Year of the
Outhouse," *Cimarron Review*, 1978, and "The
Queen of Hearts," *The South Carolina Review*, 1982.

LIBRARY OF CONGRESS CATALOGING-IN-PUBLICATION DATA
Mickle, Shelly Fraser.
The Queen of October: a novel / by Shelley Fraser Mickle.
p.   cm.
ISBN 0-945575-21-1
I. Title.
PS3563.I3530 4   1989
813'.54—dc 20   89-34121
CIP

10 9 8 7 6 5 4 3 2

Contents

PART I

For my grandmother, who,
if she were still here, would wring my neck.

—SALLY MAULDEN
MAY, 1988

I.

My Parents Return Me

That strange and crazy year began in the last hot days of August. It was a year that would stretch and spread into what would nearly be two, and yet it stayed in my memory as a single time. It was like the whole world, as I knew it, blew up and got replaced by something like a distant cousin. A hunger for change seemed everywhere. It was in me, and in the sudden jolt that sent my mother and father to a lawyer. It sat in Coldwater, Arkansas, like a cicada waiting seventeen years underground to be born and sing. It rode in the crazy, mixed-up heart of Sam Best, who told my mother he loved her one day in her kitchen while I was hiding in the pantry. And it began soon after I discovered that no one would ever love me, no one at least outside of family—and they *had* to.

It was 1959, and I was thirteen.

"Sally! I can't find them! I just can't find them."

I was sitting on the steps of my mother's apartment house in Memphis. It was one week before school was to start in Coldwater, Arkansas, and I was being sent there. "I haven't seen them," I said. My mother had misplaced the car keys— probably because she tried to file her life away in Mason jars.

"Damn!" A jar hit the floor and broke. A blast of cuss words was followed by quiet. Then the screen door opened. "You didn't hear that, did you?"

"No'm." I knew better words myself. I even knew how to

3

put them together better. When my mother moved me into the junior high in Memphis, I'd gotten put into the least-filled classes—the worst—"sucking hind tit," as Coldwater farmers would say. And I ended up sitting on the back row with already fully mature boys in Elvis hairdos and leather jackets who knew how to cuss better than anybody I'd ever heard.

"Here, sweetie, look through this, will you?" My mother set a Mason jar on the top step. For driving me to the Trailways bus station, she had on a hat, gloves, stockings, the whole works. So did I. She'd made me wear my Easter outfit—a full-skirted sundress with a jacket, one-inch heels, gloves, and a hat with streamers. The dress was made out of blue dotted swiss that, when I rubbed my hand across, reminded me of heat rash. And because the concrete step was hot enough to fry an egg on, I was having my clothes pasted to my skin with sweat. I felt like the paper doll of some berserk child who'd glued my clothes on. I'd never get to change. And yet, more than anything, that's what I wanted.

For something had happened to me. I'd learned to behave as everyone expected. I was known as "sweet." But I sat on anger. I could be right in the middle of a room feeling mean and out-right murderous, and not a living soul would even get a hint. In fact, I was as boring and predictable as the tobacco-colored spots that darkened all over my face whenever the sun came out. The only comfort in looking like a speckled bird dog, or an Appaloosa horse, was that, at thirteen, I didn't have zits. At least only a few. Apparently freckles and pimples are like termites and carpenter ants in the same house. It's hard to have both at once.

"They're not in here," I said, putting the receipts and stuff back in the Mason jar. "Try your old purse," I suggested. Earlier she had changed to a dressy one.

"Maybe so." She turned around and went inside. Then she came back and stood at the door, leaning out it. "Sally, where did I *put* my old purse?" Tears were making streaks through her powder and rouge like a water pistol shot onto a chalkboard. I stood up to follow her inside. Her crying was aimed at the car keys, but I knew it came from what was going on in her life, and also from the fact that, after today, I'd be gone.

For you see, it was not only the year I discovered I was ugly and unfit for anybody, outside of blood kin, to love; it was also the year my parents decided to try a divorce. It was the year of our Big Bust-up. Back then, divorce was worse than having both parents killed in an airplane crash, or by cancer. Either of those would have stirred up a good amount of pity. But as a victim of divorce, I felt tainted. And it seemed not so much a tragedy as wickedness falling upon us.

But The Bust-up was going to be okay. My mother said that. In fact, she said it a lot. Probably The Bust-up was just a blessing in disguise, seeing as how I was so homely and was going to have to lead an unconventional life, anyway. I could see only two routes left for me: to be an old maid or a tart—and I was leaning toward the second. So The Bust-up was just right for getting me used to not being hooked up to anybody—at least for long.

In fact, I was busy making plans on how I was going to make it in the world, alone, since as far as family was concerned I was like someone who was being put out on the side of the road, halfway to somewhere. I vowed that as soon as I got out of this family for keeps, I'd never do anything to get back into another one. Instead, I was going to go on out to Hollywood and get into the movies.

So that strange and crazy year began like the world had suddenly sped up and stopped, sending us sprawling into new, uncertain space. Something was pushing us. It was like a hunger for a food we could not name. It kept us awake and aimed us for places we did not know. And it began with me walking around in the final countdown of The Bust-up, thinking up places for the car keys. "I just can't understand how I could have lost them!" My mother's voice was one inch from a total downpour that would make us both feel worse. I quickened my search like a kid at a church Easter egg hunt.

I was being returned to Coldwater because when my parents agreed to file for divorce, they started fighting over who would raise me. I was flattered that my father would want to. Finally it was arranged that I should stay with my grandparents in Coldwater until the judge who was handling their case could decide where I should end up: with my mother or with my father. Since we'd moved from Coldwater only the year before, I'd be very much at home. In fact, Coldwater was exactly where I wanted to be—anywhere but in that stupid Memphis junior high where kids wore tiny clothespins on their collars and no one talked to me, and the homecoming queen walked around in an angora sweater over false tits with a poodle on her skirt. Lord!

My mother found her purse under her bathrobe on the bed. She dumped it out, making a nest of ticket stubs, makeup, and Kleenex. "Hot damn." She looked at me, licking tears off her lips, holding up the keys like a just-caught fish. "Well—I mean, at least I found the darn things."

So finally we were out the door for keeps, and she turned around and straightened my hat—that straw job with streamers down the back. As soon as she took her hands off it, I tipped the whole thing whankyjawed again. I would have torn everything off and prissed down the street buck naked—embarrassing my mother to insanity—but we were late already. Probably it was a good thing my mother and I were splitting up. We'd been getting on each other's nerves a lot lately.

I slid into the backseat of her car, which was a 1949 station wagon with side panels of honest-to-god wood that sadly now were turning black like a ripening banana. Soon we were tooling down Central Avenue to my father's rooming house to pick him up. He wanted to show a lot of interest in me so he'd have a fighting chance with the judge. Even though nobody special would know he was in the backseat on this day, it could be important. For instance, there could be witnesses: his landlady maybe, or the ticket-teller at the bus station.

I stared at my mother's hair, swept up and pinned on top of her head, the color like October maple leaves. She was still a glamorous woman. Her earrings were almost as large as her ears. If she ever needed a hearing aid, she would have the perfect spot for a secret installation.

"Jeez," she said, "just look at that," pointing to the passengers waiting at a bus stop. We had entered the block where my father's rooming house was, and we were stuck in traffic. She glanced back at me. "Don't you think that looks just like Tyrone Power?" My mother had an eye for good-looking men. That was one thing, she said, that had gotten her mixed up with my father. He was so good-looking he never had to do anything but stand around and get looked at, and so he didn't learn anything about being good at small talk. The wrong kind to get married to, she told me. But neither of us could help it: we stared at the bus stop.

What she'd said was both sad *and* impossible. Because Tyrone had died suddenly in Spain the year before. And my mother, of course, would know all about that. She was a singer.

She was off to revive that career, minus me and my father. Or, at least, minus my father. If she got me, I was supposed to travel with her.

There had been four other children in her family, and her father had promised each of them two years at the local teachers' college. What she should have done was teach in one of the little towns throughout the South, as every nice girl mostly did, and there marry some nice man from a land-rich family. But not my mother. She took the name Boots—Boots LaMar —and joined a Glenn Miller–type band and toured four states of the South.

One Saturday night in Vicksburg, Mississippi, where my father was at an insurance company convention, he went into a supper club and heard my mother sing "Moon over Miami." Somehow that did it. And ever since, my parents' romance kept being re-stuck and revived by that song about a city none of us had ever seen. But lately the music hadn't been working. And now we had to go and divvy up everything.

I had read four or five select passages from *Peyton Place* and every volume of *The Black Stallion* books, and was well prepared for understanding anything. *But why couldn't they get along?*

One day the summer before, when we still lived in Coldwater, I'd gone into the pantry for some jelly when I heard my mother offer Sam Best a cup of coffee. He was the richest man in Coldwater, and there was never a time when I didn't know him. He and my mother came into the kitchen; and as Mr. Best began changing the subject from what he wanted in his coffee to his desire for my mother, I closed the pantry door except for a crack. What I saw and heard came back at strange times. So maybe while I was sitting in eighth-grade geography in Memphis in October, I would see, in the map of Africa,

Sam Best's hand closing over my mother's as she stood at the stove. I could hear his deep, as-though-smiling voice saying he would love her, no matter what, and forever. He had cradled her against his large and wealthy chest while she cried out of frustration and unhappiness. She would, she said, love my father in spite of everything, and forever, too. That, she added, was the real tragedy of her life.

But why, if that day in the kitchen my mother loved my father so, would she file for divorce ten months later?

Once Bobby Watts, who was part of my sordid past in Coldwater, told me my father had the hots for some woman in Searcy. But my mother said the trouble was, my father couldn't get excited about anything—except maybe her driving. If I had known why exactly we were busting up, maybe I could have fixed it. Surely somebody could have fixed it. But nobody understood what was happening enough to explain it to anybody else. It was just an all-over outright Bust-up. Probably I should have long ago put it on my list under World Wars I and II, The Origin of Life, and Why Elizabeth Taylor Married Eddie Fisher. But for the life of me, I just couldn't. It had to make more sense than that.

I looked out at the traffic and the pavement, the people waiting at the bus stop. Nobody was busting out of line or running their cars up on the sidewalk to get away from traffic. They'd have been nuts if they had, or else downright mean and meant for prison.

I watched the people, sweating and moving with good reason—slow, but with good reason. The stoplights and the white lines and the bus stop—it'd all been planned and made sense. It came to me then that the real answer for The Bust-up was there, suddenly clear, and in the backseat with me. It *was* me. It was my fault. I was boring and plain. And there were probably a million other things about me nobody could stand to be around anymore. I should have known that. I should have known that all along. Of course it was me. Now *that* made sense. *I* was the reason.

I guess that meant, too, that even blood kin didn't *have* to love me.

"I'd given up on you," my father said, opening the car's back door. He slid in beside me and put his arm on the top of the seat over my shoulders. He was dressed in a dark suit, tie, hat —the whole works.

"We got detained," my mother said. She glanced in the rear-view mirror. We could see her lips pressed into a tight line because she was concentrating hard. My mother didn't like to pass anybody, but she loved to change lanes. Usually we just ended up riding like a sucker-fish next to the rear fender of the car in the next lane. Right now she was trying to stick us to the black fin of a Cadillac. "Go up or come back," my father said. But she told him if he didn't keep quiet she was going to put him out.

She'd threatened me the same way during all of my wiggling childhood, and never once had I had to call a cab. But with my father it might be different. I couldn't predict anything anymore. My whole past seemed now like a paper bag I'd blown up—that they'd busted. I watched my mother raise her white-gloved hand and gesture to a man in a Mack truck, then smile and gun to the space he made in front of him.

"You're going to wear this car out," my father said.

"Fat chance," my mother said. "It's already shot."

The Mack truck's air brakes farted, and it turned.

My mother glanced at us in the rearview mirror. "That's one of the things on the settlement list."

"What?"

"A new car."

"A new car?"

That was the first time I had heard a car was on the same list with me.

But my father only laughed and said he'd get her an Edsel. That was the car advertised for the man on the way up. I guess nobody wanted to admit he was only on the way up, because nobody was buying the car. My father's suit pants were losing their creases and growing small round spots of sweat. Why he and my mother had moved from Coldwater only a year before, I wasn't sure. From what I knew, my father got a job in an insurance company in Memphis, specializing in farm equipment, just about like the one he'd had in Coldwater. So his job didn't have a darn thing to do with it. The truth was, I think, my parents were hoping if they moved their marriage might improve. My grandparents did live next door to us in Coldwater, and my parents' marriage was a bit on stage. And, too, maybe my mother feared Sam Best's love for her might lead to scandal. But if my father was to raise me, I knew I would probably be returned to Coldwater. He'd move back, or leave me with my grandparents. My father *believed* in little towns.

He took me, when I was ten, to the Coldwater River that had given the town its name, and we'd gotten in a boat and fished. I knew he'd always wanted a boy. But I guess he and my mother never got together long enough to make one. So if they were stuck with me, I was willing to fish. In fact, I even found out I liked it. I got the hang of it and was on my way to a second bream until I cast my line in an oak tree and fell out of the boat and scared away the fish. We had to go home then, on account of my wet clothes and all. And whenever I asked about going again, my father always said, "Not today."

I looked at him there beside me in my mother's car. If I

could have fished better, maybe we'd all still be together in Coldwater.

The sidewalks looked hot and I watched the burnt August grass and the little houses all in a row, sickening sweet with people inside. I thought that every one of those houses with a family together in one spot, with TV moms and dads and stupid kids with names like Beaver, ought to be found out and dynamited. I folded my hands into my lap, and in the blue rash of dotted swiss I made a silent joke—a mean kid's finger play I'd learned walking home one summer from Bible school in Coldwater: "Here's the church. Here's the steeple. Close the doors and mash the people." A laugh came up and sat on my lips like a high-diver poised and counting for courage.

In no more than an hour I'd be out in the world. And on my own.

But thank the Lord! For the real truth of the matter was, I just flat out didn't need a family. And besides, I was going to Coldwater.

I loved Coldwater about like a kid loves the circus. There wasn't a road leading out of it that I hadn't at one time or another been on. The cotton fields around it, the land in summer that was as green as dollars, then faded in winter to wheat brown, lying flat—to me, it was home.

Yet there wasn't anything out of the ordinary or even the least bit special about Coldwater. I'd been driven through lots of little cotton towns and each one of them seemed to be just about like it. At certain times of year, the whole town could almost disappear under a coat of dust that turned everything to the color of putty or well-chewed gum. Some of the streets weren't paved. And there was no stoplight.

In fact, Coldwater was, I guess, just about as plain as I was.

2.

Sam Best Appears

The Trailways bus station was in the middle of a block down-town. I felt like a dummy in my Easter outfit next to the dingy benches and floors, the sleeping folks, and the sign warning: "Fifty Dollar Fine for Spitting."

"One ticket to Coldwater, Arkansas," my father said.

"One way or round trip?" the teller asked.

"One way," my mother said and pulled off her gloves. Then she looked at me and asked, "You know why?"

Sure I knew why. They were going to drop me off and be rid of me. But I guess she felt guilty about it. She leaned over and whispered, "After the trial, I'll have a new car and I'll drive over and get you."

The ticket-teller handed the ticket to my father and looked at me. He was, of course, a potential witness for my father. He was fat and his hair was gone.

Thinking about that—the trial, and the whole big mess of the fight over me—made me realize another truth. In fact, it hit me square between the eyes about like a wad of spit gum. Until then I'd been too dumb to even see it. My daddy didn't want me. Not really. He was just using the fight for me to diddle my mama. It's not like he and I really had a future together or anything. It's not like we'd spend a lot of time yucking it up on fishing trips. "Let's get a Coke," my mother said.

"How about some ice cream?" My father cuffed me under the chin as though we were members of the same team in the locker room. I didn't even need to answer. Saying nothing was as good as saying yes. Lord! we were all such good actors. I could have committed murder over being smack in the middle of a Bust-up. It was a funeral I was forced to attend. But we were all acting so damn good about it—which, if you really wanted to think about that, was sure a fine sign for me. For after going through this, it ought to be a snap to knock 'em dead in Hollywood. Then my father said he thought he'd go right down the street to a café and get us some butter pecan. After he left, my mother said: "Well then, let's just get us a magazine."

I followed my mother to the newsstand. While she thumbed through a fat issue of *Life*, I looked out onto the street. Somebody was getting out of a cab and reaching back in for shopping bags. I could see her back, bent-over and broad. The black sturdy lace-up shoes she had on seemed familiar to me. I'd watched those shoes and those exact feet, standing just like now, somewhere in my past in Coldwater. But where or why I couldn't remember.

I wasn't expecting to know anybody at the bus station. I figured my mother didn't need witnesses. Almost anybody in Coldwater would come to my parents' trial and testify that she was good to me. It wasn't really her style to plant a witness anyway. She probably wasn't even going to trial. No doubt she was planning to let me rot it out at my grandparents' until I was thirty-five or forty, and then she'd come back with her million gold records. She'd sell my story to *Modern Screen*, about how she'd had a daughter so ugly she'd had to hide her away in a cotton town in Arkansas.

"Let's get this one," my mother said, handing me the fall issue of *Seventeen*, which had a model on it in wool clothes so hot that the thought of them just about gave me a heat stroke.

While my mother paid, I watched the back of the lady in the black lace-up shoes as she hurried into the bookshop across the street. She was half covered up with shopping bags. Something about the way the back of her hair curled looked familiar too. I knew that people in Coldwater seemed to have a special talent for going out into the world and bumping into each other. Once the Second Baptist preacher ran into the owner of the Soybean Plant at The House of Vestal Virgins in Rome, and it was written up in the *Coldwater Gazette*, which started a whole new trend of people writing in to say who they'd seen where when they'd least expected it.

On the other side of the waiting room my mother aimed for the Coke machine. By now it was obvious my father was having trouble finding some place to buy ice cream. And he wasn't giving up. So we were sitting on a bench looking out the front window of the bus station, sipping Cokes out of bottles and thumbing our magazines, when somebody else from Coldwater dropped in. Only this time we knew only too well exactly who it was.

"Mercy," my mother said, getting up. "Sam!" She laughed nervously. "It's been ages." They hugged.

"Do you know how long really?" he said. "Thirteen months and three days."

"Well." My mother glanced at me. I was still sitting down, holding a Coke. "I guess that's right. We left just about this time last year." She laughed, a low bitter laugh that ended flat. "It didn't do us a lot of good though, did it?" She smiled at him and looked away. "I guess you know Hodding and I are breaking up."

"S'what I heard," he said. They both sat down, one on each side of me.

Sam Best wore a dark striped suit over a white shirt. He was tall, big through the shoulders, yet lean and sort of leathery. To me he looked like someone who rode the range, and owned it. He even had cowboy boots, dark with tooling, made out of alligator or lizard, sometimes with silvery scales like snakeskin. Today they were black and seemed new. Some people in the bus station glanced at him, then stared for a moment.

People in Coldwater said Sam Best could charm tattoos off sailors and sell you a piece of chewed gum for a dollar. A year before he'd flown to New York and been on "I've Got a Secret." He'd stumped the whole panel by being a millionaire from Arkansas. So if people didn't recognize him, they stared on general principles.

I turned to look at Mr. Best's face. He noticed me and winked, then reached into his pants pocket, while hiking himself up off one thigh to rattle his change. "I'm really sorry to hear about you and Hodding," he said, looking from me to my mother. "But then again. . . ." He smiled—a boyish sort of grin—and reached into his other pants pocket. "Might be for the best." He pulled out packages of cigarettes and peppermints. After he offered them to my mother, he held out the candy to me. He always carried mints, sourballs, or chocolate kisses that melted in his pockets, causing wads. As my mother held the cigarette to her lips, Mr. Best reached over me and flicked on his lighter.

"Sometimes," my mother said, blowing out smoke, "you just can't fight it anymore."

Sam Best shook his head. He stood up and walked to the front window. Taking off his suit coat, he threw it over his shoulder. The muscles in his back moved under the thin cloth of his shirt. In the inside pocket of his coat, I caught a glimpse of a silver flask. And then he folded the lining to hide it. He came back and took the chair beside my mother.

"I want to say something to you now that I want you to think about, *really* think about," he whispered—which sounded to me like the beginnings of something right intimate.

My mother reached for an ashtray and crossed her legs. She said, even though she didn't look at Sam: "You been over here to the cotton offices?"

He stared at her, then at me. It was obvious they were bothered by my being there. So they were just going to change the whole subject. "Yeah. Front Street," Sam Best said, getting the hint. "I come over one Saturday a month, at least. And if I take the bus I don't have to worry about driving." He laughed.

Sam Best hated to drive. He said he was scared of it, which made everyone laugh. He could say outrageous things and everybody just assumed he didn't mean it. For a while, people in Coldwater offered to take him anywhere he wanted to go. But then he hired a driver, saying he could spend time in the back seat tending to business. So my mother and I both knew he had probably taken the bus that day to see her. He could have learned from my grandfather that today was the day for returning me.

"Sally," my mother said, digging into her purse. "Go buy a package of gum." She put a dime in my hand and took my bottle of Coke and held it over her lap.

At the newsstand that was part drugstore, I picked up several packages of gum, thinking about choosing one. But the whole time I was standing there, I kept glancing at my mother and Mr. Best. He reached over and touched my mother's hand. I bought some Juicy Fruit and then inspected a bunch of digestive aids lined up on a shelf. My own stomach didn't feel especially good, but mainly I was looking at the medicines so I could stand even closer to my mother and Mr. Best, and could hear.

Mr. Best held my mother's hand and looked down at it. "You can marry me and I'll get you a maid. I'll get you a cook. I know a man in Nashville who makes records. I'll sing as a backup. Watch this." He did a ham-bone, humming all the while, thumping his thighs and chest, alternating the palm of his hand with the backside, turning his body into a set of bongo drums that sounded wonderful. I put my hand over my mouth to stop my laugh. If I hadn't been told to get lost and wasn't having to hold myself incognito in front of those damn stomachache medicines, I'd have jumped onto the middle of the floor and boogied like a crazy person. I had this thing about tap dancing. My mother had taught me how when I was little. But then she'd stopped teaching me, and I was sorry, for I don't think I'd ever seen a tap dancer who wasn't having a hell of a good time.

Mr. Best could do the best ham-bone I'd ever seen—or heard. Everybody in the whole depot stared; some tapped their feet and juked along with him. Then Mr. Best stopped as suddenly as he began. My mother was laughing, her eyes watering. She was searching in her purse for a Kleenex.

"We can go on the road," he said. "I'll buy a guitar. Say yes."

My mother stopped laughing. "Sam, you're already married."

"No, I'm not." He looked at her. "Ellen went to Little Rock. She took Julie and moved out. She says she might want a divorce."

My mother swallowed and was quiet a minute. "Oh, Sam. I hadn't heard. I'm sorry."

"Coldwater's getting slow." He grinned. "I thought you'd heard by now. She left two weeks ago." He let go of her hand. "We weren't ever married, at least not much. You know that." He pulled his eyes at the corners. "We were both Japanese— Southern Japanese. It was arranged."

My mother laughed, but sadly.

Mr. Best smiled. "We can run off together and get divorces by mail. We can take the bus to Mexico this afternoon. We'll take Sally and set up housekeeping in Acapulco. Say yes."

My mother giggled. It *was* flattering.

"We can live anywhere you want. We'll do whatever you need to be happy. I've never seen you happy."

"Sam," she whispered. Turning him down must have been awful. In his own way, Sam Best was as good-looking as my father, only he was fun and rich. She held her head to one side, crying a little. Then she laughed bitterly. "But if I married you, it wouldn't solve anything. I don't doubt you love me, but I can't return that. I love Hodding; but he can't return *that*, so we're no better off. No one would be happy. I couldn't do that to you."

"I wouldn't mind." Sam Best covered her hands on my Coke bottle with his own. "Just think about it."

My mother sat silently, then lit a cigarette and looked at the newsstand for me. I just wanted everyone around me to get what they wanted. I didn't see what was so hard about it. When I got out into the world I sure wasn't going to have a messy life. I wasn't even going to get mixed up with any man for long—which was probably going to be easy since no man would want to get mixed up with me. And I'd already decided that whenever I found out I was having a bad day I'd just get back in bed and wait until it got better.

I walked back to them with my package of gum. "Here," my mother said, handing me my bottle of Coke.

Mr. Best got up and went to the men's room. And when he came back and sat down beside me, he smelled faintly of whiskey.

"Sam," my mother said, stubbing out her cigarette and running one hand down her shin over her nylon stockings. "Do me a favor—will you?"

He smiled. "Sure, Boots. Anything."

"Keep an eye out on my girl, here." She put her arm around my shoulders. "You know she's going to Coldwater until we get things settled."

"Sure."

"And, she's never ridden the bus by herself before—have you?"

She looked at me.

"No'm."

Sam Best put his arm around my shoulders from the other side, covering my mom's arm. "Sure. We'll stick together." Then he looked at me, face-on. His eyes were dark brown, deep in the center but on the edges sort of faded like the streaked sides of pecan hulls. And in them was a blend of sadness and mischief, or if not exactly mischief, then something kin to the hope and eagerness I'd seen in the eyes of stray dogs. "You know," he said, smiling at me, "there's nothing to riding the bus. S'why I do it." He laughed.

My shoulders were cradled there on the pewlike bench between my mother and Sam Best when my father came back with three dripping ice-cream cones. He politely offered one to Mr. Best, and Mr. Best turned it down just as we knew he would—even though he might have been dying for it. We all had these incredible manners.

Sam Best kept up a running monologue about cotton and soybeans, feed corn and rice, while watching us lick that ice cream back onto the cones. When the bus pulled up in front of the station, we went to stand in line.

"Let those colored people go on around," my mother said, and straightened my hat. She reached to kiss me, and when she finished she offered her cheek to Mr. Best, who was, after all, leaving for Coldwater too. But the whole time my mother was moving into a kissing position with Mr. Best, she was glancing to see if my father was watching.

"I'd be happy to," Mr. Best whispered, looking steadily at my mother. He started a brotherly kiss on her cheek, then slid around hunting for her lips, found them and hung on.

My mother put her arms on Mr. Best's shoulders, raised one leg in a display of arousal and glanced at my father.

I sat down on my suitcase and picked my thumbnail.

If Sam Best's display of desire for my mother was supposed to uncork my father's, it fizzled. Walking over to the bus, my father leaned down and examined the drive shaft under its belly.

The kissing business took a while, so all the other passengers walked around us. "You didn't see that, did you?" My mother looked at me, embarrassed.

"No'm."

My father took my suitcase and handed it to the bus driver to put in the baggage compartment. Then my father came back to me, put his hands on my shoulders and kissed me. "Take care of yourself," he said as we walked together to wait in line behind the other passengers. While all this was going on, some colored baby was screaming his lungs out in the back of the bus. I knew he had to ride back there—at least, if people in Alabama were changing the rules of where they sat in a bus, nobody was bucking the custom in Tennessee yet—but his crying filled up the bus just as if he'd been in the front seat. I settled next to a window, and Sam Best shuffled in beside me.

By then my mother and father had moved to the side of the bus so they could look up at me and Mr. Best. They were already waving, even though the bus driver hadn't sat down

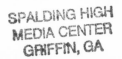

yet. Then behind them, I saw, running like an abandoned duck, those lace-up shoes from the bookstore. All along I should have known they belonged to the Coldwater librarian, Colleen Pankhurst.

"Boots Maulden!" she cried, setting down her packages and holding her hat with one hand. She hugged my mother and looked at my father. "Oh, Hodding, I'm glad to see you! Boots, there's a sale at Goldsmith's you wouldn't believe!" Then she glanced at the bus and yelled: "Don't leave me!"

The bus driver looked at her, cleared his throat, and wrote on a clipboard. He was tall, skinny, and pasty white. Gold-rimmed glasses encircled his eyes like two loops of a sprung Slinky. I didn't think he'd ever been in the sun.

"Good luck, honey." Miss Pankhurst hugged my mother again. "Next time I come over I'll call you and we can have lunch at the Peabody. Could you come?"

But there was no time for an answer. The bus driver honked the horn; and Miss Pankhurst picked up her bags and, with my father's help, climbed on.

The bus pulled away from the curb. Colleen Pankhurst and Sam Best and I waved and my mother and father waved back, standing side by side for one of the last times that year. Inside me something came up and closed around my heart, pinching it like the snap of a door spring catching on the end of a shirt. For a minute, I didn't think I could even breathe.

But then I remembered—my mother and I didn't get along. About all we had left was a mutual admiration for Elvis. And my father didn't like the way I fished.

The bus soon crossed the bridge over the Mississippi River. And with that baby screaming most of the way, we headed into the flat cotton country of Arkansas.

3.

Me and Miss Pankhurst

Sam Best slept. The baby got quiet too. And across the aisle from Sam and me, Miss Pankhurst had settled herself in. She'd spoken to me so kindly that I felt I was suffering from a disease. To her, I guess I was. If Sam Best had heard my parents were splitting up, she had, too.

"Honey, you just ask me for anything if you need it," she had said, leaning across Sam Best before he went to sleep.

"Ah, she's in good hands," Mr. Best had said, meaning his.

Miss Pankhurst was the school librarian in Coldwater, which meant she wasn't in charge of much. The library was in a small room next to the cafeteria. It had one set of the *Encyclopedia Britannica* and two shelves of fiction. All of the bindings smelled like northern beans. That's where I'd watched the back of her in those shoes lots of times while she'd been shelving books.

She was also the librarian for the Coldwater Public Library, which was open on afternoons and Saturdays. She must have closed the library for today or, more likely, had gotten a substitute, because she believed in offering culture to what she called the country people and Saturday in Coldwater was a big day for farmers. Not many of them, though, chose the library over the cowboy movies at the Ritz.

Now, while Miss Pankhurst had her head down, reading, I

studied her closely. In the last year, I'd gotten real interested in human sexuality, and started just automatically categorizing everyone I met as one who *did*, one who *didn't*, or one who *couldn't*. I decided Miss Pankhurst was one of those who *couldn't*. She was a rich old maid. She was so ugly that I decided she was one who *couldn't* because no one wanted to do it with her. And studying her profile while she read *Better Homes and Gardens*, I suddenly realized that she looked a whole lot like Gene Autry. Even in the body she was thick and not exactly right. Above the black lace-up shoes, her calves were as stout as those of someone who's spent a lifetime spurring mustangs.

According to my grandmother, my legs were one of my weaknesses, too. But mine were nothing like Miss Pankhurst's. My grandmother had this thing about thin ankles being a sign of good breeding. She thought all women should have ankle bones like thoroughbred horses or the stems on fine crystal, and I was skinny and shapeless everywhere but in my legs. I was built like Olive Oyl, with Popeye's forearms in my calves. But I could outrun anybody up through the fifth grade. I would even sprint, alone, through dust alleys on the way home from school, coming out the other end panting and windblown with the excitement of my own speed. But racing had gone the same way as marble shooting. I got sent to the principal's office for bending over a circle drawn on the playground and lining up my agate with the boys, while wearing a dress. When my grandmother found out she broke out in hives, and I was benched. If she hadn't been so determined to make me a skinny-legged debutante, my Popeye legs would probably have run me straight into the Olympics.

But compared to Miss Pankhurst's, the size of my calves was nothing. She didn't even shave hers. I remembered what Joel Weiss, one of the boys I had shot marbles with, said one day as we watched Miss Pankhurst walk across the library to check us out some books: "She's so ugly I bet she has to whip her feet to get in bed with her."

I looked out the window of the bus, watching the fields as we passed. Beside me Sam Best was breathing heavily. His head was turned slightly toward me, his face sliding into the crease between our two seats. I pulled down my skirt. I wiggled a little and popped my gum. But Mr. Best still slept. I aimed my face toward the bus window. In the reflection, my own face and Sam Best's came back. Below my shoulder, his hair, dark brown with a few traces of gray, lay clean and freshly cut. There was the smell of shaving lotion. Probably he'd stopped at a barbershop right before coming to the bus depot. His skin was tanned, drawn smooth by sleep. And, strangely, I found myself admiring his nose. It looked like it'd once been broken and was now crooked, yet on him it looked good. I liked the way his cheeks blended into his jaw.

Mr. Best had a daughter a year older than me, who in earlier times had played Kick-the-Can and Rollie-Bat under the water tower summer evenings with a group of us town kids. Then after I moved I heard Julie had been elected junior homecoming queen and had gotten stuck up. Now Mr. Best's wife, Ellen, had apparently moved to Little Rock and taken the homecoming queen with her.

Over the years my grandfather, who had been the only doctor in Coldwater for forty-two years, had treated Sam Best's father for all sorts of ailments, mostly connected with too much alcohol. My grandmother said Ed Best had "owned" Coldwater —had in fact ended up owning almost that whole section of the state. I had heard my grandfather whisper that Mr. Best had died a terrible death. His liver gave out and there had been nothing my grandfather could do for him. And soon after,

Sam's mother had died. She had lived in the large Victorian house that Sam inherited. For several years before her death she was purple from bad circulation, and children were afraid of her.

I had also heard the stories of Sam's orphans. Every year or so he would leave his business, at the cost of thousands of dollars, to go to South America to see about an orphanage he sponsored in Peru.

As I stared at the window, I watched his face, reflected against a background of August dried pastures and fields. He was sliding over to lean on me. I would have rolled the jacket of my sundress into a pillow and placed it under his head, to at least keep him from slipping. Doing that seemed only natural. But Sam Best was Sam Best, and I wasn't even fourteen years old.

"Listen, honey," Miss Pankhurst said, standing in the aisle and tapping my shoulder. "Come sit with me."

I climbed carefully over Mr. Best. And as I slid next to the window, Miss Pankhurst handed me a book named *A Man Called Peter*.

She must have just bought it. It was brand new and smelled wonderful. I turned the pages slowly, reading only parts. Then I became fascinated by the section where Peter feels he is being called by the Lord. Unconsciously I began smacking my gum.

"Dear," Miss Pankhurst said. "Do you *have* to?"

I looked up. At first I didn't know what she meant. "I guess not," I said.

"Do you like it?" She nodded toward *A Man Called Peter*.

"Fine." I said.

"That Peter Marshall was one of the greatest men ever put on this earth. And his wife who wrote the book's no small potatoes either. I finally raised enough money to buy a copy for the library. I don't like to donate my own personal books for public use. You'd be surprised at what I find in the pages of returned books." She looked at me. "Things like gum, food, fingernails . . . *nose* products." She looked away. "Oh I could go on and on." Then she looked back. "Are you glad to be returning to Coldwater?"

I said yes, because I was, though I wasn't overjoyed about having to live with my grandmother. Of course I didn't say anything about that. I hadn't said anything nasty since I was about five and said "poot on you" to some old biddy at church who'd tapped my shoulder for wiggling. My mama switched me for that. Then it seemed that whenever I got in trouble and got caught, I threw up. I even found out that when I got in trouble and didn't get caught, I would still throw up. So when I was about seven I gave up making trouble, because my stomach couldn't take it.

"It's just too bad about your parents," Miss Pankhurst said, leaning her arm on my arm rest. "They never should have gotten married in the first place."

"I guess not," I said.

"In fact, if you want my opinion, I think the greatest danger to a young person in the world today is animal lust. But, then, your mother's probably already warned you about that. Why, at the time, I'll bet not a person on this earth could have told your parents they weren't a good match. And now look. . . ."

She looked at me. She was right. I was what came from a union that was doomed from the beginning. I swallowed. And by accident, my gum went too.

"I just hope you don't come out of this crazy," Miss Pankhurst said.

"No ma'am," I said, coughing as my gum hit bottom.

She smiled. "Well, if anybody can keep you on balance, it'll be your grandmother."

If anything, I thought, she might be the one to tip me over.

"But of course, that's what Freud says," she said. She looked at me. "If you keep your fears conscious, you can lick 'em. Right?"

"Yes ma'am." I didn't know anybody in Coldwater named Freud, but what Miss Pankhurst said sounded good.

"Anyway, right now it seems your whole family's in hot water. Your poor grandfather—*and* your grandmother. It must be awful for her to see everything they've worked for hanging on the brink of a precipice." She blew a little wet spot on my cheek when she said *precipice*. I turned to the window and dried it off, as though scratching my face.

The trouble she meant was my grandfather's medicines and his trial. My family was so busy going to court that year, I had to think to keep it straight. My grandfather had invented two kinds of medicines that were supposed to make the whole human race invulnerable. One was for the inside of the body and the other was for the outside. He put some ads in magazines and newspapers to tell the world about it, with a Coldwater P.O. box where you could send for it. Then the Post Office, with the Food and Drug Administration, took him to court for mail fraud.

Almost the whole town of Coldwater came to the county courthouse and testified on his behalf. My mother and father went, too, and I heard them talking about it. The prosecutor had said my grandfather's medicines belonged in the same class as the left hind foot of a rabbit caught in a graveyard in the dark of the moon. My grandfather was forbidden to sell any more of them. If he did, he'd lose his license to practice medicine. To my grandmother, that was as embarrassing as being married to Jesse James.

In fact, when you got right down to it, I guess my grandfather was somebody my family could have been just as eager to hide as me.

Miss Pankhurst smiled, looking at me head-on. I hated being looked at that closely. It made me think *she* thought we were in cahoots and belonged together. She had a faint downy mustache, and there was a space between her front teeth that any good cowboy would have cherished as a spitting hole. "Well, anyway," she said, "we're glad you're coming back to Coldwater, even if for a little while." She smiled, and face-to-face, close-up, she looked so much like Gene Autry that I couldn't keep my eyes off her. Fascinated, I studied the shape, the similarity, the lines of her face.

"Is something wrong?" She touched her hat, rearranging the cherries on it.

"No'm."

"You know why I ride buses?"

"No'm."

"I tell people I do it so I can spend all this time reading. But the truth is. . . ." She took a deep breath. "There's something about them—their size, their strength, maybe even"—she laughed—"their smell. Don't tell your grandmother; she'll think I'm coarse."

Then she reached down between her cowboy legs into her shopping bag and brought out a burnt-orange cloche, the shape and color of a deformed pumpkin. "This is what I got for your grandmother's luncheon, the one in early November—and I wanted something fallish, in a Halloween color, don't you think?"

"Yessum."

My grandmother's Eastern Arkansas Missionary Society Meeting was looked forward to every November, and written up in the *Coldwater Gazette* about like if the King of England had come to visit.

By then we'd been on the bus a couple of hours and it stopped for a few minutes so we could all get off and rest or get a drink. As quickly as I could, I headed as far away from Miss Pankhurst as I could get. Even Sam Best woke up and came smiling off the bus to where I was standing by a Coke machine, saying that he wanted to buy me something. We put peanuts in Cokes and let them fizz and sucked the foam. Sam Best could laugh and carry on as good as anybody I knew, maybe better. I kept thinking there might still be a chance he'd end up my stepfather. I made up all sorts of pictures in my head about that, because I'd end up rich. Probably I'd even get to be the Coldwater homecoming queen, seeing as how his real flesh and blood daughter had already gotten to be it. Not that I wanted to, or anything.

We stood there, Sam and me, by the Coke machine outside a café named Pete's Place, and he showed me how to skip gravel across the highway. Then, just as we were ready to get back on the bus, I turned and saw one of the strangest things I have ever witnessed in my life. Miss Pankhurst was flirting with the bus driver just like she was Marilyn Monroe, even sticking out her lips and talking breathy like that. And mercy, if that bus driver didn't hold her arm and help her up the bus steps, with her still wearing that stupid orange hat! She was even smiling at him out of her cowboy face. She stood there right by the steering wheel and the bus driver's seat, and we all had to wiggle past her. She even left me alone where we'd been sitting and rode up there in the front seat for the rest of the trip and read aloud passages to him from *A Man Called Peter*!

Another hour went by, and then I could see the water tower that was near the back of my grandparents' house. Painted a bright silver, it glinted in the sun. When I had been small, I thought it looked like a pot-bellied man on stilts. Now it was only a water tower. But just as I remembered, only maybe a little faded, there was the large red heart painted on the front, and the words: *Coldwater, Arkansas, Heart of Best County*.

I glanced around the bus. Just about everybody but me had somebody with them. I was in the world, on my own, and left out.

Mr. Best had woken up and was reading the *Wall Street Journal*. He looked across the aisle at me and winked. One time when he'd come to visit my mother at our house in Coldwater, he'd looked up at the water tower, and after staring a minute at that heart and the words under it, he'd laughed a sudden deep laugh that pulled the edge of his mouth into a slight upward skip that was part amusement, part surprise and, without expecting any answer, said: "You ever heard a better name?" Then a beat of silence while he looked at us and grinned: "S'been right convenient."

As the bus bumped up over the railroad tracks onto the main street of Coldwater, I swallowed my stomach and then my heart. I was home!

I slid my stupid-looking hat with the streamers under my seat and left it there. Finally, no mother to dress me up with her ideas of me. And no father wishing every minute that I was some stupid boy instead. Probably every girl in America would hate my guts for being so lucky.

4.

Being Back

When the sun broke open with yellow light onto the high headboard of my bed through the open window, I heard a laugh. The room my grandparents gave me was an enclosed sleeping porch with windows all around it. And the window behind my bed looked onto the side of my parents' old house.

Only a short driveway separated the two houses. I could see across the narrow yards into my parents' old living room. New furniture was in it, and the voices I heard were coming from my parents' bedroom. Some woman was talking. When she laughed the sound was high and light like someone running a finger up the treble keys of a piano. Then a man sneezed. "You?" she said and laughed again.

I stretched out in the bed, thinking what a nice sound that laugh was. I couldn't remember my mother ever laughing like that, except maybe once. She'd dressed me up—I was about six—and put me in a county talent show. I was supposed to tap dance and sing. When she got me all done up in a ruffly pinafore (I think I was supposed to be something like a Shirley Temple from Arkansas) she shrieked and laughed and near about went crazy over how cute she said I looked. But I was homely even back then; it just hadn't gotten organized yet. And besides, when somebody's little and plain they can get by. But now I was five-foot-four and still on the rise, and even though all my life I'd heard plenty of people say somebody was so ugly she was cute, I knew I'd long since passed out of that category. Then, when my mother and I got on the stage and she sat down at the piano to play while I sang, I got stuck. Even after she played the introduction five times, and I finally got out the first notes, I sounded like somebody pulling chalk across a blackboard. Nobody could hear the taps on my shoes any more than if I'd been tap dancing at a deaf school. My mother wanted Shirley Temple and she got me. I couldn't sing any better than I could fish.

I looked up at the wood curls in the walnut headboard of my bed. Everything was different. I was a woman now. I was out in the world, alone, and on my own. Even the bed was a sign of how much things had changed. Before now, I'd been afraid of it. It was part of the bedroom set my grandmother had shipped from her family plantation in Mississippi. It had been my great-great-grandfather's and was very beautiful, except that my grandmother told me the man it had belonged to had fought at Shiloh and got shot in the stomach with a cannonball. She showed me his picture. For several years he had carried part of that cannonball in his stomach, and then he died of the flu. In his picture he didn't look as though he had a stomachache any more than any of her other relatives. Still, sometimes when I spent the night at my grandparents', I woke up in his bed sweating, his face crashing my dreams, in which he had tried to share the bed again.

But now I thought about beds differently. The year before they'd only been places to sleep, read books, and dream. Now I attributed ninety-five percent of the world's population to them, giving the other five percent to drive-in movies, bear rugs, or bare floors.

I could hear my grandmother shuffling around in the

kitchen, talking to my grandfather. She didn't sound cheerful. My grandmother was never cheerful. I think it was part of her religion not to be. I wasn't in any rush to get up and get in the middle of that.

Of course my parents had called me the night before—my father first and then my mother—to see if I'd arrived in Coldwater all right. After I'd talked a minute, my grandmother had gotten on the phone and carried on about how much I'd grown. She said I was a bona fide teenager now, and she was too old to raise one again. She told my father she hadn't gotten over raising him yet, and that he and my mother ought to cut out their shenanigans and straighten out their lives. Maybe my grandmother was just using me to push my parents, but I didn't get the message like that. Maybe she thought I was sitting there beside my grandfather watching a cowboy movie on TV and couldn't hear her. But it didn't matter, because I knew the truth. Did they all think I was some peabrain two steps from the halfwit ward at the state insane asylum?

My grandmother ended the conversation by telling my father she loved him and to not worry; she loved me and we'd get through the year somehow. Then my father told me he loved me and to also give his love to my grandparents. And then my mother called and we went through the whole business again. She hung up saying all that love stuff again, her voice sad and reeling it off like the inside of a greeting card. The whole time my grandfather sat in his chair in front of the TV, asleep and left out. But I'd just as soon have been. All that love stuff was a bunch of junk. I'd been sent away. My grandmother would never love me unless I became a bona fide debutante, and even if I broke down and agreed to "come out," the paper would probably take one look at my picture and put it on the obituary page.

I rolled over and looked out the other window. I was just going to stay in bed and never get up. They'd forget about me. A hundred years from now, somebody would come into the room, brush away the cobwebs over the Man-from-Shiloh's bed and find me as an old woman who'd never had a life anywhere outside this room. My feet would be pressed against the footboard like two old bass. The rug would have holes worn in it where I'd tap danced for eighty-six years. The story of my pitiful life would end up a legend.

Now the early sun was shining on the dew in the backyard, and I could see the orchard and the empty chicken house. My grandfather had put a pump under the grape arbor because he wanted to tap pure water for use in his medicines. My grandmother had gotten rid of the chickens because she found it depressing when the hens pecked each other's feathers off.

"Sally?" She opened my bedroom door, holding up a newly pressed dress that looked like something an extra would wear in *Gone With the Wind*. As she came in and took over the whole room, I knew that all hopes of staying in bed for life were over. I lay there looking at her while she stood at the foot of her relative's bed and looked at me, one hand holding up the dress so it wouldn't touch the floor. "Sleep well?"

"Yessum."

She was tall and her hands were twisted a little by arthritis, reminding me of the grape vines. Her hems dipped sideways until noon, when her back warmed up and she could stand straight. And maybe she was in pain a lot and just wanted you in the same boat with her—because she could drive you nuts faster than ants finding sugar. "I just don't have time to iron and cook," she said, hanging up that Tara dress on the closet door. "And Louella's singing a solo at church today and couldn't see fit to come help. She knew I had to give the Devotional to the Golden Age class, and she's dying to see you. But could she come and help?—oh, no. She couldn't pass up that solo—and I don't know why. She can't sing worth a toot."

Louella was my grandmother's maid. She could always sing better than anybody I knew. But my grandmother was hard on all of us. Most of all, she hated to cook.

We had stiff toast and walked to church.

As we went down the sidewalk, three abreast, my grandfather reached for me. "We're so glad you're here," he said, putting his arm around my shoulder. "Even if it is only because of your mother's and father's trouble." He winked at me. With his other hand he held my grandmother's elbow. Probably he'd have supported the whole world if he could. Some people thought my grandfather was a genius. And some thought he was nuts. But if he was a little crazy, to me that was what was so wonderful. Now I had to slow down my steps to match his. I hadn't seen him in a year, and I was again impressed with how large he was. His hair was white, his hands overly large and trembly, reddish, chapped, sometimes peeling —which made you wonder what they'd been into. His features were big, his eyes burrowed under white wiry ledges of brows; and his cheeks were masses of crinkled lines. But the most outstanding thing about my grandfather was that he never worried. Or at least if he did, I didn't see any sign of it. I guess he got that way from being present at an infinite number of tragedies. He knew how to stanch blood, hold hands, deliver hope, death, new life, not do much and never run out. That was bound to make him calm.

Main Street in Coldwater was calm, too. There were people like us, walking all along it to some church, dressed up in summer colors. I felt the old circus spell of Coldwater. It was like looking through the decorated opening in a candy egg and seeing there a whole scene, ongoing and contained. Because Coldwater was not only small, it was simple.

On the central block of Main Street were one feed store, one drugstore, a bank, and two groceries. And just beyond each end of Main Street was a sign that said: Welcome to Coldwater, Arkansas, Pop.: 2,309. For all the years I'd lived in Coldwater, these signs had always said, Pop.: 2,309. When someone was born, someone else died, because the number never changed.

Cater-cornered to the Best Mercantile was my grandfather's clinic, which meant he could step out the back door of his office, walk across the alley, and be at home. He thought that was convenient. My grandmother said it was dangerous. If he blew up his office while mixing his medicines, the house would go, too. Yet she also thought that might turn out to be a blessing in disguise, since she'd always wanted to move to the street near the Mill Pond.

Next to my grandfather's clinic was the newspaper office where the *Coldwater Gazette* was printed every Friday. And next to that was the post office. My grandmother stopped to admire the silver compote in the window of the jewelry store. But nothing could compare to the silver that had been passed on to her from her family's plantation in Mississippi, and as though we didn't know, she told us that once again as we crossed the street to the First Methodist Church. The bells in the tower were ringing, and around the corner, the bells in the First, Second, and Third Baptist were ringing, too.

At 5:00 P.M. those bells would be given over to recorded hymns. Every night at just about suppertime the Methodists would chime out a hymn first, and then at half past five the Baptists would pick it up and finish out the hour to six. Fortunately, the Church of Christ was quiet; their women didn't even wear lipstick, and we had heard they sang without so much as a piano. So after the Methodists reminded us that *the tie is blessed that binds* and the Baptists topped it off with *the amazing grace that saved a wretch like me*, the rest of the evening would be as quiet as we cared to make it.

I stopped on the church steps. Everybody was having a fit over my being there, anyway. My grandparents were referring to my family's situation as "my little visit," while I looked across the street at the machine shop. Tractors and combines were parked in front. On any day but Sunday there would be a fire raging inside and the sound of steel being pounded from 8:00 A.M. to 6:00 P.M., and behind it, sweaty men hunkered down shooting craps and drinking out of bottles that from April to October were a hazard to anybody who went barefoot.

Mr. Harris, who owned the machine shop, would sit beside his wife during the eleven o'clock service in our church while she played the organ, pumping the pedals with her too-large, varicose-veined legs. Then when her legs gave out, which was usually during the Doxology, he'd take over the pumping.

I went into a class and sat beside Bobby Watts, which didn't thrill me. Two other kids were in there and they were from the country. I was the only town kid that year my age who wasn't a Baptist.

Bobby Watts reached in his pocket and offered me a cherry Lifesaver. He'd sprouted a case of acne and had on argyle socks, like old men wore. When he and I were six, we'd spent some time together in all sorts of places around town, swapping visions of anatomy. Once we did it in the basement of the Methodist Church and another time in the alley behind the dime store. We were only six and I guess there was nothing to be embarrassed about now, but it drove me crazy to think I'd shown myself to someone who'd grown up to be a nerd.

I stared at the Lifesaver, balanced on the end of his thumb.

I could feel his eyes on my face. Seeing him made me realize what a bad kid I must have been. My parents had probably known all along how rotten I was.

"No thanks," I whispered, turning down Bobby Watts's Lifesaver and catching the attention of Miss Pankhurst, who was our teacher. Her Sunday school lesson for that day wasn't much different from any other time. For what was always stressed, more than the facts and memorized Bible verses, was the idea—which we saw again, if we went to the Saturday afternoon movie, when the cowboy in the white hat caught the cowboy in the black hat—that evil would get its due.

Due was something that took me a long time to figure out; there were so many dues: *do* and *dew*. But I decided they all had to do with action or something falling. And whenever I walked barefoot over our lawn in the early morning, I knew that wet feet were the mildest of all possibilities.

I thought the same way about *just desserts*. Someone got it when he deserved it, but I never ate chocolate cake without it seeming a grand sign.

So, no one in Coldwater was worrying about the state treasurer. If he was embezzling, God knew it, and he would get his due. Same with the governor and president. And just the same with Mr. Harris, who, more often than not, ran crap games at the machine shop. Pumping the organ for his weak-legged wife on Sundays would certainly help. For it was a just God we believed in, and He'd surely take into account every day of the week.

To me, that whole theory seemed simple. If you got so happy you couldn't believe it, you were in trouble. Life had to be balanced; there had to be the bad with the good. Tip the scales and all hell broke loose.

Once I overheard my mother telling one of her close friends

that she'd gone to a psychiatrist and that he'd told her there was no sense in even considering whether or not she was happy. If she found out that she was, she couldn't live through it. "Leave yourself in blissful ignorance," he had said. "It's the only way you can function. Yours is a life better off unexamined." I guess she forgot what he said, though. Now I'd lost her, and my father.

My grandparents and I walked out of the church into the hot noon sun and went home for Sunday dinner.

Ezekiel, my grandparents' handyman, was up on a ladder picking plums off one of the trees near the chicken yard. Sometimes he came to my grandparents' house on Sundays to do some yard work that couldn't be put off. And ripe plums couldn't wait. The year before, my grandparents had lost almost the whole crop to birds. No doubt my grandmother would be supervising Louella in making plum jelly all week. Probably Louella wasn't singing a solo in church so much as she was staying home to rest up.

As my grandparents and I went in the sun porch door, Ezekiel carefully placed a handful of plums in a bushel basket, while calling hello to us. It'd been a whole year since I'd seen him. I'd never talked to him much, but I always remembered the time that he'd oiled my three-wheel bike when I was little, even though we'd both overheard my mother tell a neighbor that she liked to hear the squeak of my trike so she'd know where I was. But when I was four I'd gotten a terrible itch to go farther than I was supposed to go. I'd asked Ezekiel to oil my trike, and he'd done a fine job on it. So after my mother got used to the idea of not hearing exactly where I was, I set off around the corner, with all three wheels purring as smooth as pleated satin, onto the sidewalk of Main past my grandfather's clinic and the post office and the jewelry store and the machine shop to the parking lot of the Second Baptist Church. There, I did a few fancy figure eights on the asphalt, then headed home. On the way back I caught a glimpse of Ezekiel standing in the alley, checking up on me. But when I pulled into the driveway at home, he was mowing the lawn just as if he'd been there the whole time. Neither of us ever mentioned my trip.

My grandmother was in the kitchen now, pulling out pots and pans and Lord-knows what else. She could make that whole side of the house sound like a drunk drum section in a band. We always had a big Sunday dinner after church. And while my grandmother worked in the kitchen, I helped by setting the table, being careful with the china and silver that she was also getting out.

I walked back and forth to the dining room table.

"How'd you like living over there?" my grandmother asked on my next trip to the kitchen. She handed me a tea service which she told me she would one day pass on to me.

"All right," I said.

My grandfather was reading the paper on the sun porch, which my grandmother called the solarium. It looked out onto the alley and the back doors of the buildings facing Main Street. "Well, nothing's happened here since you left," she said. She was peeling apples and dumping the ragged fruit skins into a sack. "Except of course your grandfather was taken to court like a criminal. I have dreams his face is hanging in the post office. Can you imagine! Accused of mail fraud! And the thing that's giving me ulcers is, he *did it!*" She came into the dining room, carrying napkins.

I was getting used to how the house smelled. Mostly it was like the White Gardenia bath powder my grandmother wore. That odor aged into an aroma that pervaded everything she touched. When she gave me a birthday card, even the envelope smelled like her. I never would have told anyone, but to me, when White Gardenia bath powder got old, the smell of it mostly resembled a wet poodle.

As I carried that silver back and forth, I was again amazed at how tacky my grandmother's house was. Considering her general taste and philosophy, her total lack of any decorating sense seemed abnormal. For to my grandmother, *how* to be and *how not* to be—*that* was the question. But she hated to spend money. She had inherited almost everything in her house, and if it didn't match or belong she didn't care. Even if she had liked to spend money I predict she would have bought ugly things; I don't know why. My grandmother just couldn't seem to put anything together in an attractive order, except her large silver collection. The main luxuries in the house were a telephone in my grandparents' bedroom, another one in the back hall, and one in the kitchen. My grandfather's profession prompted that.

I stood a moment at one end of the dining room, which was really part of the living room, to look at the picture of my grandmother, which I hadn't seen in a while. Honey-brown hair piled into wings on top, delicate curls rimming her face. She was standing straight and very regal in a long white satin gown, holding a rose bouquet in her arms, which were covered in white gloves with seemingly hundreds of buttons all the way to her elbow. Her face was serene, dignified, and very beautiful. She was looking away from the camera at something that only she could see; the result was a picture of total confidence, and something else I couldn't put a finger on. The angle of her head, and the expression in her eyes, reminded me of some of the people I'd seen in the bus station when the bus drove in and their relatives got off. It was, I guess, a look of excitement and hopefulness. The picture was the one taken for her debut. The one for her wedding was not very different. I stood there looking at that, and at a small picture below it on the sideboard of my mother and father in their wedding gear. I guess something had gotten spilled on the sideboard at one time, because a stain went up one side of the frame and had seeped up across the bottom of the picture. It was probably milk. It was probably me who'd spilled it, some Sunday when we'd all been together for dinner.

Behind me my grandmother was putting napkins around and bringing me up to date on Coldwater. "And the tenant your grandfather rented your house to isn't worth much. She's loud and messy and will probably tear the place up. But she's the only one who promised to stay all winter so the pipes won't freeze. And Ellen Best moved to Little Rock week before last. She'll probably get voted into the Junior League there. But then I don't think she and Sam intend to divorce, only separate. Which, if you ask me, makes a whole lot more sense than what your mother's doing. If she'd play her cards right she could be in the Junior League of Memphis. But I'm afraid she's shot her chances now; a divorced woman looks used."

I couldn't sit on my curiosity about the woman I'd heard laughing in my parents' house. "Who'd you rent the house to?"

My grandmother pshawed. Her sound of disgust reminded me of the hippopotamus at the Memphis Zoo, who would look at me, burp, close its eyes, and then disappear underwater. In fact, my grandmother's pshaw was as famous in Coldwater as that hippopotamus became when he swallowed a rubber tire some smart ass threw to him. His operation made it into the national news, and the state of his health was followed for weeks. "Oh, just somebody I don't think is fit for you to discuss," she said, going on about the tenant in my parents' house.

"Why?"

"She sings and dances. She performs every Saturday night." My grandmother rearranged a few pieces of silver in the china cabinet. "She doesn't have any talent, but what everybody objects to . . . I don't think I'll go into it."

"What?"

"She's common. You know—has no sense of what's proper."

"Like what?"

My grandmother licked her lips and glanced at me. More than anything, I think, she wanted to pass things on: her silver, her opinions, the arrangement of the world in her lifetime. And here was a perfect spot to pass me what she called pearls. "Well-bred people don't step over boundaries," she said. "At least when they do, they do it on purpose. Miss Norris does things without even knowing she shouldn't."

I think she left that intentionally vague.

Then she turned on a light in the living room because she kept the drapes closed. "I halfway hope that girl'll marry that man she's carrying on with now—and they'll move away. Though with my luck, they'll marry and *he'll* move in. Might as well—he just about lives there now, anyway. Your mother would just die."

She went on about the year I hadn't been there and how much she envied me for having left. She considered Coldwater a dump, and the tragedy of her life was having to live in it. She seemed to always be homing in on shortcomings—if not someone else's, then Coldwater's. She said it was just her luck to have to live in a place where not one person knew what the Brandenburg Concertos were or could speak a sentence without having to stop and spit a wad or suck his teeth. "I'd give almost anything to trade places with you," she said. "This town's got about as much sense as the head on a wooden nickel. I've tried and tried to get a beautification plan started and I get about as much response as Miss Pankhurst at the public library." She pshawed. "The worst thing about this town is its apathy. Why I've written four letters to the editor about that outhouse. . . ."

Suddenly my grandfather hollered outside. It sounded as if he was pulling the sides off the porch. We were finished setting the table, anyway, and we went to find out.

My grandfather and Ezekiel were bending over a crowbar set into the side of the sun porch. They'd discovered dry rot.

My grandmother rubbed her hands. "I just wish the whole house would fall down. We should have moved to the Mill Pond years ago."

"Go ahead and fix it," my grandfather said to Ezekiel.

Ezekiel nodded, while studying the side of the sun porch. There were tight swirls of gray in his hair. He was a little younger than my grandfather. His face was bluish black, thin and sort of bony. Usually he wore overalls that had hammers and screwdrivers, rulers and pencils sticking out of pockets or tied on. Today his overalls didn't have tools on them. And as long as I'd known him he'd always been called Ezekiel and not Zeke, though I'm sure at times the short form was tried— it just never stuck. Maybe that's what his parents counted on when they gave him the name of someone in the Bible who had his own book—that Ezekiel would end up to be just as he was now: proud, tall, maybe a little too skinny, but never called Zeke. My grandfather was hunkered down beside him, still dressed in what he called his Sunday-go-to-meetin' suit— a blue seersucker with a light straw hat.

"Yessir, Dr. Maulden," Ezekiel said. "Won't be soon though."

My grandmother stepped toward him. "It has to be. It just simply has to be." She smoothed down her hair that had come loose in the heat. "I've got the Missionary Society luncheon in eight weeks."

"Oh, it won't take that long." Ezekiel put up the crowbar in a tool chest. "'Bout three weeks at the most."

Thin wisps of hair flew around my grandmother's face like spun sugar. The face in the dining room picture seemed like a distant relative. "This is just the last thing on earth I need —two months before the Missionary Society luncheon—this and," turning, she pointed, "that." On the other side of my grandfather's office, where the alley blended into the back of the newspaper office, was a gray-board outhouse. "I've written four letters to the editor to get rid of that thing. But no one cares. It can smell and stink and ruin our health, but people in this town are too lazy to do anything about it. A few members of the Missionary Society wrote letters supporting my proposal. But do you think Charles Rankin will do anything? Of course not! He *enjoys* controversy. He wants to hear citizens screaming and tearing their hair out."

Apparently the outhouse was my grandmother's latest project. She was always writing letters to the editor to point out how Coldwater citizens could improve themselves. And apparently she and Charles Rankin, the newspaper editor, who also owned the outhouse, were having a knock-down-drag-out battle over it.

We stared in silence at the outhouse. Disappointment put a hitch in one side of my grandmother's lip, and when she moved her mouth to speak the crease stayed. "We might as well eat," she said and headed for the porch steps.

My grandmother told me to go take off my good dress and

put on the one that she'd laid out on the bed. A lot of good it'd do. The whole stupid closet was full of damn Tara dresses. I turned the key in the lock of the bedroom door. It probably hadn't been turned in half a century. It'd be just like my grandmother to come busting in while I was undressed, saying she just wanted to check on me.

I put on a sundress that had yellow flowers on it. It was one my mother had made. It had attached petticoats that made me look like a damn lampshade.

I studied myself in the mirror of the dresser that went with the Man-from-Shiloh's bed. He probably hadn't used it much. I didn't know why men needed mirrors on their dressers, anyway. To mash bumps or pick turnip greens out of their teeth?

I looked awful in yellow. In fact, my ears were sticking out. My chin was shaped the same as my grandmother's, and the color of my eyes was hers. She was as evident in my face as in the dining room picture. I grinned at myself and stuck out my tongue.

I turned the key, and then the knob; but the door wouldn't open. I leaned against it, jiggling the lock and beating on the doorknob. I was too embarrassed to yell.

I sat down on the bed to think. I could feel my stomach getting all the old signals that I was in trouble. But I kept telling myself I was too old to throw up. Then I could hear her voice. At first it was normal, but it soon rose to a very high decibel on the last syllable of my name. And the terrible sound of her clumping down the hall began.

As I sat there, the thought came to me that if I was so bad as to cause my mother and father to bust up, living with my grandmother was probably my due. Soon as I got out of that bedroom, I really ought to have a talk with the Lord about that.

5.

Betty Jane Norris and Joel Weiss at the Rexall Drug Store

"Sally, is something wrong? Are you sick?"

"No ma'am."

The door knob wiggled. "Well then, open this door."

"I can't."

I turned the key in what I thought was a display of its uselessness. "Oh good Lord!" She pshawed very loudly and then I heard her say down the hall to my grandfather: "Horace, she's locked herself in the bedroom."

My grandfather didn't even hesitate. More than likely he was eating the Jell-o salad or stirring his tea. "Just don't tell her she'll miss your lunch. She may never come out." Then he added: "Maybe that's why she did it."

"Horace, would you come here?"

I sat on the Man-from-Shiloh's bed and picked my fingernails. "I didn't lock it on purpose," I said. "I mean I did, but . . . I'm not unlocking it because I don't want to."

Apparently my grandfather was still sitting in the dining room, because my grandmother was yelling. "She's depressed, Horace! I knew this divorce business would ruin the child! And now look."

"I'm not in here because of my parents," I said.

"Call Ezekiel, Horace! Tell him to bring his tools! We'll have to get her out of here by force!"

"I didn't do this on purpose," I said, sort of loud.

"Of course you didn't." Apparently my grandfather had gone for Ezekiel and my grandmother was now leaning on the door, breathing in my direction. "Anyone who has to leave their parents and come to a town like this is bound to lose control. Just don't do anything rash."

I took the key out of the lock.

"Are you moving around? What is that you're doing?"

Through the big rusted keyhole I thought I saw my grandmother's eye.

"I'm trying to get a nail file to open the lock."

"Oh my Lord!" She pressed against the door and yelled. "Ezekiel, Horace, would you two hurry! She's going to commit suicide!"

I filed the key for a minute, thinking that by removing some rust it might work. I put it in the lock and slid the nail file through the door. I tried to work the key and began sawing the lock at the same time, more as a sign of my mental health than a belief that I could let myself out. But the best thing was that the sharpness of the file made my grandmother step back.

I heard Ezekiel come down the hall carrying the tool chest; when he walked, the tools clanked. I stopped my sawing and moved in front of the dresser. "Won't be but a minute," Ezekiel said.

"Yes," my grandmother whispered, "but it only takes a minute to kill yourself." Then: "Sally! What are you doing now?"

"I'm just standing here," I said.

"There hasn't been anybody in this house," my grandfather added, "with a body worth locking up in twenty years. You want me to help you, Ezekiel?"

"No sir. It just seem the hinges so rusted I gonna have to oil them to pull out the door pin." I could hear him move away.

"Everything's going to be all right, Sally. Believe me." My grandmother must have been leaning on the door; she sounded very close. "You're going to have a good year with us, I promise." My grandfather chimed in behind her: "We can put you a dog house out back and get a poodle."

"Nonsense." My grandmother must have looked at him, her voice sounded muffled. "What do we need a poodle for?"

"A girl needs a dog. Everybody knows that." My grandfather leaned on the door and yelled through the keyhole. "You'd like a poodle, wouldn't you?"

"I guess," I said. At least along with all the old Gardenia bath powder, you wouldn't be able to smell it in the house.

"Which you want—," he asked, "white or black?"

"Think of the fleas it will leave in the rugs." My grandmother's voice sounded aimed at him and not the door. "We'll have to have the house fumigated before each Missionary Society meeting. As if the outhouse weren't bad enough."

My grandparents might have just been fooling around, but I was sick and tired of being smack in the middle of a fight. "I don't really need a dog," I said.

Ezekiel came back and squirted oil on the hinges. He pounded on them with a hammer and nobody could say anything. Behind me I heard something tapping on the window. When I turned to look at what it was, I saw my grandmother looking in at me. "Just stand still and talk to me, " she yelled through the glass. She must have been standing on a stool or something. She looked shaky and was holding onto the windowsill.

Ezekiel lifted the door off its hinges and broke the lock. They found me sitting on the Man-from-Shiloh's bed, filing my nails, while my grandmother watched me through the window and recited all sorts of stuff off a boring list of things she planned for us to do that year.

When we were all in the dining room again, my grandmother put her arm around me. "Now you won't do that again, will you?"

"No'm," I said, meaning it.

We ate our lunch, which was something congealed called Sunrise Salad—meat and vegetables with carrots rising to the top. My grandmother seemed to have hundreds of recipes that could harden things together in a jell. While we ate, she kept up a running conversation. My grandfather rarely joined her, but my grandmother talked at him anyway. I think Emily Post taught her how.

"This is weird," he said, holding out his fork with the salad shimmering on it.

"Don't talk about your food, Horace," my grandmother said.

My grandfather took a bottle of his Inside Medicine out of his back pocket and poured some in his iced tea.

"Oh good heavens!" My grandmother stood up and looked at him as though he had just stripped naked. "What are you doing?"

"I'm going to need this after this lunch."

She moved close to him and pshawed with such guttural participation that I thought she was sick. "Horace!" She leaned over him and breathed fire. "You know you're not supposed to be doing anything with that medicine."

But my grandfather remained calm. I was awed at his display of courage. My own flesh was puckering just from the nearness of her breath. "They mean I can't sell any," he said. "It doesn't mean I can't use it on my own family." He took a drink. "In fact, I guess that includes you." He poured a little into her glass.

At this point, my grandmother may have considered divorce herself, except of course she would have jeopardized her membership in too many organizations.

My grandfather walked around behind her as she cleared the table. He was sipping from his glass, telling us that fifty years from now everybody would be laid up with emphysema and heart disease while he was out catching largemouth bass on some sweet riverbank. Unless of course he won an appeal on his case and could offer his medicine to the whole human race.

I was the only one still sitting. I didn't want to get up and be noticed.

Then my grandfather walked into the real dining room, which my grandmother called the den, and he told me to follow him. When my grandparents bought a TV they moved the dining room to the living room because it was low-class to have a TV in the living room.

"Now," my grandfather said, sitting back in his recliner and reaching over to switch on the TV. "After a lunch like that we need a rest."

I didn't want to sit in my grandmother's swivel rocker, so I sat down in a straight-backed chair that had been a dining chair at the banquet table on my grandmother's family plantation. It made me sit up too straight and was hard.

My grandfather looked at me. "She'll go rest in a minute and we can do whatever we want." Then he turned on the TV and we found an old Gene Autry movie. We could hear my grandmother still shuffling around in the kitchen, and my grandfather nodded in her direction. "Anybody who doesn't drink my medicine will poop out and have to go to sleep." Then he winked. "We might even go out and buy a poodle."

When my grandmother looked in on us to say she was going to lie down, my grandfather was snoring. The afternoon was a hum of lawn mowers and car doors banging shut and the occasional low voice of someone passing on the street. I sat

listening to my grandfather breathe. The room was so quiet
and dark with the drapes drawn, it felt that no one in the
whole world was near. Inside me was something hard, settling
down on the inside of my ribs, under my heart. Against the
background of my grandfather's breathing, a loneliness spread
through me like I was a hollow egg, blown completely out,
painted and empty. It was the craziest thing in the world—
to be right there in the room with someone alive and breathing and to hear people outside moving around talking, and yet
have a loneliness take me over with a pain so sharp it was
worse than moving ice against a sore tooth. I got up and went
out onto the front porch. For a while I just stood there studying
the bushes against the house and the grass all the way out to
the street, seeing how everything was dry and wilted. For no
reason I could name, I felt scared. Being in the room with an
old person doing nothing but breathing would probably make
anybody feel scared. I stood awhile on the porch, watching
Ezekiel load up his wagon, putting a bushel of plums in it that
my grandmother must have given him. He had an old mule—
she looked old to me, anyway—to pull it. As he drove off he
waved at me.

I headed toward Main Street. Everywhere there was dust.
The earth was so fine that it left with whatever breeze came.
The ground was like sifted gray chalk, always eager to move. I
remembered being little and sitting at the edge of our unpaved
road and building dust castles. But that earth wouldn't stay
in any one shape for long. And I remembered sitting in the
bathtub, bone-tired and my skin covered by dust that soaked
off in the tub and made the water the color of chewed gum. My
mother would lean over and run the washrag up my back and
drip water over my legs like rain. "Mercy!" I could hear her say,
"You sure are good at getting dirty." I could remember what it

was like: the warmth of the water. The smell of the room with heat and soap. And of being loved. But I'd ruined it.

I headed for the Rexall's drugstore. It had always been the gathering place for most of the town kids every day after school. We'd giggle in the booths and twirl on the stools, buy Hershey bars and Cokes and long new yellow pencils that smelled wonderful and had chaste, flat erasers. On report card day, Mr. Barber, the pharmacist, served cherry Cokes on the house for anyone who'd gotten nothing lower than a B. He kept us at a high level of achievement and cavity-prone. If we didn't go on to college, at least we kept the dentist fat.

I sat on the first stool at the soda fountain, just beside the cash register. Mrs. Barber was the soda jerk, and when she saw me she let out a high sound that I guess was supposed to be delight. "Lord a-mighty!" she squealed. "Sally Maulden, is that you?"

"Yessum," I said. Since the petticoats under my dress wouldn't let my skirt drape over the stool, I pushed at them. I was just thankful nobody I knew was at the soda fountain—nobody except some country people. To them I probably looked like the daughter of a Rockefeller. The truth was, I liked pretty clothes; I just didn't like extraordinary clothes that caused me to be stared at. And I didn't like being dressed up in a Tara dress, like a miniature of some lady I wasn't sure I especially liked, either.

"Well, don't you just look darling!" Mrs. Barber said. "I heard you were coming back. I'm sorry to hear why, though." She smiled sweetly. I felt like a poster child with a disease.

"That's very kind of you to say," I said—which was a really stupid remark. But since I'd been brought up to have a sparkling personality, by those rules silences were awful.

"Well, anyway, we're glad you're back." She asked me what I

wanted, and I ordered a cherry Coke. I twirled the stool a little
and looked in the mirror behind the soda fountain. I looked
hot and my hair was a mess. Soda fountains with mirrors were
probably put in drugstores so when you looked at yourself
having a soda, you'd get up and buy a bunch of cosmetics or
drugs.

Mrs. Barber leaned over the counter toward me, opened one
of the ice-cream vats and started scooping around in it. She
had just had her hair permed into sausage-shaped ringlets,
and when she got close the curling chemicals made her smell
like a cat box.

"Your grandfather's misfortune sure is helping our business." She shook her head. "I hate to say it on your account,
but the government putting the quietus on his medicine's been
a boon to us." She smiled and handed me a vanilla cone. "On
the house," she said. "A little coming-home present."

I was nearly through with the ice cream when the door was
opened by a woman I had never seen in Coldwater. At first I
glanced over when she came in, more of a reflex than anything
else. But then I didn't want to look away; and if I hadn't been so
well-bred, as my grandmother said I was, I would have stared.
I was struck by how much she looked like my mother—or like
my mother had tried to look when she had been younger. Their
coloring was similar and they were the same height. From a
distance, one could have been mistaken for the other if they'd
been dressed alike. They stood the same, straight but with
their shoulders bent forward a little, as though any second they
could reach out, touch you, and wanted to. But this woman
was younger and prettier than my mother. In fact, she was the
most interesting woman I'd ever seen.

She stood a moment, looking around, then went to the newsstand. She didn't flip through the magazines; she just reached

down and picked up one and came over to the cash register
with it. I caught myself staring, so I turned the other way,
putting the whole tail-end of the cone in my mouth, which
would have been disgusting for her to see anyway.

Mrs. Barber couldn't come to the cash register because she
was waiting on somebody else. And then suddenly I felt something touch my skirt.

"This is really beautiful."

When I turned around the woman was sliding the hem of
my skirt through her fingers and smiling at me.

"Thanks," I said.

Now I could study her without looking as though I were
staring. Her hair reached halfway down her back and was the
color of brownish red that reminded me of pennies. It was a
color so rich and rare, it sang. My mother's was almost like
that, but hers came out of a bottle, while nothing about this
woman seemed unnatural or planned. Her hair hung mostly
straight and thick with a few waves. I doubted that she had ever
even rolled it up. Whenever mine had been long my mother
had twisted it up on rags so when she combed it out, I had
long curls like corkscrews. And always the humidity undid my
mother's handiwork. Frequently I heard my mother tell her
friends that the good Lord had given her a little girl so that
she could play with her hair. But somewhere along the way my
mother got frustrated and gave up.

"I've never tried that vanilla. Is it good?" She didn't talk
like anyone around Coldwater. She sounded Southern, but her
voice was low, raspy. She didn't have a whine to it. Instead, her
words seemed coated, held low in her throat before they were
let go.

"Yeah. It's right good." I didn't seem to feel the need to say
"ma'am" to her. She looked so young. And, too, there was some-

thing about her that didn't seem to require it. She looked at me. "You visiting someone in town?"

"Yeah. My grandparents—the Mauldens."

She laughed—that same laugh I'd heard while lying in the Man-from-Shiloh's bed. She took her hand away from her throat. The stone she'd been twirling was blue. "So you're Dr. Maulden's granddaughter. I'll bet you're going to be surprised to hear this." She leaned toward me, smiling. "I'm living in your house." She waited a second, watching my face, and laughed again. "I'm renting it. Your grandparents gave me a lease until your family comes back or . . . whatever." She smiled again.

Her face was so beautiful that I had trouble thinking about what she'd said. Strangely, none of her features were fine or perfect. By themselves her eyes were too small, her nose was big, her mouth was usual and plain until she smiled. But together all her features worked to make her beautiful, almost exotic. And there wasn't a freckle or bump on her whole face. Even though she was more of a redhead than anything else, she didn't have the complexion that usually comes with one. My mother and I weren't even true redheads; and yet when the sun came out we looked like Howdy Doody. I forgot myself and stared.

Her eyes were a grayish blue like the stone she wore, and she had a full skirt with pockets. It fell loosely around her legs, and her blouse was a simple white sleeveless one. But best of all, when I glanced down out of the embarrassment of her catching me staring at her, I saw she had on black single-strap shoes like dancers wore.

The strangest thing about her face was that her front tooth was chipped. It was crazy—on anybody else it would have looked awful. But on her, it made her look like a tomboy who'd grown up and gotten appealing. In fact, as I categorized her quickly, I knew that she was somebody who *did* it, and *liked* it.

"You going to be here for a while?" She was opening her purse and taking out money.

"Yeah, I guess."

"You'll have to come over. I didn't move anything in your room. I didn't have any furniture for it anyway. But it's such a pretty room. Your mother must have spent a lot of time on it."

"Yeah," I said. "She likes dressing me up—even my room." I laughed a little. She was smiling at me.

"I'm Betty Jane Norris," she said, placing her hand across her shoulders as though claiming herself. Then she smiled again. "Most people call me B.J. And isn't your name Sally?"

I shook my head. "I guess everybody in Coldwater knows everybody else—even before they meet."

"Well," she laughed, "everybody knows your grandfather. Anyway, I lived outside of town on the other side of the Soybean Plant for a while, so I knew something about Coldwater even before I moved in. There aren't many places to rent around here. Nothing nice anyway."

"I guess not," I said.

Mrs. Barber came to the cash register and punched a key that made the drawer fly open. "Will that be all?"

"Yes." B.J. handed Mrs. Barber a dollar.

"Well, thank you and come back." Mrs. Barber handed B.J. her change. Before she turned, B.J. looked back at me. "It was nice to meet you." As she walked away, I stared at her shoes. In them she barely made a sound.

"She tell you she's renting your house?" Mrs. Barber was looking at me.

"Yes ma'am," I said.

"Well, your grandmother's not too happy with that. But I

hear Miss Norris was the only one willing to sign a lease that would make her get out on a day's notice if your parents came back." Mrs. Barber wiped the counter in front of me. I'd let the ice cream drip all over. "I guess it's better than leaving the house empty. Last winter the pipes froze and leaked. But you probably know about that."

I nodded. I already had down pat the signal to say that I understood even if I didn't. And I also knew how to keep Mrs. Barber talking. I rearranged the salt and pepper. "What's my grandmother unhappy about?"

"Oh, . . ." Mrs. Barber wiped in circles. "I don't think it's fitting for a girl your age to know. Especially since you might move back into that house and spend the rest of your life there."

"I don't think I will," I said. Obviously Mrs. Barber saw me as a potential old maid like Miss Pankhurst, who lived in her parents' house because no one asked her to live anywhere else. "What's wrong with Miss Norris?" I asked.

That, of course, was the right question for Mrs. Barber. Now she didn't think about what she was telling anybody. She bore down on B.J. like a buzzard onto a starving dog. "Well . . ." she started. She rinsed out her rag. "She came here with Sam Best when he returned a few months ago from his orphanage in Peru. She'd supposedly been working down there. But if you ask me, no nuns would even let her near an orphan. She was probably the cook, though I doubt she can boil water. Anyhow, Sam said he hired her to run his jewelry store. Now Ellen probably thought otherwise; that might just be one reason she up and left Sam and moved her and Julie to Little Rock. Though Sam's a good man and's never done wrong by Ellen. But Mr. Allgood *did* die last winter, and we haven't had any place to get wedding gifts. So Sam really did need someone to run the jewelry store. But someone from Peru! She doesn't look like no Peruvian to me. Does she to you?

"Anyway, this Betty Jane Norris, or B.J. as she likes to be called, took over Mr. Allgood's business. 'Course Sam owned all the merchandise anyway. Then lo-and-behold if she doesn't take up with a man working on the pipeline. So if Ellen moved out because of B.J. coming to run the jewelry store, she might as well come back. They say all sorts of things go on in that house of yours. And that girl doesn't seem to give a hoot about anybody seeing what time a day that man comes and goes. It's driving your grandmother nuts. And to make matters worse, the girl's started singing and dancing—if you want to call it that —at the Silver Moon. She's the midnight show and believe-you-me I hear she's a good one." Mrs. Barber pshawed on her last word, which sounded a lot like a gigged frog. I'd heard there were strippers at the Silver Moon, and I guessed that was what Mrs. Barber was talking about. She looked at me. "Now tell me how your mother is."

"Fine."

"She going off to cut a record?"

"I guess," I said, thinking how ugly Mrs. Barber could make recording a song sound—like maybe it was something nice people didn't do.

When Mrs. Barber walked her swirling rag farther down the counter, I got off my stool. I stood looking in the mirror a second. I didn't like my face, but I stuck out my tongue more on general principles than anything else. What was wrong with going off to make a record, if that's what my mama wanted to do? And what was so bad about getting rid of me so she could do it? My mother'd probably already be famous and singing on TV if she hadn't had to stay home and make me get in the bathtub so I'd look halfway decent when I hid in the alley behind the dime store and swapped naked peeks with Bobby Watts, who my mother probably already knew would end up a loser.

I went outside and was just about to take the long way home when someone pushed my shoulder from behind. " 'Cuse me."

I stepped back and moved against the drugstore wall. Joel Weiss passed in front of me carrying a bundle of newspapers. He put them in his bike basket. While I'd been in Memphis, he'd obviously gotten the job of delivering the *Arkansas Gazette*, which was the only daily paper people in Coldwater could get. The *Coldwater Gazette* came out just on Fridays. So every day on a bus from Little Rock the daily paper came. But before Joel pushed his bike around the corner, he stopped and looked at me. He had on shorts and a T-shirt with the sleeves rolled up, which showed off his biceps nice. His legs were hairy and tan and he wore short socks. He grinned sort of crooked and shook his head slowly. "Aren't you hot in that getup?"

I lifted one shoulder. I tried curling my lips real cute as if saying, *So what, I can't help it.*

He turned around and rode his bike across the street. In the year I hadn't seen him, Joel had grown as tall and good-looking as Bobby Watts had grown pimply and ridiculous.

I walked down the street, and every once in a while I'd catch my reflection in a store window. Inside my chest the knot was like a melon, swelling up to bust. I turned into the alley behind the dime store and the Mercantile, and in the indentation where Bobby Watts and I had done our sordid business I leaned over and grabbed the bottom of my skirt. I hid my face in it, catching a hint of Tide and Niagara Starch. My mother had made that dress. And that lady named B.J. had said it was beautiful. But what did she know? It was a lie. I took the hem of my shirt in each hand and tore a line straight up the middle of it.

When I got home, I told my grandmother that I'd gotten caught on a barbed wire fence running away from a bull. She had to take paregoric and go to bed. Then I sat, mean and quiet, beside my grandfather, watching "Lassie" on TV. I could have shot everybody on that show—even the dog. The ball under my ribs came back and took up its spot like I was its nest.

Pretty soon I'd probably have to hitchhike straight on out of town. It was just in my nature to ruin things.

6.

An Afternoon at the Mill Pond

Misery crawled on my skin like bedbugs. I'd gotten out of my family and had no one to mess with me but grandparents so old they ought to have been easy to outsmart. I couldn't put my finger on one minute of fun. My grandmother even insisted on those Tara dresses for school. And now I had to walk around with my shoulders humped, making me look even more flat-chested and ugly, to hide the knot that had taken up permanent residence in the middle of my chest. The world was a greased walkway. It was not any kind of a place I could trust. I was so bad that the sidewalk might open up to swallow me whole as I walked home from school, taking the slow route down Main. Ordinarily I'd have gone on down to the Rexall's. But every-body there was dumb and silly and didn't know anything about real life. Maybe this was the day I ought to hitchhike on out to Hollywood. But somebody as plain as me might not get a job right off. Still, there was no doubt about it, magic was out there. Somebody as big and fat as Kate Smith could end up looking half good. At least a lot of people seemed to love her, and yet if you knew her up close, she might turn out to be a terrible person, a real bona fide asshole. But she was famous and loved.

Passing on the street in front of me was a truckload of Mexi-cans. I stood by the Mercantile to watch them. Every fall, they were driven across the border to towns like Coldwater, for cotton picking. Their coming had no announcement and no forewarning. I would hear about it one day in school when one of the farm kids whispered: "They're here—done come in the night." This meant that particular kid wouldn't have to stay out of school anymore to spend every afternoon picking cotton himself. When the cotton was all picked, usually sometime in early November, just after Halloween, the Mexicans would be loaded onto the backs of trucks and driven out of Arkansas as quickly as they had come.

Now as I watched them riding past in the back of that truck, it seemed to me they were having a grand time. One of them was young and good-looking. And when they were halfway down Main, I stuck out my thumb for a ride. The one I'd liked was sitting near the tailgate, and he saw me and smiled. He had gorgeous teeth—so white they reminded me of the whirl of lights at a carnival. Then the truck turned.

They might come back to hunt me up looking for a good time. On Saturday they'd be back for sure. Every Saturday all the migrant workers came into town and filled the stores and went to the cafés and ate turnip greens and cornbread and the Mexicans talked the whole time in a language that no one else could understand. They stood on the streets and rode up and down Main in the backs of trucks, and some people, like my grandmother, didn't much like the Mexicans being there. They were good for the economy, but my grandmother thought of them as something like a lower form of evolution. It'd been heard that out on Hersham's Farm, which was the biggest in our county, that they'd relieve themselves almost anywhere. It was talked about at the bridge clubs and the Missionary Society, though not much at the Rotary Club; the men didn't seem to care. But it was said that if you went to the fields during the day and you stayed there long enough, you were bound to see several of the cotton pickers walk to the edge of the field and proceed. Sometimes they would even use the lawn of their employer. But they always left the field; it seems they had that respect for cotton.

I didn't much blame them. I'd picked cotton a few times. It must have been about when I was in the fifth grade. Walking home from school, I'd seen a couple of my friends working in the long rows in one of the town fields that came up to the back of the ball field. I'd always heard a lot of talk about how much a person could pick—forty, fifty, sixty pounds. A hundred was real good. I was curious to see what I could do, so I took one of my friend's bags and joined in. It wasn't a damn bit of fun. The bag was heavy; it fit over my shoulder and dragged on the ground. The rows seemed endless, the sun outright mean. Pretty soon my mouth was so dry it felt about like I'd been sucking on the damn cotton. If I'd had to go to the bathroom, I wouldn't have walked all the way back to some bunkhouse, either.

Now, after I'd cut loose and given one of those Mexicans my most dazzling smile, he was probably going to come back looking for me. I guessed I'd just go on back to Mexico with him. Might be I'd end up with a house full of Mexican babies. I could send my grandmother Christmas cards with a picture of all of us on it. It'd be too far away for my parents to visit, which they wouldn't mind. Or I could just go on out to Hollywood and send those Mexican babies to my grandmother to raise. I ducked into the dime store and walked up one of the aisles.

Mr. Weiss, who owned the store, was sitting on a stool behind the cash register with his sleeves rolled up and his dark oversized forearms coming out like hairy pipes. "How're you?" he asked, looking up from a magazine at me.

"Fine."

"You glad to be back?"

"Yessir."

"How're your folks?"

"Fine."

"You heard from them lately?"

"Yessir. They write me a lot. And they call." Which was the truth. But I wasn't opening the letters. I was fed up with phony stuff about how they cared about me. I didn't want to hear junk that wasn't the truth. It was a waste of my time. I was stuffing their letters in my suitcase under the Man-from-Shiloh's bed. "My mother's making a record," I said, which might be the truth. "She's probably gonna be on the 'Dinah Shore Show.'" I could even lie good.

"Well, wouldn't that be fine."

"Yessir."

"You'll let me know when, won't you?"

"You'll be the first to know." I smiled.

Mr. Weiss was bald and the dome of his head glistened. "Anything I can help you find?"

"No sir, I'm just looking."

"Make yourself at home then." He looked down at a magazine again.

The floors were scuffed hardwood, and creaked. I guess he could know exactly where I was every minute. He was Jewish, and there were only two Jewish families in Coldwater. The other one was Guy Levy who owned the bank. And since there was no synagogue within two hundred miles, I wasn't sure what arrangements they had with the Almighty Powers, or even what they believed in.

I used to see Guy Levy sitting in his walled-off cubicle whenever I went to the bank with my mother. Everyone called him

Guy, but we all knew his real name: Eshek. That sounded so much like "oh shit" that for a while my friends and I used it as a substitute for swearing in public. Then I found out that Eshek was listed in one of the begot paragraphs in the Bible. My grandmother said Jewish people usually gave their sons names from the Old Testament, not only because they didn't believe in the New Testament, but also because they thought there was the possibility their first-born son would be the Messiah. Well, Guy Levy had a son, Benjamin, who was three grades ahead of me; and he had dark curly hair and a large nose and wore glasses. I would sit in the school cafeteria, looking at him and comparing him to Jesus. Frankly, I couldn't believe it.

My grandmother had already passed me several pearls about Jews. She said they were big eaters and were oversexed. She told me that I must not ever get into a car with one. Guy Levy was wealthy, though—very wealthy. He owned a lot of the town and most of the houses people rented. My grandmother said that if Benjamin Levy ever stopped the car for me, it would be all right to get in. In fact, she encouraged it. But Joel Weiss, Mr. Weiss's son—now, he was a different story.

I walked down the makeup aisle and stood politely thumbing through the nail files. In front of me was this picture on a poster of a gorgeous girl with auburn hair and a smile that could melt taffy and inch-long fingernails like my mother's, painted ruby. My fingernails were bitten off. I walked down all the other aisles and came back. And after I glanced to see if Mr. Weiss was still reading his magazine, I slipped a tube of lipstick in between the pages of my math book like it was a pencil marking a spot.

"Bye," I said, walking out.

Mr. Weiss looked up, smiling. "Didn't find anything you just couldn't live without?"

"Not this time."

"Well, you come back now."

Outside in the hot sun I made a getaway toward the Mill Pond. The stream was the one that had given Coldwater its name, and it emptied into the river where I'd gone to fish with my father. The bank rose in a long graceful curve, perfect for manicured lawns. Everybody who lived on that street was rich. That's why my grandmother wanted to move there. That was one of the things about the outhouse that was rubbing her raw. She was the only person in Coldwater who had to look at it all the time.

I walked along the street, studying the houses. There were only six. Three of them belonged to parts of the Best family and one was Eshek Levy's. The others were Miss Pankhurst's and the Coldwater Funeral Home. I stopped and hid in some bushes near Miss Pankhurst's house and opened my math book. The tube of lipstick I'd swiped was some dumb color called Purple Midnight. It'd look awful on me.

Coming around the curve, and thumping some of the houses' front steps with a thrown folded paper, was Joel Weiss. I stood to one side of the huge house that was the funeral home and hid myself in an azalea bush. Joel was a year ahead of me in school and always spent a lot of time at the Lucky Lion, a pool hall at the edge of town, which his father also owned. All through primary school, Joel's mother would pack foreign foods in his lunch box. I knew what they were, because for a while Mrs. Weiss set up a counter in the dime store. Everyone who went in came out with something kosher. It was Mrs. Weiss's hope to start a deli, but the farmers' tastes were already too set on turnip greens and salt pork. Once I saw her talk a man into trying a bagel, and when he got outside he threw it down, saying he had no use for a stiff donut so old the sugar had fallen off.

I watched Joel weave his way down the street past the hearse parked in front of the funeral home and take a short cut at the end of the street through a car lot. He scooted under a streamer that said YOU AUTO BUY NOW.

I stood to the side of the funeral home. Just as I was about to leave my hiding spot, the door opened and Tommy Walters came out. I'd heard he'd gotten a job at the funeral home, driving hearses and learning the inside details of the business. Everybody was real happy for him. His mother was a widow, very poor. And it was a fine setup for him, everybody said. But I had also heard he couldn't get a date anymore.

I didn't want to be seen, so I sat down behind the bushes and leaned over, easing the pain in my chest where the knot was like tight fingers squeezing my shoulders together. Probably that was one reason I wasn't too worried about getting caught stealing. Something worse was going to happen. This thing inside me was a tumor, a cancer. It would spread. It was only a matter of time before I'd probably be in the funeral home with Tommy Walters working on me. It made me sick to think about that. But maybe if I wouldn't know about it at the time it might not be so bad. And I could see my parents coming to my funeral. They'd be relieved I was gone. Yet they'd cry and grab each other for support, putting on a good show and all, and then they'd get back together. I'd die and they'd get back together over it. I'd have done it. I'd have made everything all right. Tommy Walters got in the hearse and started the engine. And I watched him drive off.

Crossing the street was someone who for a minute I didn't recognize. And then she half-trotted, or almost skipped, into the field beside the funeral home. Overgrown with bushes and tall weeds, this field had once been a pecan grove. Even though I didn't see her face, I recognized B.J.'s clothes and also the way she walked. I had never seen anyone move like that, almost as though she didn't touch ground. I also thought that I would have to be paid to walk through a field like that in shoes like hers, because of the snakes. But before B.J. reached the end of the field and turned onto the path beside the Mill Pond, I was tromping down knee-high Johnson grass and stepping on rotten pecan shells, trying to follow her. If I stepped on a fat moccasin, surely I would black out before he bit me.

By the time I got through the field, B.J. was halfway down the path behind Miss Pankhurst's house. I stood a minute and looked across the Mill Pond. It was very shallow here. Some kids had built a footbridge out of planks, flattened cartons, and a couple of juice cans. On the other side, a bunch of long-horned cows and their calves grazed under trees. I set down my books and sugar-footed it across the makeshift bridge, then walked a little way to some bushes, where I hunkered down, folding my skirt around me, to watch as B.J. went up the long sloping backyard of Sam Best's.

Until the cow came toward me, I hadn't even noticed her. But then I saw she wasn't looking at me too kindly. And in another second she was coming at me full force, her head lowered and the horns curved like ice tongs aimed for the middle of my Tara dress. I took off in the opposite direction and nearly bumped into the cow's calf, who must have come up beside the tree I had been hiding behind. I twirled around on my Popeye legs and headed sideways. I had to get anywhere else except between the mother and her calf. I headed straight for the railroad trestle that went over the Mill Pond.

I climbed onto one of the concrete footings that held up the bridge and spent a while just breathing. Then I leaned out to look at the cow. She was standing near the water. "Asshole!" I said. Her calf loped up beside her and started nursing.

Now I could hear the sound of people talking on Mr. Best's

back porch. Then the screen door opened and Gill Williams, Sam Best's driver, along with Sam Best and B.J., came out. They went to the patio on the lawn. B.J. leaned her head toward Mr. Best and rested her hand on his arm. The patio was almost hidden behind a clump of gardenia bushes beside an oak tree. If I hadn't been sitting under the train trestle I couldn't have seen them. B.J. was talking, but I could only hear the tone of her voice. Then Gill brought a tray with drinks on it. I'd heard my mother talk about Gill; he'd brought her tomatoes and stuff out of Mr. Best's garden. Sometimes Gill had sat out in the yard with us at night, cooling off and swapping stories. His chest was sunken because he'd lost a lung in the war. He'd been a pilot, and whenever the weather was cool he wore a leather aviator's jacket. His face was the color of a baseball glove and looked about as punched as one.

I heard B.J. laugh. She talked to Mr. Best the whole time she sipped her drink. Then after a while she bent down, put her glass on the tray, and kissed him. That seemed odd to me, seeing as how Sam Best loved my mother and B.J. was supposed to be carrying on with some man who just about lived in my parents' house. She smiled at Mr. Best and walked to the Mill Pond path to start back the way she'd come. Sam Best watched her go. Then he leaned his head back and closed his eyes.

When I looked into the Mill Pond to compare my face with B.J.'s, the big flat-pointed head of a moccasin was coming downstream. My breath sucked in so loud that the cow stopped grazing. I stood up and flattened myself against the concrete, and the cow snorted. The snake saw me, or smelled me— whatever the hell it is that snakes do. Maybe he only liked the dry spot where I was, but he sure seemed businesslike in my direction. I stepped out of my hiding place and climbed up the embankment to the top of the trestle, grabbing clumps of bitterweed to help pull myself up with. The snake crawled onto my former spot and stretched himself out to dry. "Shithead!" I called down to him. Then I stood up on the railroad track and looked around.

Sam Best seemed asleep, and the cow lay down in the shade below me. Across the highway at the Dairy Dip I could see Joel's bike propped against the side wall, and farther down the highway the tin roof of the Lucky Lion glinted in the sun that now was lowering in the sky behind Mr. Best's house.

The railroad track smelled like creosote. It was too late in the season to think of anything as being green or lush, but the dryness of the earth and its toning down was a sort of lushness, too. Spring might be the catchy season, but knowing what I knew now—being a woman—fall was also a sexy time. The whole earth was lying back, looking as though it were going to drop its fruit and sleep a while, yet quietly underneath it was scattering seeds like crazy. And standing up there, it seemed that all the colors in the world were overripe, fierce, and too bright. It was said that when you were dying, things got special—colors got bright, minutes could swell into hours. Then I realized that I was mad as hell about that. All this shouldn't be happening to me. I probably ought to tell my grandfather about the knot. I probably ought to let him or somebody else cut it out. When my parents found out that I was dying, surely they'd do something special about it. It seemed that every kid I'd ever read about who died got to go to Disneyland first. Hell!—why couldn't they get back together in Disneyland?

I stomped a little on the railroad ties, and then I hopped onto the rail in a sort of step-ball-change that started both feet flying out in a rhythm that in another minute settled into a tune. I twirled my skirt and as it lifted from my waist I saw it as an umbrella, and in another two seconds I was doing "Singing in the Rain" up and down the rails in the driest season of Arkansas. Next I added the words with a full orchestra in my head; and the magic of it was even greater than on the big screen at the Ritz. I could have danced all over the stage at the county talent show and won the whole damn thing. But I was nearly fourteen years old now, and dying. I was bad enough to bust up a family and steal from a dime store. It was only a matter of time until I landed up in the State Reformatory School. But I wouldn't have to stay there long. The Coldwater Funeral Home was next. And while the sun turned the color of a peach and burst open behind the high peak of Sam Best's house, I twirled toward the highway and looked straight at Joel Weiss, who was standing beside his bike behind the Dairy Dip watching me. "Oh shit," I said, and turned away, facing the sun. Below me Mr. Best was watching me too. And beside him Gill was in the seat B.J. had been in, eating potato chips out of a bag. His eyes in his baseball-mitt face were like two knuckleballs aimed on my Popeye legs that had gone crazy under the Tara dress. "Damn," I said. No doubt the cow and snake were watching too. The only sure way out of this would be if I got run over by a train.

Almost in answer, something rumbled through the rails, and the light switch down the track signaled green. When the feeling of thunder came up through my feet, I jumped off the side of the trestle straight into the Mill Pond. And not a sound came out of my throat.

I hit the water holding my nose so the muddy stuff wouldn't go up it. But my head didn't even get wet. My feet went straight into the deep muck on the bottom, and I stood chin-deep in the Mill Pond staring at the moccasin. He probably didn't want me any more than I wanted him. Though maybe he'd been sent for me. Even if he was my punishment for being so damn rotten, I sure as hell wasn't going to sit still for him.

I stepped out of my shoes on the bottom and swam in an

Esther Williams breaststroke, with my lips pinched together. The snake was going upstream, but he didn't seem to be moving against the current and I was sure he and I would end up together no matter where I aimed.

"He ain't after you," someone said. A leafy branch fell on the top of my head. I put my hands in the leaves and looked up to the bank at Joel. "You sure can dance." He pulled the branch toward him, with me hanging on it.

"Let's get her out on this side." Gill was on the opposite bank, holding out a garden hoe in my direction.

Standing a little behind him was Mr. Best. And he was staring at me. "You're as pretty as your mama," he said, his eyes still on my face. "And when you sing, you sound just like her."

Above us there was a clattering on the rails. I grabbed the end of Gill's hoe, and we all looked up. A little cart with railroad workers passed over, two of the men pumping the thing down the rails as if they were seesawing. They waved.

"You're gonna smell awful." Joel laid his tree branch down. "I bet your grandmother won't let you in the house."

I was out of the Mill Pond now, standing on the bank with Gill and Sam Best. Joel was on the other side with the trestle between himself and the cow. I was dripping water the color of coffee, and I smelled dead.

"Gill, take her up to the house and get her a towel," Sam Best said.

"That's all right." I looked down at my feet. Holes were in my socks and weeds were stuck between my toes. My grandmother would really give me the business. I'd lost my shoes. They were stuck in the bottom of the Mill Pond and would probably stay there unless they popped up and floated like something dead. "I'd better just go on home," I said.

"I think that dress looks better wet." Joel was wiping the mud off his shoes. "Before, it stuck out like a tent."

"Don't make fun of the girl," Mr. Best said. "You don't know anything about fashion. Gill, get her a towel."

Gill pulled me up the sloping bank and I trotted to the back door. Sam had gotten a towel and was wiping my arms. Joel walked back to the highway.

"Where'd you learn to dance?" Mr. Best was squeezing water out of my hair, using the towel as a blotter.

"I didn't," I said.

He shot my feet with water from a hose.

"You know how, just naturally?"

"I guess. My mother taught me for a while. But then she quit. And my grandmother said I shouldn't do it anymore."

He turned off the hose. "Why?"

"She says it'd develop my calves. And they don't need any more developing."

Gill came and put a towel around my shoulders and another one around my waist. My hair was like mud-coated strings. "I think I'd better go on home," I said.

"No need to walk." Sam told Gill to drive me. Then he reached for the end of a towel and wiped my face with it. "I'll go call your grandmother and explain what happened. If I was you, I'd want to warn her before I just drove up."

My head was down, but I could tell he was still looking at me.

Gill put newspapers in the backseat of Sam Best's Land Rover and I slid in, making crinkling noises as I did. It looked like the kind of car somebody would drive in Africa. Yet I was too much of a mess even for it.

Then, before we drove off, something so very strange happened it was as if the afternoon stopped. It was like a minute had been caught, taken and framed to hang in my mind. And it began with Sam Best reaching into the back window and touching my hair. Yet this time he wasn't wringing it out, and he wasn't worried about me being wet.

He looked at me, and then still looking at me, he laughed. But it wasn't a laugh like somebody making fun. It was instead a low sound that felt to me as warm as sun stirring around in the dark of leaves, or something like that. And I laughed too. With my mud-coated hair and memories of the snake, I felt like the Medusa. I could see by the way he looked at me and by his laugh, which now met mine, how funny it all had been. It hadn't been so awful. It wasn't even quite so embarrassing anymore. And then Gill put the Land Rover in gear.

As we drove off, I turned around to see Sam Best still standing, watching. The way he had looked at me was there on the inside of my eyelids when I turned around and looked out at the street and the houses going by, and then the magnolia in front of my grandparents' house. And it may have been the world I was looking at, but inside my head I was seeing the way Sam Best had looked at me, where it was stuck now like a photograph. The trail of cuss words I left, that never got past my mouth, was as blistering and mean as the aimed barrel of a bazooka. Because Hell! why was it *me* who had to die to make everything all right?

7.

The Return of Foster Collins and the Poodle Substitute

In the next few days I nearly died from the fear that my mother was dead and nobody knew it. Or that my father had gone out to some farm to see about some equipment to insure and had gotten run over by something like a combine. They were crazy, unconnected fears; they made no sense. And because I couldn't sleep or do much of anything else but wonder if my parents were alive—I even failed a P.E. test—I got out the letters from under the Man-from-Shiloh's bed and read them. They didn't say much. Just day-to-day stuff about what my mother and father were doing. It was night and my grandparents were asleep, and I went into the back hall and called my mother from the phone there. It took my mother five rings for her to answer.

"It's me," I said.

"Sally?"

"Yeah."

"Is everything all right?"

My damn heart was beating like a bongo, and the fist inside my chest was swelling up. For a minute I thought I'd die on the spot. My grandparents would find me in the morning, dead in the hall. But at least *she* wasn't dead. "I just kind of wanted to talk to you a minute," I said. "You going to Jackson Friday?" Her last letter had said she was.

The conversation went on about like that—with me saying a few things about what I was doing, and her telling me about the places she was going to sing. Then, since I thought I'd save my grandparents the cost of another long-distance phone call so I could check up on my father, I told my mother that my grandmother had said my father was sick and that it was serious. My mother laughed. "Nanny Maulden tends to blow up everything. He's probably just had a little cold. I really wouldn't know. Haven't you heard from him?"

"No'm," I lied—at least I hadn't read his letters until in the last few minutes and they hadn't said much of anything. And the only person in the whole world who ever called my grandmother Nanny Maulden was my own mother and father when they were talking to me about her.

"Well, he's just been traveling a lot, so maybe that explains it," she said.

There was this minute of silence. She was smoking a cigarette; I could tell. I was dying to tell her about the tumor in my chest. I knew that it would scare the peedoodle out of her. She'd probably cancel her rehearsals and even call my dad. I'd be the center of attention; and then I'd start feeling guilty over that, even though I'd probably get a real bang out of it. At least if I was the center of attention again, it wouldn't be because I was in the middle of a fight. In fact, when somebody was dying didn't everybody get real quiet and sweet? I stared at the pictures over the phone table in the hall. "You ever thought about going to Disneyland?"

She laughed. I'd made her laugh. But I hadn't meant to. "Lord, honey," she said, "a trip like that would cost a million dollars. And I'm in the middle of rehearsing for a record. I couldn't go even if I wanted to."

"But isn't it out near Hollywood?" I picked my thumbnail.

"We could kill two birds with one stone—you know what I mean?"

She laughed again. I'd turned into a goddamn comedian.

We shot the bull a little bit longer. I even said that I was probably going to fail P.E. She told me all about the songs she was going to sing on the album. (She really was going to make a record!) She even hummed a few bars on a couple of them, and then we both hung up.

But they weren't dying. My mother and father weren't dying. *I* might be. And I was bad and mean, and I thought mean thoughts. But at least it wasn't going to be a triple funeral. Anyway, ever since I'd fallen in the Mill Pond everybody had been treating me like I had a bad disease—and it had nothing to do with the knot inside my chest, which nobody but me knew about. I'd waked up with Louella leaning over my bed. "Sugar, your grandmother says you jumped off a railroad track and nearly got bit by a snake." Louella was Ezekiel's niece. She was skinnier than I was and still a head taller. She'd been married once but she said it wasn't sweet for her, and she sure didn't plan to do it again.

"But I thought a train was coming," I said. "Only it turned out to be just one of those little fix-it carts."

Louella handed me my robe. "Well, shoot, I'd have jumped too."

"And I wasn't jumping off the bridge to kill myself like my grandmother thought."

Louella studied me. She wore a white uniform, with plum juice stains on it, and tennis shoes that had cut-out holes for corns that she always put my grandfather's medicine on.

Getting thrown out of a family can make a person look suspect. My grandmother sure didn't want me to look crazy. And I wasn't crazy. I told my grandmother I wouldn't have been up on any railroad trestle for any other good reason than to get away from a cow.

Louella walked out talking about French toast and bacon, squeezed juice and fresh plum jelly. Then she stopped and looked back at me. "I so glad that train didn't run over you or you get gored by no bull."

Louella was the only person in my family who still might love me, I thought. For according to my grandmother, Louella was blood kin since the whole Negro race was descended from Noah's son Ham. My grandmother had told me many times that story about when Noah came off the ark and he had three sons: Shem, Ham, and Japeth; and since everybody else was dead from the flood, from these three the whole earth was peopled.

She would read me Genesis 9, 18–27—all that stuff about Noah running a vineyard and one day getting drunk and falling asleep naked. She would tell me how Ham saw his father and told his brother. If Ham was giggling, neither my grandmother nor the Bible said. But anyway, the story goes that Shem and Japeth politely took a blanket, laid it on both their shoulders and walked backward to cover their naked father with it. All the time, they were turning their faces away so they wouldn't see Noah in his embarrassing position.

So when Noah woke up and found out what his youngest son Ham had done (and the Bible doesn't say either if Shem and Japeth told on Ham) he was furious. He put a curse on Ham's son, Canaan, saying all the children of Canaan and his children's children would be slaves forever. And supposedly this was Louella's distant relative, which also meant that she was related to me—and also to my grandmother, which my grandmother totally overlooked.

But I found out that Noah didn't have Ham until he was five

hundred years old. No doubt he was burned out from childrais-
ing and his sons had driven him to drink on the day he woke
up cursing. My grandmother should have been sympathetic to
that. And the verses say nothing about Ham or his son Canaan
being black, yellow, or any other thing. I decided that was the
part that was magic. It seemed that words could be found written down somewhere to support anything. You could lift them
off the page, and by themselves they could mean whatever you
wanted them to.

So, according to my grandmother, everybody descended
from Ham was supposed to be a servant. She said they enjoyed
it—proof of this was just listening to them sing. But plenty of
times I'd heard Louella in the bathroom cussing out the rings
on the tub. She was embarrassed when once I'd come in on
her. She cut down on her cussing after that. It just seemed to
me that my grandmother could never see Louella as someone
like herself. To her the Negro race was something like negative
prints to God's original design.

My grandmother also had told me that anybody who was not
Protestant and white liked sex better than almost anything.
So Protestants had to work doubly hard to keep Jews, colored
people, and Catholics from outnumbering them. Of course
Jesus himself was a Jew, but for that my grandmother forgave
him. Besides, he wasn't just any Jew, he was the King. In ad-
dition he had blue eyes, which made his heritage suspect. She
knew about this because on her grandfather's plantation there
had been some blue-eyed slaves. It proved they weren't all one
thing or another; something had gotten mixed in. Anyway, it
didn't matter if Jesus wasn't a blueblood, because the fact that
he had risen to be King (and even above) was in the best of
the American tradition.

I could remember her looking at me and asking me point-blank just how could any Christian like Jews for what they had done to Jesus? I'd always stare quietly back and switch my gum from one side of my mouth to the other. I didn't have an opinion on that, but I didn't want to just take hers. I'd already decided that somebody had to die to make the story of going to Heaven so good and lasting. If Heaven were supposed to be true, somebody had to test it, and in that case Jesus was the first guinea pig. It also made sense to choose somebody who was always pushing you to be better than you were. Socrates did and he got it. Indians scalped missionaries for teaching them about sin and making them feel so darned awful. And thinking about how she pushed me, always seeming to be dissatisfied with who I was, I began to wonder if maybe my grandmother might have to be sacrificed.

I heard her voice in the kitchen: "Now what in tarnation does he have?"

I went in and stood watching Louella flip French toast in a black skillet. My grandfather was coming down the alley from the direction of the post office. As he passed in front of the outhouse we saw he was carrying a wide, shallow box with holes in it. The cardboard was the same color as his hat and his pants, and he was smiling.

He came in the sun porch door and lay the box on the kitchen table. We heard high pinging sounds coming from it, like corn popping. "Well, girl," he said to me. "Maybe not as good as a poodle, but just about as cute." He grinned, took off his hat and wiped his head.

I looked into one of the holes on the side of the box. Inside must have been fifty baby chickens peeping like crazy and falling all over each other.

Louella looked through another hole. "Lord, they're cute,"

she said. "Can't be but a few days old."

"Closer to six." My grandfather stuck his finger in one of the holes. "And there's seventy-five of 'em."

When I took the lid off, my grandmother swallowed the air that ordinarily she would have breathed in.

My grandfather was talking fast. "Got 'em for nothing. Somebody ordered 'em and forgot to pick 'em up." He grinned. "The post office gave 'em to me just to get rid of 'em. One more day in the P.O. and they'd have died."

"Oh for Pete's sake." My grandmother closed her eyes. She smelled like coffee and her hair was loose.

My grandfather was looking at her. "If the girl can't have a dog she ought to have something."

My grandmother opened her eyes and said we'd have to take the chickens back.

"Can't." My grandfather looked at her. "If they go back to the P.O. they'll die. We have a chicken house; we can keep them till they grow up and sell off the ones we don't especially like."

"I don't like any of them," she said.

Louella and I put our hands into the yellow peeping mass, and Louella set one of the chicks in her palm and lifted it out of the box. "Ain't nothing cuter 'n a biddy," she said. They were the color of pale lemons and softer than cotton. I held one and rubbed it against my face.

"They must be hungry," I said.

My grandfather picked up the box. "They've got a little water and corn mash in the box." He started to the backyard and I followed him. "You don't have to be bothered," he called back to my grandmother. "Sally can join the 4-H now if she wants to."

My grandmother walked out the door and down the steps after us. She stopped in the alley near the outhouse. "I've already signed her up for the Daughters of the American Revolution and Children of the Confederacy. She's eligible for those through *my* family."

My grandfather stopped beside the garage and looked back at her. "4-H can't hurt."

My grandmother pshawed.

By late morning my grandfather and I had gotten all seventy-five of my chickens settled in the vacant chicken house. I'd gone uptown and bought a big sack of mash to feed them. Now my grandmother was calling us in to lunch. It seemed as if everybody was wanting to give me something to make sure I wasn't going crazy. My grandmother had told Louella to do up a big ham and make a chocolate cake, just for me.

When I went into the bathroom to wash up, the phone rang. It kept ringing and I guessed that my grandmother and Louella were busy setting the table, and my grandfather was still outside with my chickens, so I picked up the phone in the back hall. Just as I did, my grandmother answered the phone in the kitchen and I heard Miss Pankhurst talking breathlessly. She was shooting out words faster than I could think, and every one of them was about somebody named Foster Collins, who turned out to be the bus driver who'd driven us from Memphis.

I couldn't hang up; the click would tell them I'd been listening. So I just put my hand on the mouthpiece and listened some more. Foster Collins had turned up on Miss Pankhurst's front doorstep with the latest best-seller and they'd started trading books. He had told her that one reason he'd become a bus driver was so he could spend all those hours in hotels between trips indulging in what he called his habit. He read everything from Western fluff to *The Ugly American*. And then, on the bathroom phone, I heard Miss Pankhurst giggle.

In what she thought was only my grandmother's ear, she whispered that Mr. Foster Collins was not a handsome man, but he had a certain animal magnetism. She'd even invited him in for a cup of coffee. Then in a normal-sounding voice, she informed my grandmother that Foster Collins was on the way to our house with my hat with the streamers that had been left in the bus.

Before my grandmother had time to hang up, the magnetic bus driver was standing on our front screen porch. My grandfather had just come in from the backyard and he answered the door. Mr. Collins handed me my hat and my grandfather invited him to see my chickens while my grandmother invited him to stay for ham.

"Lord, they're cute," Foster Collins said as he knelt down and picked up one of my chicks. "What kind are they?"

"Don't know." My grandfather told him there was no information on the box. When the P.O. tried to reach the man who'd ordered them, the closest people with a phone said he'd moved.

Foster Collins squinted and turned the chicken over. All those chickens were supposedly mine, and I felt a little maternal. "I don't know much about chickens," Foster Collins said. "But I was raised on a farm. Separating sexes is an art. Not much to go on at this age. But right now, I'd say you have a good chance of owning about seventy-five White Leghorn roosters."

My grandfather leaned over and picked up a chick. He turned it over and rubbed his finger across its belly. "I don't see how you can tell."

Foster Collins laughed. I was a little embarrassed with the way he and my grandfather picked up one chick after another to examine their undersides. "They look like hens to me," my grandfather said. "But of course when I went to medical school, I didn't take chicken anatomy." He laughed and set down the last furry body, and Foster Collins stood up and said to me: "Well, a month from now you'll know."

My grandfather and I walked Mr. Foster Collins to the front yard. As he rounded the corner, I thought that Miss Pankhurst was uglier than I was, and if somebody could fall in love with her, it could probably happen to anybody. But then that cranked up another whole new mystery, because for the life of me I just couldn't imagine Miss Pankhurst as an object of desire.

After supper I went into my room and got that tube of Purple Midnight lipstick and gave it to Louella. It'd look better on her, and giving it away might even out my chances of staying out of Hell.

The fist in my chest wouldn't loosen its hold and let me go to sleep. It was probably close to midnight. Outside my window it was so dark that I could see only my own face, reflected on the glass from the nightlight my grandmother left on in the hall. The fist had worked its fingers all the way around to my back. I could barely breathe.

I went into the bathroom, feeling my way through the dark. I used towels to cushion the sound of my opening the medicine chest. Just as I hoped, there was a big bottle of my grandfather's Inside Medicine on the bottom shelf. I took two big swigs, forcing the swallows down, reminding myself of Mat Dillon in Kitty's saloon. I wasn't sure if I should put much faith in the stuff. But it was worth a try. I sat down on the closed toilet seat, waiting to see if my windpipe would open up and for the medicine to hit bottom. I could hear my chickens outside the window, their peeps soft and sweet-sounding. I thought about them sitting in the P.O., starving and not belonging to anybody. And now they did. All those seventy-five biddies belonged to me. Knowing what a sucker I was for anything small, soft, and pitiful, I'd probably even end up loving them. Damn stupid lucky chickens.

I can't say for sure if it was my grandfather's medicine or the sound of those chickens, but soon after I got back in the Man-from-Shiloh's bed, the fist loosened its hold in my chest and let me go to sleep.

8.

Going to Rathwell

In the morning the sun was a ball of fire I would have gladly shot out of the sky with a bazooka. I was sick of people thinking I might be crazy. And I didn't want to die. But if I didn't, how else would my parents get back together?

I fed my chickens and hit my hand against the hen house. So what if my parents did? What good would it be if I did die and my mother came to the funeral in a new black dress looking sexy and sorry? And my father came in a dark pin-striped suit, rumpled, half-shaven, looking loose with grief and feeling rotten and loving me and seeing my mother on the other side of the coffin looking sorry and sexy, and he falls in love with her all over again? *I* wouldn't be there.

My chickens had eaten up all the mash. And now about all seventy-five of them were trying to climb on top of my shoes, peeping and carrying on. I put the empty water bucket over my head and yelled, "Shitass!" so loud that the echo made my ears deaf.

What in hell are families good for anyway?

In my bedroom, I put on a ruffly blouse so the ruffles would fill in my chest when I pulled my shoulders forward to ease the pain of the fist. As I walked in to breakfast, my grandmother reminded me to not slouch over.

Right before I left for school I went into the bathroom, closed the door, and pounded on my chest. I drank half the bottle of my grandfather's Inside Medicine and refilled the bottle with water tinted with Listerine.

Suddenly I felt dizzy. I felt so funny and light-headed I got worried that maybe I'd drunk something out of the medicine cabinet that wasn't my grandfather's medicine. Maybe I'd poisoned myself, and I was about to die even sooner than I thought. I checked the label on the bottle I'd drunk out of. It said Maulden's Medicine on the front of it along with four big words as part of the ingredients and 14% alcohol. I walked to school. And, strangely, everything that happened there that day seemed fun. I tap-danced in my head through World History and took a trip to Japan during Study Hall. And then the rest of the day started off as being as ordinary as me.

I was walking home after school was over when I looked down the street to where my grandparents' house was and saw a Land Rover was parked out front. Sam Best and my grandmother came down the front porch steps. They looked toward Main at me, and then they both raised their arms and pointed in my direction. In another few minutes, the Land Rover came on down to the end of the street and met me.

Sam Best leaned out the back window: "Wanna go for a ride?" Gill Williams was driving, and he looked at me too. They both had on straw hats, the kind that almost all the men in Coldwater wore when they were out in the sun for a long time. Mr. Best held the door open for me. "I got to go out to Rathwell on a little business. We'll be back before supper. And your grandmother said yes."

Anything was better than an afternoon spent with my grandmother—especially since she'd already started polishing silver for the November Missionary Society meeting and made me help. I climbed in the Land Rover and settled myself on the leather seat beside Mr. Best. The cushions had papers and files stuck between them, and paper clips and pens were in the ashtrays.

We drove past fields of cotton where Mexicans were hunched over, trailing cotton sacks, stuffing them full. And while Sam Best asked me all kinds of stupid things about school, Gill bumped the Land Rover through land that Mr. Best owned, along paths barely wide enough to let us through.

Sam Best would study his crops of cotton and soybeans and rice, and sometimes he'd get out of the Land Rover and pick some, or stand at a fence rail and look at his cattle. The dust was so bad we had to keep the windows of the jeep closed to even breathe.

There's only so many cows and soybeans a person can look at and appreciate. And I was about ready to open up my geometry book and get a head start on that when Sam Best asked Gill to stop the car beside a cotton field. "Come on," he said, grabbing my hand and half-pulling me into it.

Mexicans were at the other end of the field, leaning over, dragging cotton sacks. They glanced up at us and then kept working. The dust made a film against the horizon. I was just on the verge of saying that I was about ready to go home. My grandmother would have a hissy fit if I wasn't there in time to eat, and it must be getting close to supper. And, too, I was so bored I could have spit.

Across the road were two shacks with colored children sitting on the porch watching us. A litter of puppies was rooting in the ditch. Gill had turned on the radio, and the weather report was rolling out of the Land Rover as if some man with a John Wayne voice was lying under the hood.

Sam Best reached down and picked up a clod of dirt and then hurled it down. The way he did made me jump. He didn't use any cuss words, but he let it be known that he was mad as hell just the same. It was the dirt he was mad at, or at least he said it was. Mad at it for being dry. For holding back. For playing him, and everybody else who depended on it, false, like a fickle woman who could never be pleased. I'd never seen such anger—coming quick, shooting out. It scared me, and yet I wanted to be with it. I could have reached down and thrown dirt myself.

But just as quickly as his anger had come, it left. He looked calmly down the row of cotton, then he looked at me and smiled. His face was so boyish; there was a white line just under the edge of his sideburns where the hair had been freshly cut and the skin hadn't been tanned by the sun yet. On either side of us, the cotton spread out in straight rows, and he waved his hand across it and looked at me. He was studying my face, smiling. "Looks just like jack rabbits playing ostrich, doesn't it?"

He picked some of the white hairy fiber out of the gray boll beside me and rubbed the seeds out of it. "Just like a jack-rabbit's tail," he said, reaching over, grinning and dusting my nose with it. I could smell shaving lotion on the skin of his hands. His pants were a dark khaki, almost the same color as the soil, and he wore a white shirt with the sleeves of it rolled up high onto his forearms. He was still watching my face. "I don't know about you," he said, "but I got a fine need for something cool. A Coke maybe, or a cup of ice cream. You won't tell your grandmother, though, if I ruin your supper?"

His head slanted a little, and he was watching me with a smile that looked as if any minute he was going to bust loose with a laugh. "Well? What is it? Coke? Ice cream? Or both together? And you won't tell your grandmother on me, will you?"

For a minute I couldn't think of anything to say. It was as if we'd been walking in this hot field and suddenly the sky had opened up and let loose with a shower. And this man who seemed like a whole piece of music, who could move quick from one part to another—from one mood of anger so hot it seemed murderous to a quiet, calm one two minutes later— had just asked me to play a trick on my grandmother.

"You're safe with me," I said.

He laughed and slapped his knee and made me run back to the Land Rover. The whole afternoon changed. It was as if Sam Best and Gill had gone in cahoots to punch a button on some crazy machine. Gill rolled down his window and took off his hat, and Sam Best did the same, and they started beating the side of the Land Rover as if we were part of a posse. They hooted and hollered and the dust rose in clouds, and we coughed and laughed, and Gill made that jeep zigzag down the road better than any ride at a carnival.

Sam and I were slipping around on the leather backseat, laughing and hollering like country bumpkins on the county fair Tilt-a-whirl. Then we turned the corner onto the only road in Rathwell. Gill slowed down, and we sat up in great dignity. We were sputtering laughs out the sides of our mouths like a bunch of kids tickled in church.

Rathwell was only a stopping place at a crossroads—a filling station, a store, and a church. I'd heard people say that it had soil so poor the Lord covered it over with dirt to hide the entrance gate to Hell. We walked across the porch of the store, which was lined with old men in overalls, rared back in cane-bottom chairs with their faces as wrinkled and brown as tobacco leaves. Inside, newsprint covered the walls; you could read an item from twenty or thirty years ago while buying a loaf of bread, if you cared to stand awhile. The air smelled musty, except for a trace of cinnamon candy and potato chips. Lined up on the counter was a train of tomatoes as red and ripe as the cherries on ice-cream sundaes. Sam knew everyone there: the clerk, the men on the porch.

Three colored children stood barefoot, barely able to see over the counter at the candy jars, and when Sam asked their last names, he said that he knew their families and gave them each a nickel. I went to the bathroom, a closetlike room at the back of the store with WHITE ONLY printed on the door. When I came back, Sam reached into a huge red cooler, his whole arm disappearing into ice water. "You ever think what it would be like if you couldn't use that?" He nodded toward the bathroom and pulled out an ice-cold dripping bottle of grape soda that he popped the cap off of and handed to me.

He walked across the store and bought pork skins and two beers, which he shared with Gill. He pulled his wallet out of his pocket, and as he paid I saw snapshots of Ellen and Julie in the little plastic slots in his billfold. The one of Julie seemed to be the yearbook picture from the time I hadn't lived in Coldwater. Having your picture in a wallet, looking good, and in a pocket like his would probably be pretty wonderful, I thought.

He led us across the dirt street into the pine-needle yard of the church. The late September light was dappled from the trees. The rust-colored dry ground smelled like pine-needle smoke. Gill sat down at one of the picnic tables that dotted the grounds. The white frame church, with "Mt. Olive" painted over its door, separated the yard from the high-grass field where I could see headstones with the faint color of wilted flowers on some of the graves.

"You going to tell about the murder?" Gill sat down on a picnic table and propped his feet on the bench. His Adam's apple was so big it gyrated when he talked, like a fishing bobber. He wore black aviator boots and the pork skins crackled as he ate them.

"Come here," Sam said to me and walked into the high-grass cemetery.

He pointed to a gravestone: Obidia Tews, 1803–1855. Beside it was Thomas Jacob Spade, 1811–1855. Linking them was a footstone, "Here they rest in peace."

We walked back to the church yard, and Sam smiled and suddenly lifted me to a table under a pine tree. I looked down at him, with the dry rasping sound of crickets and cicadas tuning up in the weeds behind us.

"It was a hundred years ago." He smiled. "You want to be the good guy, or the bad?"

I stood there like a dummy—a stupid dummy who couldn't talk. The question was simple. Then I got the idea that we were getting ready to act crazy and put on a play right there in the church yard. Yet I didn't know how to answer what he asked. I knew the truth: I was bad. I never told anybody off. I didn't make trouble. But inside, I was murderous.

For a minute, even though I was looking at Sam Best, I wasn't seeing him. I guess I was too busy seeing what was going on inside my head. Then I felt Sam Best touch my hand, and my eyes came back to focus on him. I knew I must have looked like a person in the middle of a stroke, or else frozen by craziness. But he didn't look at me as if I were pitiful or crazy. Instead he smiled, and then he put his arm around me and laughed. "Well, actually both of these guys was bad—so maybe, just for fun—you and I don't really have a choice." He went on then and told me the story of how Obidia Tews had been shot dead one day at a church fishfry by Tom Spade, in a quarrel over wages; and while he did he poured an imaginary drink into my half-empty soda bottle.

The trees stood breathless in the late afternoon as Sam Best came swaggering up, packing a make-believe pistol and yelling at me: "Get yor fishy smelling face over here!"

Gill hooted. The men on the store porch set their chairs down on all four legs to watch what they must have thought were two town people going crazy in their church yard.

We shouted insults and shadowboxed. We used sayings we'd grown up with and heard all our lives. "I'm going to cloud up and rain all over you," Sam said, his eyes squinted and mean.

I yelled: "Why don't you walk west until your hat floats!"

Then I danced around on the picnic table and suddenly Sam pulled his pointed-finger pistol from his belt and shot me. When I shot back, he fell instantly. He lay sprawled on the pine-needle ground; and then, like a dummy, I realized I had forgotten to fall dead myself.

His eyes were amused, and aimed steadily into the center of mine. I was so busy thinking about the chances of him ending up my stepfather that I just stood there, holding my arms around a make-believe wound and thinking about my mother. I could see her in my head, running off, chasing something like a hunger she could not name. Hell! couldn't she make a record and keep me and my father at the same time? But she had thrown me away—all of us. And Sam. And even though I knew that I was bad enough to deserve being dumped, I was still so mad about it that it would probably have been easy to commit murder for real.

"Isn't it about time you fell dead, or are you going to rewrite the script?" Sam looked at the imaginary bullet hole I was clutching in my middle.

When I fell beside him, we lay, our eyes open like grotesque dead people's are supposed to be, looking up at the sky. He said out loud: "You see that cat in that cloud there?" He rolled his head over to look at me and lifted his hand to point. In place of the anger I'd felt at my mother, there was a feeling so warm and fine now that it was like the afternoon was not close to October and growing dark and cool. It was a fine thing indeed that my mother had let Sam go. And me. I was free, lying on the pine needles beside him, his leg stretched out and touching mine. I knew every second that his chest went up with breath and came down, alive, beside me. And even if it was only his love for my mother coming toward me like a creek dammed and changing course, I didn't care. I was willing to settle for that.

"We got to go," Sam said and sat up.

There was a crisp, distant sound across from us that made me think of pine fat catching fire in winter. When I sat up I realized that the old men on the store porch were watching us and clapping.

Sam swung me into his arms and began a dance around the skinny pines, whose needles were dropping. The old men on the store porch laughed and changed their clapping into a rhythm, setting a beat that Sam Best and I, then Gill, danced to, laughing too, hooting at the cotton-white sky like three people gone berserk, wonderfully.

Twirling me to the side of the road, Sam stopped. "We got to hurry," he said and trotted back to the Land Rover.

I sat on the backseat beside him. I could smell the heat and the drying sweat on our skins. I glanced at him and the new sunburn on his arms and cheeks. If this was what my mother called love, and what she was making her life a mess over, I could see now what maybe all the fuss was about.

I didn't care where Sam and I went or what we did, as long as we were together.

9.

Sam and Me

The sun hadn't been up long. I sat at the Man-from-Shiloh's dresser. It must have been about seven. I'd just fed my chickens. I could hear them outside peeping and scuffling around on the ground, looking for more corn mash.

I pulled rollers out of my hair and smeared on Freckle Fading Cream. I sprayed on hairspray, making my hairdo stiff and disgusting, holding my nose so that the damn stuff wouldn't go up. Whatever good looks I could come up with had to last at least until three. Sam'd be there then—outside, in the Land Rover, under the magnolia tree. He always was.

The Land Rover would roll onto the grass beside the sidewalk in front of my grandparents' house. There in the shade, while Sam wrote business letters in the backseat, and Gill listened to the radio or slept, they would watch for me walking home from school. My grandmother always let me go with Sam. Nobody viewed it as a date. But it was a well-known fact to just about everyone: me and Sam were a couple about town. He was seen as a substitute father for me. And if he was a substitute for me, I was one for him, too. Yet, while I didn't especially like that, and knew he probably didn't, either, neither one of us wanted to spend time with anybody else.

Sam and I would go all over the county to the roadside restaurants or feed stores or car dealerships that he owned, and while he went over the books or talked with his managers, Gill and I would eat ice cream or buy gum, or get in all the new cars and push the buttons.

Now I could hear my grandparents moving around in their bedroom, talking. I didn't have much to do with them any-more, except for the stuff they made me do. Every night my grandmother put me up to doing some ankle-reducing exer-cises that she'd read about in some damn women's magazine. I decided the main reason that she thought thick ankles were so bad had nothing to do with thoroughbred horses, except maybe how they got born. For what she was actually wanting me to do was to get ready to attract the opposite sex about like I did my chickens when I walked into the chicken yard with a bucket full of mash. And apparently thin ankles were going to help me do just that, because they were so sexy. Of course, once I got to looking sexy—if I ever did—I'd have to deny I wanted anything to do with sex. In fact, almost all the women I knew who belonged to the category of those who *could*, *pre-ferred not to*. And here I was: learning to look like I wanted *it*, while all the time *it* was supposed to be the farthest thing from my mind. I felt sure that was a practice which, in the long run, could make a person crazy.

I walked down the sidewalk. The sun was still warm even though it was October. In the distance, I could hear my chick-ens peeping like the faraway sound of bells. It didn't mat-ter what happened at school. Nothing would bother me. The secret of Sam and me was like the fist, swelling inside me —only Sam's love wasn't squeezing me, and taking away my breath. Instead, it was like a warm sun, spreading out, melt-ing the fist, making it let go. It seemed that I wasn't going to die, not anytime soon at least. And the secret of thinking that

I would soon be dead gave way to the secret of my and Sam Best's love. Only this time, my secret didn't just set me apart from everyone else, it made me special. I could even pull the secret out and throw it around a little.

I walked home at three with a bunch of kids heading for the Rexall's, half of them country kids staying late for a ball game that night. I was beside Lucy Calhoon, who had an awful case of zits. "You going to the ball game?" She was looking at me, her poor face peppered like she'd fallen face-down in an ants' nest.

"Na," I said. "I got a date."

"You *do*?"

"Yeah. I'm serious with somebody, and he doesn't like ball games."

"Where do you go?"

"Just out—usually somewhere like a nightclub."

That, of course, set old Lucy Calhoon off. "What color hair does he have?"

"Dark," I said. "With light streaks." The light was the gray part, but I wasn't going to get specific.

"Is he romantic?"

"Always."

Lucy Calhoon was panting and rubbing her zits. And I was able to go on talking about Sam without anybody knowing who I meant.

Most afternoons Sam and I drove through some of the land that he'd inherited. Sometimes his voice would get so full of anger that I would sit quiet and still, half-scared but loving it. He'd rail against the ignorance of men, the capacity for cruelty, the poverty of so many lives, the ignorance and stubbornness of the South, and yet how much he loved it. Usually I didn't understand much of what he was saying. It was the shape of his mouth and the way it moved that took my attention. Once he'd laughed and then fumed about the sign in front of the Little Rock High School two years before, when colored kids had tried to go there: *This school closed by order of the goverment.* "G-o-v-e-r-m-e-n-t," he said, spelling it out. Then, "Dern!" I knew he was tempering his language for me. "If you're gonna fight with the government, you ought to at least spell it right." He seemed as embarrassed as if his mother had shown up at school with her slip showing.

At the corner on Main Street, I stood for a minute, looking at what I knew I would see, the Land Rover under the tree where it always was. As I stood, Sam saw me in the rearview mirror and leaned out of the back window to wave at me. He opened the door, got out and yelled, waving a Dixie cup in his hand. "You got to hurry up, girl, this is meltin'!" Drops of ice cream were dripping off onto the sidewalk, and Sam was dancing around them like a movie cowboy getting his feet shot at. I laughed and crawled in the Land Rover beside him, and we drove on out of town.

A cloud of dust covered the back window. Thick woods came up to the edge of the road on the right, and on the other side there was a wide deep field of cotton, full of Mexicans dragging cotton sacks behind them, some stopping to wave. We drove down that dirt road for some time. On the other side of the woods was the Silver Moon, that nightclub where B. J. worked, and then beyond that as the woods ended and more cotton fields began, a farm that I knew belonged to some colored people named the Jenkins.

We pulled up in front of the house, which was painted white, and Gill parked near the front walk. It was lined with colored bottles, their necks stuck into the ground in front of blooming marigolds. Behind it, an unpainted barn with a tin roof sat, slightly lopsided. On the other side of the field, I could see the tin roof of the Silver Moon glinting in the sun.

I knew the story of Ella Jenkins because Louella had told me about her. When she was about my age, she had joined up with a band that had come to the county fair and had traveled around the country with them as a singer. Then ten years later she had come back to Coldwater to settle down, and now she sang at the Silver Moon on Saturday nights.

We went up the walk. A bunch of kittens looked at us from the damp cool dirt under the house, then ran out and attacked our ankles.

"Mercy," Ella said, leaning out the door, her face the color of dark caramel, smiling. "Sweetest sight today." She held the door open for Sam, and he leaned over to hug her.

Inside, the room was small, with homey patched furniture and braided rugs, mixing every color of shirt and skirt anybody in that house had probably worn since they'd been born. An old woman, who I knew from what Louella had told me must be Miss Lu, Ella's mother, sat in a rocking chair dressed in solid white, her face the color of fudge and her eyes covered over with cataracts as white as her clothes. Miss Lu was ninety and practiced a form of magic which she'd picked up in New Orleans, where she'd lived until she followed Cab Jenkins to Coldwater. He'd died before I'd been born.

"Let me see, Mr. Best," she said, holding out her open palm with a perfumed lace handkerchief dangling from her blouse cuff. The inside of her hand was smooth and the color of dust.

He placed his hand in hers. "You're looking good, Miss Lu."

She stroked his palm and traced the lines with her trembling finger and began in a voice as soft and crackling as a wireless message from halfway around the world. "Been doing good for folks. I see that. Been eating well. You're full of hope."

Then she shook her head and clicked her tongue. "Been drinking too much. You going to run out of yourself, Sam Best. You going to. . . ." Suddenly she dug her finger deeper into the center of his palm and cried out: "Oh Sweet Power of God! What's this I see?"

Sam tried to pull away, laughing. "Don't tell me bad news, Miss Lu." Then, with the toe of his boot against the rung of her chair, he pushed, pretending to be trying to pull away. But in doing that, he purposely rocked her faster and faster until her head wobbled.

"Cut that out, Sam Best!" Miss Lu was holding onto the rocker, laughing and yelling: "You going to give me a heart attack and mess up my reading! Hold still. I got to see what this is." She traced over the line in his palm. She aimed her half-blind eyes at him and said in a low, serious voice: "Who's this living over in Little Rock supposed to be living with you instead? Your own wife and child. Now just what other women you need?"

Sam pulled away. Then he yelled as though in pain, complaining over Miss Lu's finger being too sharp to stand. He looked behind him, where I was. Then he reached for me, putting his arm around my shoulder and pushing me forward. "This is the only new woman in my life." He said my name. Until then I'd been left out.

Ella Jenkins poured me lemonade. "Child," Miss Lu said, reaching for my hand and stroking it. She whispered my name as soft as a prayer. She told me she was running out of my grandfather's medicine and could I get her some more.

"I don't know," I said, so timidly that I felt ashamed of myself in front of Sam. I said that no more could be sold.

"Damn government!" Miss Lu screwed up her lips and banged the arm of her chair. "The Outside Medicine's all allows me to rock this chair. Without it, my legs freeze up and won't bend." She leaned over my hand. "But I see here for you a long and happy life." She felt my palm and looked into my face with her white eyes and sucked her lips a minute. Then she whispered, which I was grateful for, since she started on my future sex life.

"A nice, curly-headed husband and *many* children," she murmured. She paused. "But you won't be rich. Instead you will travel, dance, and become a queen."

I didn't put much weight in her reading. Everybody in Coldwater knew that Ellen Best had taken Julie and moved out of Sam's house. Miss Lu wouldn't have needed to read that in his palm. And Sam's hair wasn't curly like the man she'd said that I'd marry. I wasn't sure what Sam and I would be up to, but I figured we'd be traveling around the world, and there wouldn't be time for a bunch of kids.

Sam patted her shoulder. "We couldn't get along without you, Miss Lu." He reached in his pocket. "We also came for some of your homemade relish."

Ella, who had been sitting quietly, smiling, on a piano bench across the room, stood up. "Want it super hot, Sam, or medium?"

"Couple of both." Sam followed her to the kitchen. He stood outside the door and placed a twenty-dollar bill on the dining table. He wouldn't take change.

Ella Jenkins handed him the relish in big Mason jars. She touched his arm slightly and said softly, "You look good." As we turned to go, she sat down at the piano and traveled her fingers over it like vines blown by wind, tinkling an introduction to a song as if it were the first patter of rain. Her hair was swept back and tied off her face. Her Negro features blended into a strong face with rounded cheeks, like the polished mahogany in my grandmother's living room. Her eyes were light brown and her mouth, when quiet, seemed to be hiding a smile that at any second could flash like fireflies at the edge of dark woods.

Ella rolled her head back, bending her neck. "I taught B.J. this song. She might do it next week." She moved her left hand over the keys, playing a hard deep bass. "Only I'm making up my own words for right now." Her voice, low, laughing, started to sing: "You like my relish? You like it, hon. Well, if you like my relish, there's plenty more where that comes from." She added a wink and a sound low in her throat, sexy and teasing: "Umhummm." Her voice, laughing and warm, changed to an old Negro spiritual. And I knew then what my grandmother had meant when she had said that B.J. Norris stepped over bounds. In my grandmother's opinion, as well as almost everybody else's in Coldwater, what Betty Jane Norris did that was as bad as stripping off her clothes in public, or maybe worse, was singing with Ella Jenkins.

She followed us out of the house to the Land Rover. A crow screamed overhead, then stopped on a dead oak limb to caw at us. Now the sun was almost lying on the fields, sending pink-orange streaks through the rows of cotton where the Mexicans were dragging their bags to the field road to load on trucks that would take them to weigh in their day's work.

Gill fished his keys out of his jeans, which lay so narrow over his thin hips it seemed that he was trying to inch into an envelope without crinkling it. Ella said, smiling at me, teasing, but probably serious, too: "Can't I give you one of these kittens to take home?" She reached down and picked up the one rubbing her leg. She handed it to me, and as I held it against my chest, it started purring as loud as a bee backed up to a microphone.

"I'll ask," I said seriously, yet knowing my grandmother

would have a fit if I moved a cat in right after all those chickens
—who probably wouldn't like the cat, either. I handed it back.

"Take care, Ella," Sam said.

Gill started the Land Rover's motor, which turned over and
caught with a grind as loud as an airplane. We drove off with
Ella Jenkins watching us, while a couple of cats lay in the grass
watching her.

We'd stayed late and Sam was worried that my grandmother
might be waiting supper for me. "I should have called her," he
said.

We'd gotten good at spoiling my dinner with Coke floats—
pouring Coke over ice cream till it bubbled up and flowed over
the top of the glass like lava. We'd always cut up, doing all
sorts of things my grandmother would pshaw over. But we had
never been late. If Sam was concerned, though, it wasn't anything like the worry the Land Rover gave us when it sputtered
and drifted to a stop about half a mile from Rathwell.

Gill pumped the accelerator, turned the key, kicked the dashboard, where everything from the fuse to the starter shorted
out from humidity sometimes, and then he got out and raised
the hood, to gawk and wonder at the engine. I was the one who
found the puddle in the dirt of the road under the Rover's back
end. "Shit," Gill said, apologizing to me immediately after he
said it.

As we looked back at the road from where we'd just come,
we could see a thin trail of gas that was still dripping through
a hole in the gas tank.

Sam pushed up his sleeves and tied a handkerchief around
his neck, saying he'd go for help. But Gill and I didn't want to
sit there doing nothing, so the three of us started off, and after
a few minutes of tromping through the thick loose dirt on the
road, Sam burst out singing "Follow the Yellow Brick Road"

—skipping, singing, going crazy all over the narrow dirt lane like it was Broadway. Then Ezekiel's mule turned the corner near Rathwell. Half a dozen of his grandchildren were riding in the back of the wagon. They caught Sam and Gill and me in the middle of our number where, along with the Strawman and Lion, I was skipping my way into Oz. "Ho," Ezekiel called, which the mule seemed to understand meant stop.

Behind us in the distance, the Land Rover twinkled in the sunset, and Sam pointed to it. "Just laid down and wouldn't get up," he said. "And we got to get this lady home." He smiled and nodded at me.

"No bother." Ezekiel nodded at me too. "I got to drop off all this lumber at her place anyhow. Might as well be now."

I crawled in the back with the grandchildren and the lumber, and Sam and Gill climbed up front with Ezekiel.

The mule walked slow, it was pulling so much. The grandchildren and I silently stared at each other. Then one said: "The mule name Kate."

Another one said: "Name after my granmomma."

The youngest one grinned, showing me a front row of missing teeth with gums as pink as bubble gum. "Can't have no babies." He was still grinning, proud of his knowledge and his missing teeth.

I figured he was talking about the mule, and not Ezekiel's wife, though it may have been true about both of them.

He smiled at me again and went on: "She come from a horse and a jackass and can't have no more like her. Mules got to be made from scratch—like biscuits."

The rest of the way we talked about Kate, her likes and dislikes, her personality quirks and pedigree. Her brown haunches kept a steady beat until we hit the streets of Cold-water. Then Sam sat up straight and let out a cowboy-type

"Ya-hoo!" and Ezekiel slapped Kate's rump with the reins, and she started trotting. Gill laughed, his Adam's apple gyrating, and the grandchildren pointed and laughed at that.

Sam started waving and bowing to everybody on the sidewalk, and we turned our suppertime rescue into a small town parade. We headed toward my grandparents' house. By the time we turned the corner, my grandmother must have heard us coming and was standing in the yard.

While Gill and Sam helped Ezekiel unload the lumber for the sun porch, she stood on the porch steps, too flabbergasted to say anything. I stood beside Kate, feeding her grass that I pulled out of my grandparents' yard, and I kept petting her head.

Finally Ezekiel drove off with the grandchildren waving at us, and Sam and Gill got ready to walk home. But first, my grandmother moved into the yard to speak to Sam. He was dusting the dirt off his pants leg and rolling up his shirtsleeves another notch. "Sam," she said, coming up behind him. "I just don't like the sight of my granddaughter riding around with a bunch of little Negroes in the back of a wagon."

Sam looked at her. "Well, I know, Emily, but I knew you were keeping supper warm, and my car was broke, and I just didn't see much point in sifting out who came to help." He put his hand on her shoulder and grinned at her. "I don't 'speck it'll happen again." Then he turned halfway around and glanced at the outhouse. "I've been reading all your letters in the paper. You're sure doing a fine job. And I think you're exactly right— it's time we all got rid of these old things and moved on."

My grandmother then started in on the pig-headedness of the newspaper editor, Charles Rankin. Gill stood quietly under the magnolia tree. I listened from inside the sun porch.

Sam walked my grandmother to the porch door. His voice

became as deep and warm as something melted, and my love for him was so big inside me that it was as if I could feel it pushing against my skin, and I was growing, becoming new. "You're sure a credit to this town, Emily. You're truly one of the most exceptional women I've ever met. And it's our good fortune that you live here." He smiled at her and held her elbow as she walked up the steps.

By then, if my grandmother had had tattoos they'd have been lying on her shoe tops, totally charmed off. After she came inside, we both stood on the porch, watching Sam and Gill walk off.

The sight of Sam moving away, the fast way that he walked and the tilt of his head, the shape of his back and the distant sound of his voice, could be my grandmother's or anybody's. But that's as far as it went. He was mine!

We would marry and live together forever, and neither of us would ever fight. I'd never need to see my mother or my father again. I'd never have to leave Coldwater. I was Sam Best's, and he was my family. He wanted me.

PART II

10.

My Grandmother and Elizabeth Taylor

Every day was like Christmas morning. I'd wake up in the Man-from-Shiloh's bed and think about Sam. It was the craziest thing in the world how I could take one short minute spent with him and make it like one of those caramel candies on a stick you could buy at the Ritz and suck on, for days, in private. Whenever I'd be with him, I'd be hoping the minute would never end; and, at the same time, be antsy as hell to get home, or somewhere alone, so I could think about what he'd said and how he'd said it.

Being in love was—if you really thought about it—a lot like dying. My whole life got real intense. But what I felt wasn't dark or mean or lonely. In fact, I seemed to tickle Sam every minute he was awake. He laughed at a lot of what I said, and whenever I talked he listened as if what I said was the most important thing in the world. I was, after all and finally, lovable. Lord! that was a relief.

It was Wednesday afternoon when he came to convince my grandmother that I should take dancing lessons. Louella and I were in the kitchen, fixing iced tea. "What's Mr. Best telling her?" Louella handed me mint leaves to put in the tea.

"The weather, his rice crop, the cotton," I said.

"Oh, but he's working up to something." Louella looked at me. "You been in trouble?"

I guess she suspected that I hadn't bought that Purple Midnight lipstick out of a pitiful allowance as an act of love. She also knew that Sam and I had been spending a lot of time together. "No," I said. Then we heard Sam mention my name. And since it was what I really wanted, he told my grandmother that I should take tap dancing.

My grandmother was sitting in a wing-backed chair, emitting White Gardenia whiffs as Sam tried to convince her that exercise wouldn't increase the size of my ankles or anything else. "Well, I don't know," she said. "It seems the only people tap dancing these days are in minstrel shows."

Sam only smiled, and then he socked my grandmother with what he knew she couldn't resist. He told her he'd just bought an old house down on the highway near the Soybean Plant, and he was opening up a dancing school. What would she think about the idea of me taking a little toe-dance? Sam was a damn genius.

Of course, my grandmother was real quick to tell him that dancing on one's toes was called *pointe*. Then she added that if he found somebody to teach *that* she might consider it—at least it'd help to make me graceful.

So that Saturday I was sitting on the front screen porch, waiting for Gill and Sam to pick me up. Sam had convinced my grandmother that a *pointe* teacher was definitely in the works. I held the money my grandmother had given me to order "ballet shoes and a tu-tu," which I thought meant she'd gone senile and was talking dirty. But tu-tus were what my grandmother associated with ballet, and that was more than I knew about it. Along with everybody else in Coldwater, I thought of ballet as toe-dancing. But I didn't give beans about who called it what. Sam Best had bought a whole dancing school just for me! He wouldn't have done that for anybody else—except maybe my mother.

Over the past weeks almost every one of my chickens had grown more long-legged and long-necked than a chicken that planned to lay eggs. One, though, was smaller than the rest, and calmer. It was either the runt or a misplaced hen, and I'd been teaching it to walk up my arm and sit on my shoulder. For two days, I called it Colleen, after Miss Pankhurst; but then I changed its name to Taylor. When its sex became evident, I'd call it either Robert or Elizabeth—a plan I considered practical.

By the Saturday that Sam was coming to get me to work on the dancing school for its grand opening, all my chickens had lost their yellow down to white feathers and all but one had the beginnings of large combs. So I knew that my Taylor was an Elizabeth. I was also now a full-fledged chicken farmer and had joined the 4-H. To compensate, my grandmother insisted I learn a lot of facts about chickens. She said that all women should know obscure and unusual things to keep themselves fascinating. So I knew that Romans considered chickens sacred to the God of War and that roosters are symbols of courage. The crowing cock had, at times, symbolized the resurrection of Christ. Also, unless hens are trained they will lay eggs on the ground or almost anywhere. But the most fascinating fact was: chickens are polygamous. And when mine came of age, I was eager to see how Elizabeth liked *it*.

I sat in the swing on the front porch, watching down the street for Sam. Inside, my grandmother was watching the World Series. Baseball-watching was patriotic for her. It also fit in with her Saturday afternoon beer and cigarette. She said the cigarette opened up her sinuses, and the beer kept her arteries clean. And during the World Series in October, she never missed a game. Los Angeles was playing Chicago. I could hear her calling the pitcher a ninny. She liked to comment on which players looked like "sweet boys" and then, when the camera came in for a close-up, she criticized all the batters' haircuts.

Rounding the corner beside the bank, slowing down to keep from hitting some walking Mexicans, was Ezekiel in an old GMC truck. He pulled into the alley and parked beside the sun porch and got out.

I went to meet him and ask about Kate. When he told me, I didn't think I could ever forgive him. Kate had been traded for the truck.

Ezekiel stepped from the running board, gazing back, proud. He held open the door, admiring the inside. There was a dent in one fender and the tires looked bad. But the truck body had been polished into a ruby black, until I could see the reflection of my clothes in its paint.

My grandmother had let me wear jeans, since Sam had told her we were going to be painting and cleaning up. I studied myself in the hood: "Where's Kate now? Anywhere close?"

Ezekiel was admiring the hood too: "Just down the road from my place. A man near Rathwell had this truck."

I couldn't believe any truck could be worth Kate. I stepped onto the running board and crawled halfway onto the seat for a closer look at the old dials and rubber floor and the plastic knob—big as a ripe plum—on the end of the gearshift.

"Sally!" My grandmother stood on the porch, holding open the door, motioning for me. When I got close, she reached for my arm and led me inside, while saying that obviously Sam had been tied up with business and was running late. I ought to stay on the porch and be patient. Then she added, her voice semi-scolding and secretive. "Don't you know it's not proper for a young lady of your age to be standing around with a Negro man?"

Behind us, the TV crowd cheered for a player who'd just stolen a base. I sat down for what seemed like an awful length of time until Sam would come and rescue me. Every once in a while, I'd glance at her. When a commercial for Budweiser beer came on, she got up and shuffled to the icebox. The light behind the bottles of milk and stuff fell across her face. She looked so disappointed—but it wasn't connected with anything in the icebox. And suddenly it seemed that I knew something —like a secret—about my grandmother. She brought out the beer she was looking for; and as she shut the icebox door, closing out the wedge-shaped yellow light, the silhouette of her, hunched, bent-over, was like that of someone who'd been stood up and jilted.

I suppose that, unlike me, she never questioned all the stuff her family passed on. Maybe she thought that if she did, she might damage her love for them. She had told me many times the story of her and my grandfather's romance. And whenever she had she'd raised her eyebrows, as though my choice in a husband could ruin everything. Sometimes she pulled out old college fraternity pins to show me how many choices she could have had. But her family had lost a lot in the Civil War, and they'd taught her that wealth and aristocracy don't always endure, but a doctor would. When Horace Maulden went into Mississippi to visit a dying relative, Emily Matthews met him at a church supper. She could, of course, charm anyone; and in a matter of weeks Horace was hers, if she wanted him— forever, too, if she cared to consider it.

Somehow my grandmother thought that Horace Maulden was on his way to becoming a famous physician who would someday specialize and be greatly thought of in the state capital. I guess my grandfather got carried away with courting and threw in a few juicy pieces that led her to think that. She dreamed of living in the city and doing all of the cultural things she'd been brought up to do. She thought Horace talked of his little practice in Coldwater as a mere stepping-stone; and when she considered the prospect of living in the stepping-stone— it was too far away to visit before the marriage—she assumed it wouldn't be for long. Living in Coldwater and then finding out that she would be permanently stuck there—where no one knew anything about opera or ballet or could say a correct sentence or much of anything without sucking his teeth or spitting a wad—was her version of eternal punishment. I guess if she thought as I did, she must have been wondering what exactly she had done to deserve it. And maybe that was why she was so angry. Because maybe the only answer she came up with was *nothing*. She was being punished for *his* inadequacies, not hers. Which of course made me know even more about how dangerous marriage can be.

A pink Cadillac turned the corner and floated like a boat to a stop under the magnolia tree. While the Land Rover was getting a new gas tank, Gill was swapping cars every week at one of Sam's dealerships, following his whims in colors and fins.

My grandmother came out onto the front porch to wave me off, and I got in the backseat beside Sam while Ezekiel hammered on the sun porch and the Cadillac's motor turned over. The car was shiny and new but already marked with Sam's things: his pipe, office files between the cushions, a pair of glasses he wore when he read the small print on legal documents. The upholstery even smelled like Sam—cherry tobacco and candy mints, shaving lotion and traces of whiskey. No Cadillac was nearly as much a part of Sam as the Land Rover. It couldn't leave the roads and bump up onto the fields he owned. But he'd left a little of himself on it already, and I breathed it in, looking stupid, probably making my nostrils flap like Kate's when a fly landed on her.

We rode only around the corner, because Gill stopped the car near my parents' house and walked to the back door. Then he and B.J. Norris came across the lawn, and she slid in beside me and Sam.

"Shoot!" She tossed the hair off her neck. "It's hot." She grinned. "Whenever the weather gets crazy, I think the world's coming to an end. This heat in October's not right." She looked at me. "How're you?" Her voice was low and sweet, like it was carrying us a secret. Sam introduced me, saying my name in a way I recorded to play inside my head forever. And B.J. and I both laughed. "Oh, we've already met," she said. Across her shoulders were white ruffles from her blouse, leaving her neck bare, tanned and filmed over with powder that smelled as sweet as jasmine. She had on blue jeans like me, only hers were rolled up over her calves, leaving her ankles bare, tan, perfect, and sexy. Her hair trailed between her shoulder blades, and when Sam got through looking at her, he glanced at me. "B.J.'s going to be our first employee," he said. "She's specialized in tap and something else we're going to call modern movement." He laughed. "In fact, she's got a Ph.D."

B.J. poked Sam's shoulder and laughed too. If anybody besides me could have seen the way that Sam looked at her as they eased back against the cushions and stopped laughing, they'd have been sure there was more between them than the business of running a jewelry store. Sam sometimes looked at my mother like that. Until then I'd thought that maybe B.J. and I were supposed to be stand-ins for my mother. But now I wondered if both my mother and I were supposed to be stand-ins for B.J. I wasn't worried about my mother taking Sam away from me, because supposedly the truth was—and I believed her—that she just flat-out didn't want him. But with B.J., it might be different. With her—well, I might just have to kill her.

She reached across Sam and smoothed my hair. "I've taken dancing a lot, but I've never taught it," she said.

Her voice was a coated guitar wire, twanging, humming, rubbing our ears with rhythms that even though I hated her I could have listened to the rest of my life. I had never met anyone so willing to like me, and seemingly for no other reason than I was there. Her eyes bathed me with interest while she asked me where I'd lived before, what I liked—anything, as long as it was about me. And I answered her, thinking that maybe I'd have to get my grandparents to kick her out of my parents' house and make her move away. But at the same time I was stretching out in the warmth of all that attention she was giving me.

When I glanced at Sam, I was embarrassed by his smile, tender, private, aimed at her—but also at me. I guess B.J. and I did look a little alike. Every once in a while, B.J. would slip with her English, which showed she was a dumbo and totally unfit for a life with Sam—yet it sounded so natural, I liked it. "I didn't never think I'd be going to a dancing school—and in a Cadillac! She rubbed the pink cushy seats, laughing. "And here I might even end up being the main teacher. You sure you ain't teasing about that, Sam?"

He laughed. "I consider you qualified to teach anything you want to."

We all laughed at the sound of that, and with the general sense of the good fun we were in the middle of having. At the end of Main Street I saw my grandfather standing with some farmers, and one of them was holding open his collar and showing him something on the side of his neck. My grandfather held as many street hours as office hours. Then we bumped up over the railroad track and headed down the highway. B.J. rolled down the window and stuck her head out and let her hair fly back like a wild string cape. She was patting the side of the car and singing "The Wabash Cannonball"— her voice hoarse and jerking on the ends of the words. We were all laughing with her. On one hand I was hoping maybe the Cadillac's door would fly open and she'd fall out onto the highway, while on the other I was wishing I could move in my old house with her and copy everything she did.

As we got beyond the city limit sign, B.J. twirled her hair up into a knot, fastening it with pins from her purse. She asked Sam to switch places with me, and we had a grand time cutting up and pushing and poking on Sam while he half stood up, and I slipped under him so I was in the middle. B.J. reached over and touched my hair, and I let her. She arranged it the same way as hers, pinning it as if I'd been a doll. And yet I didn't want to cut her hands off or hope for a wreck that would only mash her side of the car. Instead I sat still, at first embarrassed with her hands stroking my hair. As she and Sam were both admiring me, I laughed and let her spin my hair up any way she liked, especially if it looked like hers.

"Well, here it is," Sam said, as we drove up in front of a big old white frame house that I'd always thought of as the George Best house. It had belonged to one of Sam's uncles and had been built as a showplace, with even a wrought-iron fence around it and a grand gate. But the uncle had died and the widow moved, and no one could afford to keep it up. Sam had already had a big sign painted that sat on the porch, ready to be nailed up: THE BEST DANCING SCHOOL. We stood and looked at that and laughed and hugged each other and teased and cut up like a bunch of goofballs on a field trip.

Gill got a box of rags and buckets of paint out of the trunk of the Cadillac, and he and Sam rolled up their sleeves. The tan on Sam's arms and the way his shoulders moved under his thin white cotton shirt looked so sexy to me, I was hoping B.J. wasn't watching.

It was a hot dry October afternoon, and as the sun moved lower toward the fields, we stood on ladders or scooted around on our knees and painted woodwork and porch rails. Catalogues of dancing costumes and shoes were lying on a table by the door. A record player was already plugged in beside it.

"Let's take a break," Sam said after a while. Gill had been suggesting one for some time. Sam asked us if we didn't want to drive back to town for a Coke or go over to the Dairy Dip. But B.J. said she wanted to stay there and go over the catalogues and weed through the records. She laughed and said teasingly, though we also knew she was serious, that she was a little nervous and wanted to do some homework, since it was her who was going to have to get the dancing school off to a start.

"I'll just go across the road a while, then," Sam said, meaning the Soybean Plant. A group of men could usually always be found there, especially on Saturday afternoons. But first he went into the bathroom to clean the paint off his hands.

B.J. picked up a record and put it on the turntable. In no time flat she was doing some kind of fancy dance step across the new floor of the living room. "Ain't this a gas?" she said, glancing at me. She twirled, doing some fast steps that made her feet sound like castanets. Obviously she knew what she was doing, and when she moved you couldn't take your eyes off her. To me, that was talent.

Sam came in, rolling up his sleeves another notch and watching us, his face giving away his pride and affection. B.J. tapped her feet and curtsied. I looked back at Sam and smiled. Then B.J. and I just stood and watched him walk out, his neck tan and strong. We heard the motor of the Cadillac start and the crunch of its tires on the gravel driveway.

B.J. filed through the stack of records and put on one with a fast beat and began doing leaps and turns and making her arms like a train, choo-chooing up and down and back and forth. She was grinning and laughing while her feet went wild beneath her. "Come on!" she cried. I tried to follow. Pretty soon I forgot myself and copied everything she did.

The record kept going, and our feet kept going, and when the music finally stopped, we fell back against the wall, listening to the needle scraping against the empty end of the record. Then B.J. reached over and hugged me, grinning: "Shoot, honey, you and me are damn good already." Maybe I was. Maybe all along I could have danced like my mother had wanted.

We went into the kitchen and drank water straight out of the faucet with our hands. The sun was already low, the light across the back field turning the dry tall grass to the color of wheat. There was a big maple tree near the old garage, half-naked with its red leaves lying on the ground like a dropped robe. "I guess we better start closing up this place," B.J. said, looking around at all the work we'd done.

We'd raised the big heavy windows to get out the paint smell. B.J. went over to one on the front wall and reached up over her head to pull it down. In another second there was a sound like heavy wood falling, and I heard B.J. yell. She was calling my name. When I got in there close enough to see, I saw the window had come sliding down so fast, it'd caught both her thumbs under it. The sash ropes in the frame were broken and rotten and there'd been nothing to stop it. "Lord," B.J. said.

"Get it off me." She was trying to laugh at her predicament and yet saying all the while that even though it looked funny it hurt like hell.

I had to scoot in front of her with her arms around me and push and heave on the window, but it was a good five feet tall and weighed more than half of me. I couldn't budge it. I felt like a dumbbell. The thoughts I'd had earlier about getting rid of B.J. seemed crazy. I couldn't have caused this. And yet, earlier, it seemed that I'd almost been wishing for something just about like it to happen.

I stared at her swelling thumbs, pinched below the window, and felt tears no more than two inches from my own eye rims. If I'd thought about it much more, I'd probably have thrown up —which wouldn't have helped anybody. "I'll get Sam," I yelled, running out as if I were being whipped.

The yard was big and a good way from the road. I ran across it, not even slowing down to look both ways, but just kept on, turned my head right, then left, and decided I could make it and darted across the blacktop. Somebody in a blue car whizzed by, blaring the horn and looking out at me as though I were crazy.

The Soybean Plant was a good quarter-mile down the highway and set back. But I never stopped because I knew that I couldn't. If I had done anything but run my all-out best, I'd never have been able to live with myself. And while I was running, the mean small suspicion I'd been sitting on all afternoon —that Sam had started up the dancing school as much or more for B.J. as for me—no longer mattered. It was a dead idea that I promised myself I'd never think about again. I didn't care who bought what for anybody, or why, as long as I wouldn't lose Sam—or B.J. I wanted them both.

He was sitting with five other men, some standing around

him as he sat in the office of the plant. A glass with liquid so clear in it that it seemed empty was in his hand. He had a look on his face that I had never seen. His grin was lopsided, and his cheeks were red. Everyone there looked up, hearing me coming; and Sam smiled.

Everyone was watching me. The silence was like frozen air, and I was afraid of it. If I spoke, whatever I said would hang in that silence. As his eyes focused on my face, his grin straightened up. The lopsided, scary part of it moved into only what I recognized. I could see his face looking at me, waiting, blushed red with alcohol—and me. His love was so evident that it was as if he were drinking the sight of me; and I couldn't look away. All I could feel was something warm and red too turning me inside out. "We've had an accident," I said.

My voice shook. I panted and my chest went up and down as I sucked in a whole mouthful of air after all that running. Then I just practically yelled it out, making, of course, a total ass of myself: "I need you!"

II.

An Arrangement for the Outhouse

Only one of B.J.'s thumbs was broken; the other was badly bruised. My grandfather put one in a cast and the other one in a bandage, and the opening of the dancing school was put off for another week. Sam had to go to Little Rock on business anyway. So that next Saturday, I was sitting on the sun porch watching Ezekiel paint the new wood he had nailed to the sides. The day before had been my birthday. I'd turned fourteen. There'd been quite a to-do about it, what with Louella cooking me a cake and all. Sam sent me a card signed from "Your Secret Admirer," but I recognized his handwriting right off. And just about everybody gave me money. But now things were back to normal, and my grandmother had put me to work polishing silver dessert forks in preparation for the Eastern Arkansas Missionary Society meeting.

I was set up at a card table on the sun porch, and I could think of a hundred things I'd rather have been doing. My grandmother had already pointed out that she planned to pass on those silver dessert forks to me. I could think of nothing I would rather have less than a bunch of silver dessert forks. But I thanked her anyway.

She went to the sun porch window beside Ezekiel and looked out it for some time. The millions of crisscross lines around her eyes and the looseness of her skin made her face seem the softest thing in the world to touch—if I could ever have brought myself to touch it. But her face tightened now, and anger gave it a healthy blush. "Mr. Rankin is a prime example of ill breeding. Why, he has no intention whatsoever of moving that thing! Shows every bit of his upbringing." She went into the kitchen and I heard her pick up the telephone. I knew she was worked up about the outhouse. Her letters to the editor had been mysterious, aimed at businesses cleaning old appliances off their lots; still, everyone knew exactly what she'd meant.

The telephone dial whirled back into place and then, "Mr. Rankin, please." I leaned back in my chair, swirling the cloth that was over my finger in the silver polish, and considered giving all the forks a spit shine.

"Are you going to ignore my letters? You've printed them. Why don't you act?"

Mr. Rankin must have said something that didn't mean much. My grandmother's voice got louder: "We've got to do this for the sake of Coldwater. It's not sanitary. We can't go around having outside toilets in the alleys. They don't have any use anymore."

Then he must have said something that wasn't nice because my grandmother pshawed and yelled out his name. I'd heard people say the outhouse was good for the drunks to use when they'd come down the alley every once in a while. And Mr. Rankin had probably brought that up.

"Mr. Rankin!" my grandmother said again. "This is no time for impertinence and crudity. I propose that you move it. And move it quickly. I'm having the Missionary Society luncheon in a few weeks. There's no reason why all of us have to sit here and look at your wooden cubicle from my window."

I guess he said something again that wasn't nice. Because my grandmother pshawed again and came out with the best insult she could—on the spur of the moment—think up: "Mr. Rankin . . . I have always known you are a mule in a dandy's clothing. But you are certainly now showing your true colors."

She hung up.

My grandmother walked into the sun porch and looked at me. "That just goes to show you," she said. "You can't depend on anyone doing anything for you. But in this case, it's for himself too. That toilet is a health hazard and that's reason enough to get rid of it." She walked then toward her bedroom, and I figured she was going to take paregoric and lie down a while.

Ezekiel closed his paint bucket and took it outside.

The phone rang. I answered it in the kitchen just as my grandmother answered it in her bedroom. It was Mr. Rankin. And since I figured she'd want me to hear firsthand the way somebody with ill-breeding sounded—so I could, of course, avoid it—I just kept listening. Mr. Rankin apologized. He said he knew he'd been rude, but at the time he couldn't help it. He did, though, want to be a good citizen; and he believed in improvement for Coldwater. He then suggested that they work together. He promised my grandmother he would hire some men to haul off the outhouse if she would take care of covering up the hole underneath. And it was also agreed that the outhouse would be burned—not only for health reasons (which my grandmother said she cared about) but because Mr. Rankin said he didn't want it sitting in the dump with his name on it.

Finally, it seemed, the long-awaited arrangement for getting rid of the outhouse had been made. And even though Mr. Rankin was swapping hauling and burning the outhouse for covering up the hole underneath it, my grandmother, by this time, was willing to settle. Filling in a hole didn't seem too much to give.

There was a knock at the sun porch door. I laid the phone

receiver down on the kitchen counter and put a dish towel over it to stifle any sounds from my end.

A man in overalls was standing there holding a straw hat. He seemed nervous and excited.

"My boy's done stepped on a nail. I need two dollars of Dr. Maulden's Outside Medicine."

I opened the door so he could step inside. Then I heard my grandmother coming down the hall. I quickly hung up the phone, and when she came into the kitchen I told her that the man standing in the sun porch had come to buy some medicine.

"It's against the law," she called to him. "Don't come back. We don't have any."

The medicine buyer took a step forward. "Oh, Miz Maulden, please. My boy's done stepped on a nail. We got to have that medicine."

"Go buy some iodine." My grandmother turned.

"That's not the same thing!" The poor man tried to follow her, leaning, reaching out. But he stopped. He held his hand as someone does who's been roasting a marshmallow and accidentally drops it into the fire, wanting it but thinking twice before going after it. "But Miz Maulden . . . it don't work like the Outside Medicine. Did you hear about my brother's pig? He got cut up in a baler and laid for days with his legs half off. My brother poured a whole bottle of Dr. Maulden's Outside Medicine on him; and in three days, the legs grew back and the pig got up and walked."

"Yes, well, that's nice. But we're not selling any more."

"Oh, Miz Maulden. Please!"

My grandmother walked past him and held open the sun porch door. "Absolutely not. If we sold a drop we'd all end up in Alcatraz."

The man shuffled off, and she closed the door and said to herself, as though thinking out loud: "Now I've got to see about that outhouse hole."

"I'm through," I said quickly. "I'm going out in the yard a while."

My grandmother glanced at the table where I had left the forks and nodded absentmindedly. I knew she would be too busy thinking about the outhouse to worry about the forks. I was already out the door and starting down the alley, leaving her standing at the window.

Ezekiel was near the garage, cleaning his paintbrush in a tin can of turpentine. He looked up and saw me. "'Lo."

"Hi," I said, heading to the chicken yard to look for Elizabeth Taylor. In my pocket, I'd put a handful of Wheaties. As I trailed them behind me, she and half a dozen of her roosters followed me, pecking at the cereal on the ground. I'd taught Elizabeth to walk up my arm and sit on my shoulder. She'd also learned to flap herself onto the roof of the chicken house—to get away from all her roosters sometimes—and then even flap herself onto a fence post and jump down into the alley. I knelt in the grass and let her walk up my arm and sit on my shoulder.

Outside the gate I set her down on the ground near Ezekiel and fed her some more Wheaties. Ezekiel had some of my grandmother's dining room chairs sitting on papers beside his paint buckets. It looked as if he were going to reglue some of the broken rungs and touch up the mahogany finish. We'd all been put to work by the Missionary Society luncheon.

I planned to ask Ezekiel if I could help fix the chairs. Anything would beat polishing forks. But something in one of the newspapers under the chairs had caught his attention. He was hunkered down, reading it. I don't think that he was even aware I was there.

I could tell that it was the *Coldwater Gazette* under the chair, and it seemed that he was looking at the editorial page. Maybe he was reading one of my grandmother's letters to the editor. The editorial page seemed to be getting a lot of attention from almost everybody. Usually when people mentioned Charles Rankin's editorials they sounded mad and irritated. But when Sam did, he'd laugh so much, I thought he'd lose his breath. From what I could understand, it seemed that Charles Rankin, after nearly a lifetime of thinking one way, had suddenly changed. He'd begun slanting his editorials in favor of integration. Sam called them slants like the tilt of an air bag that could, in a second, pop back straight if punched. He said that old Rankin had gotten excited when this man named Harry Scott Ashmore won a Pulitzer Prize for covering the Little Rock school mess. And now Mr. Rankin had told Sam that he thought he was going to go after one of those prizes for himself.

I watched Ezekiel stick his paintbrush in a can of mahogany stain and test the color of it all over the newspaper. In a little while, he began gluing a leg on one of the other chairs and I asked him if I could help.

I strained to keep the chair rung in its socket as Ezekiel showed me, feeling the sweat begin to trickle down my neck.

"It's sure hot for October," I said. "My grandmother says it's the sun that makes us healthy. But it takes everything out of me. I don't believe what she says, do you?"

Ezekiel didn't answer. Elizabeth Taylor clucked softly and pecked on the ground.

I chatted on like a loony; I was so sick of being quiet inside the house. I kept fishing for more criticism of my grandmother and was even ready to mention Sam so that I could talk about him for a while.

"There." Ezekiel rearranged the chair. "Now here." He pointed to another rung for me to hold.

I heard the back door bang and saw my grandmother come toward us across the lawn. Ezekiel glanced up. I made a low moan of dread. "Don't say nothing," Ezekiel said. "You'll say more."

I looked at him, not understanding what he meant. But understanding that my grandmother wouldn't like what she saw, I stood up and pretended to be chasing Elizabeth Taylor across the yard.

"Ezekiel?"

"Yessum?" He looked up.

"I've got a proposal for you. You see that eyesore?"

She was pointing to the outhouse. "Well, when Mr. Rankin moves it, I want you to fill in the hole underneath." She waited then and looked at him. "I'll pay you two dollars," she added.

Ezekiel looked back at the chair rung. "I only do fixing, Miz Maulden."

My grandmother's hem jerked. Elizabeth Taylor pecked around her shoe.

Ezekiel went on, very slowly. "No moving. No hoeing. No picking. Just fixing and yard work."

My grandmother pshawed. "Well, wouldn't you say that shoveling dirt was yard work?"

"I don't know, ma'am. It's a big hole."

"Well then, five dollars," she said. Ezekiel squirted a large amber blob of glue onto the chair. "Might have to buy dirt," he said. "And then of course I got to haul it."

"Seven dollars." Ezekiel didn't look up. There were a few moments of silence. "Ten dollars."

Ezekiel raised his head. "Well, let me see what I can do."

I lifted Elizabeth Taylor over the fence and set her down with her roosters. My grandmother headed for the house, motioning me in. Then she called back: "Ezekiel?"

Ezekiel looked up.

"I'm depending on you."

"Yessum. I know it. I know you is."

We went into the kitchen, and behind us my grandfather came in through the sun porch door wearing a lab coat with large ragged holes in it. Doing what he did, he frequently spilled chemicals on himself, and his clothes were eaten through with quarter- and dime-sized holes. To my grandmother the coat was a sign of weakness and wrongdoing. Furthermore, she thought that as long as he wore that coat, his patients' would see him to be as much of a quack and crackpot as she fully suspected him to be. One of her pearls was that if you can't be good, you should at least look like you are; half the time nobody would know the difference.

"What's for lunch?" My grandfather was cheerful. He was always cheerful. That was one of the things that irked my grandmother.

She put a loaf of bread and a jar of peanut butter on the table.

"Oh, Lord," my grandfather said. "This. Again?"

"Louella will be here tomorrow to cook," she said. "And until then we'll just have to do the best we can."

"Well, not me," he said, but opened the bread. "What about you?" He looked at me. "Are you up to this?"

I said I supposed so.

While he was making a sandwich, my grandmother filled him in on the history of the peanut, then told him that another one of those farmers had come to the house here for medicine. She looked at him. "I guess you know."

"No, I didn't know."

"Well, I saw him sitting at the side of your office just a few minutes ago. You didn't give him anything, did you?"

"No. I've been seeing a few emergencies and working on the books."

"You don't look like you've been working on the books."

He took a bottle of yellow liquid out of his pocket and mixed it with a glass of water.

She pshawed.

"After one of these lunches," he said, "I have to have this." He stirred a little more of the medicine into his glass. Then he took a bite from his sandwich, and his tongue began chasing the peanut butter off his teeth.

"You're going to get us all in trouble," my grandmother said. "And then you won't have enough sense to get us out."

My grandfather turned to me and asked me what I planned to do with the afternoon.

When I told him that I was going downtown to a show, he gave me some money and told me to be sure to bring him back some Milk Duds. Then he took my arm. "Come on," he said, "I'll walk you toward town." Then he called back: "Go lie down, Emily. You need a nap."

My grandmother was washing dishes with her shoulders humped. I guess that if it hadn't been beneath her, she could have gone on TV and been on "Queen For A Day" and won prizes with the story of how awful her life was. But maybe after she told it, having to live in Coldwater and being married to what she thought of as a nincompoop wouldn't hold much water next to fire, hailstorm, and cancer.

The man who had wanted to buy the medicine was sitting on the side steps of my grandfather's office, cracking a boiled egg and peeling off the shell. He and my grandfather both went in the door to his office, and I walked on down the sidewalk.

I was at the corner of Main Street when some Mexicans stopped, looked at me, and laughed. My dress was unbuttoned, I thought. Or I had peanut butter on my face—or something worse than that. Then I heard Elizabeth Taylor clucking behind me. She was pecking along on the sidewalk, looking for more Wheaties. I had to pick her up and go back to lock her in the chicken house. Doing that made me late.

I decided to cut through the alley behind the Mercantile to the Ritz. I walked as fast as I could across the street to the side of the Mercantile, past the public water fountains, one marked *colored* and one marked *white*. In Memphis, I'd noticed that all of the department stores had water fountains like that. I turned into the alley. There were a lot of weeds against the back of the stores. A pair of legs in blue jeans stuck out into the first rut of the half-gravel, half-dust alley.

I wasn't going to look. I wasn't going to slow down. I was going to trot on, pretending the body was not there.

"Hey!"

I was silent except for breathing.

A rock skidded across my path.

"Sally."

The voice saying it was young. I stopped.

"Where you going?"

It was Joel Weiss. He had a stack of *Arkansas Gazette*s beside him, folding them into cute triangle-delivery shapes.

"The Ritz."

He laughed. "That's a bunch of junk."

"It's Mitzi Gaynor and Alan Ladd," I said. "I wouldn't call that junk."

He laughed again. "I bet you've got the hots for Ladd. I bet you wish you looked like Mitzi. I bet you crave her name."

"Not me," I lied.

"Don't tell me you're not thinking about being a Mitzi yourself."

I turned my head and looked at a brick wall.

He scratched his nose. His fingers were black with newsprint. "You'd want to be a Mitzi just so everyone'd look at you and you could tell them to kiss-off."

I didn't have a comeback. I stood watching him as he threw the folded papers into a pile.

He handed me a stack of unfolded *Gazette*s. "Do you know how to do this?" I sat down and copied him. He asked me if I wanted to know who the best actor around there was. He was quiet a minute. Then, "your grandfather," he said. I didn't have the slightest idea what he meant. But I didn't have to ask, because he went on and told me. According to Joel, my grandfather was the best thing that had ever happened to the country people. "They don't have anything else to look forward to but boll weevils, maybe a little pneumonia, a few heart attacks."

"Are you talking about his medicines?" I asked.

He laughed and looked at me. "Yeah."

He stuffed the folded papers into his canvas shoulder bag. If he had let it, his hair would have curled over his head in big loops. Before I moved away the year before, Joel's hair had been cut in a GI with just enough to comb and jelly-up like the bristles on a toothbrush. Now he was sculpturing the long loops into an Elvis ducktail, which might have been a little late fashionwise, but everything was late getting to Coldwater. And Joel's hair now was the sort of stuff to make my grandmother's skin crawl and lead her to describe him as looking like a hoodlum. Right away I was attracted to him.

"M'ere," he said, motioning to the indentation between the dime store and the Mercantile Co., where seven years before, I had gone with Bobby Watts.

Sitting down with his back against the bricks, he leaned around and worked at loosening one. He pulled out a pack of cigarettes and offered them. I didn't smoke, but I took one.

"You going to be here long?"

I raised my shoulder, tough; I looked dirty.

"Well, if you are. . . ."

Upward, I blew smoke. My head felt dizzy. I thought I saw wings of something, beating in the sky, then gliding, moving at the edge of the bricks over us. At first I thought maybe it had something to with the satellites, the Russian ones and ours, shot up there the year before. I'd heard a patient in my grandfather's clinic say if God had wanted men to be alive in Heaven, He would have sent a chariot for them. Alive, men would have to eat and cause laundry. But America couldn't just sit by and watch Russia junk up Paradise. On TV I had watched three rockets aimed for the moon from some beach in Florida fizzle and die like giant wet firecrackers. And passenger jets had started flying to Europe. My grandmother said anyone going that way didn't think much of himself. I pictured planes full of jilted lovers, their faces pressed to the windows looking down at the ocean. I took another heavy drag on the cigarette. What I'd seen on the rooftop was only a candy wrapper, flapping in the wind.

"You're green," Joel said.

"No, I'm not." I hadn't heard a thing he'd been saying. I pulled my knees up under my skirt and put my head on them, dizzy from cigarettes.

"Well, anyway. You want to go next Saturday to the Ritz with me?"

Joel was smoking fast. I stubbed out my cigarette and buried it with the toe of my shoe. I thought Joel was interested in me because of my family. Not because of who we were but because none of us were normal—at least at the moment we didn't live in a normal state. And from all my grandmother had told me, and as far as I knew, maybe abnormal families were attractive to Jews. Then, too, what if Joel thought I was a fast woman? What if Bobby Watts had pumped up his story and blabbed it around town? And, besides, I couldn't go. I was Sam's.

I threw back my head. "Nope," I said. "I can't." I told him I was going to be busy at the dancing school.

Joel hid the cigarettes and got up and went into the back door of the Mercantile Co. He bought Listerine. We used it, spitting it on the dust of the alley. Then we laughed. Since now I'd missed the beginning of the show at the Ritz, I went back to Main Street. Joel went to deliver the *Arkansas Gazette*s.

I walked in the Mercantile Co. and used my birthday money to buy a tight green tweed skirt with a slit up the back that was the shape and size of a tight, open-ended tube. In it, I felt sexy and slick.

I was going to wear the skirt home, but chicken that I was, I went back in the dressing room and put the skirt my grandmother had picked out over my tweed tube and walked home.

In my room I knelt down beside the Man-from-Shiloh's bed and from underneath, I pulled out my suitcase. Inside it, I kept all the latest letters from my parents. I hadn't opened any more of them since that time I'd been afraid my mother and father were dying and I'd wanted to see if they were all right. I hid the green tube skirt on top of the unopened letters. I ought to be out at some nightclub in that skirt, living it up with Sam. But he was away. I opened the window behind the bed and lay down to listen for sounds of B.J.

12.

My Grandfather and the Lone Ranger Liver

Louella had just cleaned up and gone home after serving Sunday dinner. My grandparents were both lying down when I went into the kitchen to get another piece of Louella's pound cake. As I was taking a dish out of the cabinet, I was startled by my grandfather, who'd come up quietly and was standing behind me. Patting his hair down, he smiled. His face had sleep prints on it.

"Do you know anything about coenzymatic dismutation?"

I held the empty cake plate. I told him I'd never even heard of it.

"How are you in math? Do you pass?"

"Barely."

"Have you had any chemistry?"

"Photosynthesis." In Memphis, I'd taken biology and learned how plants made food, but I wasn't sure if that counted as chemistry. Since Sputnik there'd been a run on science, but nobody in Coldwater could teach it.

My grandfather leaned back against the kitchen table, staring at me. He was often quiet. But occasionally something would come over him and he would let loose thunderous chains of words, with opinions on everything. When he did that, my grandmother accused him of drinking. But I suspected that when he was quiet he was just retrenching. Silence wasn't his normal state, though he liked to sit in it a lot. He reached onto the middle of the kitchen table beside the salt and pepper and the sugar bowl where he kept a bottle of his Inside Medicine. He poured some in a glass.

"Go ahead," he said, handing it to me.

By then I didn't especially need it. The fist inside my chest had let go, and I suspected that me and Sam loving each other had more to do with my good health than my grandfather's medicine, but I drank it anyway.

Through the bottom of my glass, I saw him watching me. "Doesn't taste good, does it?" He looked wistfully at the half-full bottle. He reminisced about how it had gotten Mrs. Hobbs's son through the Korean War and brought Turly Caine sleep. He laughed. "I've known this to help homesickness, lovesickness, nighttime headaches, and worms. Even your grandmother's liked the money it's brought." He leaned the bottle over, watching the liquid slide up into the neck. "What bothers her now is that she thinks the world has proved me to be the fool she's always suspected me to be." He laughed a little, but sadly. "She hates going public."

He motioned for me to follow him into the living room to the corner where he had a big leather-top desk. He pulled a chair out beside it and, right away, I got sleepy and felt my brain ooze into the shape of Swiss cheese. I thought that whatever he said would slip through my mind like water being poured over it. But a lot of what he told me stayed. And it did, I think, because the more he talked the more I realized, with growing horror, that he was preparing me to be the next medicine-maker in the Maulden family.

He started in the 1800s and worked himself all the way up to the importance of the liver. He explained that a hundred years ago, everybody thought food had one nutrient that kept life going—so overeating became a national habit. My grandfather laughed. "Shoot! anybody who sold a cure for indigestion could become a millionaire."

Outside, some kids whizzed by on bikes, and down the alley, from the direction of the Second Baptist Church, somebody was rehearsing her voice for a Sunday night solo.

He said that even the Civil War was financed by a tax on medicine. But it was repealed because doctoring yourself was considered a national right, guarded by law. And that was fertile ground for medicine-makers. "Did you know that even Benjamin Franklin's mother sold a remedy for Itch?"

I shook my head, no. And scratched my arm. The Baptist soloist had missed the note and started over. I thought about Sam and tap dancing and Hershey bars.

He went on, telling me about vitamins being discovered in the early 1900s, then germs and miracle drugs. He picked up another bottle of the Inside Medicine from the back of his desk and made the liquid whirl against the thick, greenish glass. He said miracle drugs made everybody think health was something that could be bought. We'd always believed in a right to do-it-yourself healing.

"Someone would come to me, you see, and he'd want penicillin, or sulfa, or streptomycin, or God-knows-what-else the drug companies were coming out with and advertising in magazines and newspapers. Right now there's a market for a drug before it even hits the shelves. The drug companies are the biggest industry in this country. Over 500 tons of tranquilizers were prescribed just this year. And it got to the place where I couldn't tell anybody they didn't need sulfa or penicillin or whatever; they'd get well without it. They wouldn't believe me."

Outside, a newspaper plopped against the front screen porch and through the sheer curtains, I saw Joel go by on his bike.

"You see, I began practicing medicine in 1920. By the time

I was thirty-three the Depression was coming; I didn't have sulfa, penicillin, or any wonder drug. I made this." He nodded toward it, then glanced at me. "Or my first version of it. But now. . . ." He got up. "I want to show you something." He rifled through the stacked papers on top of his desk and showed me a picture of the human liver. "There's something happening now that's made me revise my formula—and my intentions."

Stacked up on the floor were copies of the *Atlantic Naturalist*, *Hearings from the 81st Congress* dated 1950, *Sport Fishing*, *Public Health Reports*, and *Journals of Agriculture and Food Chemistry*.

"I want you to understand this." He handed me the book with the liver picture in it. I set it on my lap—it must have weighed ten pounds. I sensed that even though he was looking at me, he wasn't talking to me alone. My round freckled face was the focus of his concentration like a yogi who'll stare at anything when he sits on nails. Pretty soon, I understood that I represented the whole world and posterity to him. At his trial the judge had said that the Maulden Medicines had been labeled and sold to treat conditions that medical science did not recognize. And I guess he thought that if he couldn't make me understand, no one else ever could.

He pulled out a yellow legal pad and drew circles on it. He explained that the Germans during World War II tested chemicals for killing men, on insects, and found out their man-made formulas were terrific on bugs. "Now watch this." He made circles on the yellow paper rain onto a liver he drew beneath it. He was a pretty good artist, and I followed the liver spots on the back of his hand as he drew circles. "You with me?" he asked, looking at me. I blinked. Around the liver he drew a man. "These are synthetic insecticides," he said, giving the raindrops names.

"You see, their intention is to destroy enzymes. Their target is the nervous system, inside a bug or wherever."

He drew a line inside the man's arm. "This man's arm moves because a chemical goes from one nerve to the other. But if the chemical doesn't disappear very quickly, the nerve keeps firing." He drew the arm waving and gave it the shakes with squiggly lines like in a cartoon.

"Now," he said, "here comes the Lone Ranger." He drew a horse with a man on it running up and down inside the body. "This is an enzyme called cholinesterase. If this nerve-firing chemical decides he likes the limelight and wants to hang around, cholinesterase shoots him out. That way our fellow here never gets the shakes or acts drunk or has a seizure, or worse. And guess where this fellow lives?" He pointed to the Lone Ranger, who now held a gun my grandfather had drawn in his hand. Before I answered, he penciled a barn right in the middle of the liver.

"These new insecticides are just like the poison found in a deadly mushroom. They kill the enzymes that keep the firing chemical under control.

"So," he said, "think about this. What if the insecticide is used only strong enough to kill bugs but not men?" He drew a whole new set of balloons floating in the sky over his man with a Lone Ranger Liver. "There're things all in our world that can make these have stronger effects." He pointed to the insecticide bubbles. "That's what's hard in my line of work. It's already known that these poisons make some drugs more powerful. For instance, sleeping pills will last longer. Somebody could spray the earth with malathion and send down sleeping pills and we'd wake up like Rip Van Winkle in a new century. And," he smiled, "our wives'd be gone.

"You think I'm crazy?" He looked at me hard. He flipped

up pages of articles onto his desk, pointing out passages he'd underlined. "You know what the farmers are pouring on our crops? You know who's breathing air from the bomb we dropped on Japan? Did you know people in New York would buy fans to blow all the pollution south, if they could?" He laughed. "Nobody's ready to admit there's poison around us, so how can they admit my medicine will fight it? DDT right now is in milk, in eggs, in the feed fed to cows. Mosquitoes sprayed with DDT for several generations have turned into strange creatures called gynandromorphs—part male and part female. One of the special things the liver does is keep a balance between male and female hormones and prevent one getting the better of the other. What do you think that means?"

I stared at his face and said nothing. All I knew about DDT was that it was said all the time in junior high as a cool way to tell someone to drop dead twice.

"If the next generation isn't dead from cancer or lung disease or something else because of synthetic insecticides, they might be half-women, half-men, good for nothing. And nobody knows this. People don't even know the tobacco they're smoking was probably sprayed with arsenic."

He got up and put his legal pad down. "My medicine now includes agents for supporting the liver. And if the U.S. government insists on not letting me sell it, at least you'll be made aware of what it's intended for. And then," he looked at me, "who's to say years from now, long after I'm gone, the government won't be trying to make something like what I've got already here. So it's important that if I'm beaten—if in my lifetime I can't repeal my case and make people see and use this —well . . . we'll just have to get around what you don't know about chemistry." He grinned. "Least if your mother and father can't get things straightened out, you and I can." He patted my shoulder and turned toward the den. He walked slowly, his height hunched somewhat by the downward curve of his shoulders. "In a little while, we'll go over to my office and start a batch. But right now, you want to see this TV program on Chinese bears?"

"I don't think so," I said.

I walked onto the front screen porch. For a second I stared at the crepe myrtle bushes that grew against the house, seeing the picture of the future my grandparents wanted for me: a ballet dancer who mixed chemicals in a secret laboratory somewhere. On weekends I'd have to drive into some city and come out at debutante balls. That's the thing about a family that can drive you absolutely nuts—how they can wrap you up in their dreams and their lives and shoot you off in directions you don't especially want to go. I sure didn't want to be a doctor, a pharmacist or anybody else connected with medicine. Frankly I cared about as much for the Lone Ranger Liver as I did for my grandmother's silver dessert forks. But I loved my grandfather—I'd sure never want to do anything that would disappoint him. Or hurt him. So just how the hell was I going to turn down this family business?

13.

B.J.'s Story

That next Saturday, B.J. taught me and half a dozen other kids at the dancing school. When it was all over, Ron, the guy from the pipeline who B.J. had supposedly taken up with, came to pick her up. It was the first time I'd seen him up close. I got the idea that he didn't like B.J. being connected with the dancing school. Or at least the Best Dancing School. He hadn't spoken very nice to any of us. And he'd escorted B.J. to his pickup and barely nodded to Sam.

Sam and I drove out to one of his farms and on the way back stopped at a café. When I ordered coffee, he didn't say anything like maybe I shouldn't do that; and we sat in a booth while Gill told us stories he'd heard when he'd been a pilot. I played a bunch of songs on the jukebox that had words I wished I could say straight-out to Sam. Then he dropped me off at my grandparents' house in time for supper.

That night I sat in my room listening to my chickens changing roosts in the dark. The whole house seemed full of my grandparents' snoring. When I got old, I wasn't going to snore like that. I looked out the window at my parents' house.

B.J. still had a cast on her thumb, and I figured she wasn't going to be dancing at the Silver Moon that night. But Ron's truck wasn't parked in front of the house. She'd probably gone to be with the band, anyway. I thought of how nice it'd be to just walk through my old house, to see it again. So I slipped out of the back door and went over there, taking care not to be seen by anyone who might be passing by.

The spare key was still taped to the bottom of the water meter, and I let myself in the back door. The few pieces of furniture my parents had left were mixed with B.J.'s. My mother hadn't taken the end tables, and we hadn't taken our beds either. Mine had been my grandmother's when she had been a child. Anyway, we'd bought new single beds in Memphis, for fear the old ones might have gotten scratched in the move. Since my parents had been after a new life, I guess they thought that new beds might help. But they hadn't.

I walked down the hall. Empty houses always feel spooky. In my bedroom, I stood by the door and turned on the light. Except for the junk I'd packed away or taken with me, the room was just as I had left it. The bed had been my grandmother's when she had been a girl, and it stood in the center with cherry posts pointing toward the ceiling like raised arms. My mother had sewn a bedspread and curtains to match. B.J. was right; the room was still pretty.

Under the bed I'd always kept a sack of sardines, along with a flashlight, a few books, and some toothpaste. I guess being born when I was—near the end of World War II—put war on my mind. If the Russians came or the Koreans or anybody else I heard Walter Cronkite mention as a possible enemy, I planned to hide under the bed and wait it out. Now I lay down on the floor and slid up under the springs near the headboard. My war sack was still there. It was old and frayed, but it was still stuck in between the springs. Little did I know that the main battle I'd be in the middle of was the one between my parents. And no damn sardines could help with that.

I left the war sack where it was and went to open the closet.

Some of my boxes of old school work were stored on the floor, but they had been pushed aside to make room for hanging a row of brightly colored capes and robes. I pulled one out—a purple job with sequins on the sleeves and neck. There was enough material in it to drape a horse. But underneath were bloomers, a striped pair with a puffed-sleeve top like women wore on the beach in old photographs. When I peeled it away, there was a one-piece swimsuit like Miss America wore. And underneath it was a two-piece affair women wore now. A bikini was tied to the coathanger under that. Apparently B.J. hung her costumes here, and she did some sort of dance that showed the history of the bathing suit. A clever strip, I thought. Some night I wanted to sneak into the Silver Moon and see it.

Putting on the cape, I did a few dance steps up and down the room, then twirled until the hem spread out like a dark puddle that I was in the middle of. Suddenly through the open window I heard a sound, and I reached quickly for the light switch.

Ron and B.J. came into the house, laughing. Lunging for the closet, I closed the door and balled myself up in a knot on the floor. I draped the costume over my head and leaned against the back wall of the closet, my legs drawn up under my chin and my nose propped there, smelling my own knees and the mixed sweetness of B.J.'s costumes. I could hear the shower running and then voices in the kitchen. They scraped chairs around. And every once in a while I stopped worrying about getting out. I thought maybe I could just stay there until B.J. and Ron went to sleep or left.

Then I heard them come into the bedroom where I was. I could feel my stomach move as though crawling up into my throat, and my skin was so wet with sweat that my hands slipped on my knees. I couldn't even imagine what they'd say if they found me. Now I could hear them teasing each other and messing around, and then the closet door opened. I jumped and was sure I'd given away my whole damn hiding place. The cape I was under probably looked like a giant heap of dirty clothes, moving. But before B.J. could rake the costumes around and find me, I heard Ron come up behind her, calling her Babe and telling her to come to him, and a bunch of stuff like that that thank goodness B.J. listened to, so that she pushed the closet door half-closed and moved farther away from me into the room. He must have hugged her, pulling her onto the bed. I could hear the old springs creaking just as they'd sounded through all of my childhood whenever, before I went to sleep, I'd lean over to check under the bed to see if my war sack was still there. Giggling and laughing, B.J. and Ron rolled around on my and my grandmother's childhood bed, then got quiet.

With the cape draped over my head, I had to breathe like a fish, opening my mouth for a gulp of air near the floor under my knees. Then in a moment I began to hear sounds that at first I couldn't understand. Then I did. And I couldn't believe they were doing *that* on *my* bed!

From inside the closet, I listened to them make love. I could hear them panting and groaning, rolling around as if they were in these death agonies and at the same time, going outright crazy with something too delicious to name. Making love seemed to be a strange business. My neck and head were sweating as if I were squatting on the equator. I kept my eyes closed because all I had to look at were the dark underside of the cape and the hairy stubble on my knees. I kept moving my eyelids, squeezing them tight, then letting go, because they were the only things I could move. Unless my ears, straining forward like fly-eating orchids and then shrinking like the fly, were moving; I didn't know.

Now B.J. and Ron were silent, and I wondered whether they

had fallen asleep, and maybe I could sneak out unnoticed. But I was afraid to try it, and then I heard Ron say something and walk out of the room. B.J. started moving around. She turned on the overhead light, and the closet door opened. She pushed the coat hangers on the rod, humming something. Then she picked up the cape that was covering my head.

She sucked in her breath. Then she laughed. "Well, damn!" She offered her hand to pull me up. "How long you been in there?"

"I don't know."

I thought I'd die from embarrassment. B.J. was a little flushed too. Then she looked closely into my face, her hands on my shoulders. "A while?" she said, raising her eyebrows, shaking her head yes and smiling. I shook my head yes in reply, and we did the whole shebang all over again:

She: "A while?"

Me: "Yes."

She: "Yes?"

Me: "A while." And then like a force we couldn't hold back, we hugged, laughing—me to her, and her to me. I grabbed her at the waist; she was holding me with my head pressed to her shoulder, laughing, laughing, sweating and laughing.

"You must have been burning up," she said, brushing back my wet bangs and unwrapping the cape from me and laughing again. She hung up the costume. "How does your room look?"

"Fine," I said.

"Not different?"

"Not really."

"Bet it will now." She smiled and rubbed her tongue through and over the chip in her front tooth, then turned to the closet, thumbed through the costumes and pulled one out. She used the cast on her thumb like a tool, and I saw she had drawn red stars on it. She was wearing an old robe that my mother must have left behind. I recognized it when she turned around and I saw the circle of paint my mother had gotten on it when she accidentally backed up to a wet chair she'd been redoing. B.J.'s hair was pinned up, and she was twisting the parts that had fallen down.

"Come on in the kitchen," she said, reaching for my arm. "Ron and me drove down to colored town and got the best ribs you ever put in your mouth!"

Ron was sitting at the kitchen table; and as we walked in, he looked surprised at seeing me. But B.J. put both hands on my shoulders, nudging me with her cast, and pushed me forward. "Sally's come over to see her old room."

She and I laughed again a little, but not so much that anybody would think anything about it. For all Ron knew, she could have just let me in the back door.

B.J. reached in front of him, hugged him quickly across the shoulders and picked up a rib off a plate on the table. She handed it to me. "See if that's not the best thing you ever put in your mouth."

While I ate the crisp meat, the sauce stuck to my lips and fingers. Ron was drinking beer, and he picked up a rib, too. He smiled, saying: "Nobody else can make ribs like this. "Then he got up and reached into the icebox and set a grape soda on the table for me. His upper arm tightened—his shoulders were heavily muscled from outdoor work—as he took a bottle opener and popped off the cap. Underneath the short, creased sleeve of his shirt, his arm was pale, as white as flour; and the line where it had been protected from the sun was as sharp as if it'd been drawn with a pencil. His hair was curled, with the ends lighter; and he'd wetted it to hold it down, with the comb leaving traces like a plough on a field. His face was so

evenly balanced—the features like whittled hard wood—it reminded me of the face of a statue. But the whiteness of his
skin where it had been covered from the sun was what stayed
in my mind; that, and the definite lines in his still-wet hair
before they dried and could no longer be seen. They made him
seem so desperately eager to do things right. But the fact was,
he was the sexiest man I'd ever seen. In some ways he even
had Sam beat.

"So," he was saying, waiting for my answer as I licked the
sauce off my fingers and the rib bone. "You ever had anything
that good?"

"No sir," I said. "I guess I haven't."

He threw his head back with whoops of laughter and glanced
at B.J. "Hey, hon, you hear her call me sir?" He sat down
opposite me and looked at my face.

"I told you she was sweet." B.J. was dancing around, holding a rib and pouring wine into a big glass. She turned on the
record player and the opening song to *West Side Story* filled the
kitchen softly. B.J. sang along with it, punctuating the words
every once in a while with a dance step or a fast move. Then
she turned the music up and did a fast mean dance waving
a table knife in her good hand and holding up her cast like a
shield, whirling around the kitchen and sticking her legs out
of the open slit of my mother's old robe. She tossed the knife
to Ron, and he caught it. Holding it like a sword, he lunged at
her a few times and then, as though they had rehearsed it, he
stood with one leg bent, offering his thigh as a springboard as
B.J. danced to him, stepped up over his knee, and sprang off.
She did it again. He caught her, twirled around, holding her
by the waist, and then she leapt off. Just as the record ended,
she ran behind me, grabbing me across the chest to use me as
a hostage; and then she stuck her cast out toward Ron from
beneath my arm like it was a weapon, daring him to come

near. When the record ended, we all leaned over, catching our breaths, laughing. B.J. and Ron were sweating, breathing heavily, and they each opened a beer. "Shoot! I'd give anything to be in a musical like that." B.J. reached over and kissed Ron on the cheek. "If I am, you going with me?"

He caught her hand and held it, rubbing his mouth against it, setting the edge of his teeth against the ridge of her knuckles while looking at her silently. His look held me almost hypnotized; watching such a show of feeling I felt embarrassed and turned away. "You know I am," he said, his voice low, almost a whisper.

B.J. licked her hand where Ron's teeth had left a thin red line. She didn't act this way with Sam; she wasn't this free. "Come on," she said, touching my back. "You can help me get ready."

Until then I hadn't really thought she'd still be dancing at the Silver Moon that night. "Could I go see you?" I said, getting up. "Dance, I mean."

She stopped where the hall opened into the kitchen. "She could, couldn't she, Ron?"

When he looked at me, I wasn't able to keep my eyes still. He was sizing me up, his eyes going over my face and then my body, traveling down to my feet and then back up to my face. Finally he said, "I don't think we could pass her off as eighteen."

B.J. looked at me, chewing the side of her lip. "We ought to be able to come up with something." She wiped her face with a dish towel. "I hate to admit it, but the Silver Moon's not a place my own mother would want me in. But it's the only chance I've got to dance. I sing a little. I don't do nothing indecent. I know people think I do, but my dances are clean. Aren't they, Ron?"

He laughed. "You don't even have to move to have people

look at you. But even so, you're good. Anybody can tell you're the only one there with talent—real talent."

She smiled. "You're laying it on thick. But I like it." She reached for his wrist, turned it over so she could read his watch, and then she kissed the back of his hand. "Come on," she said to me, touching me at the same time. "You can help me get ready, or I'm gonna be late."

I followed her into my parents' bedroom. "After that horsing around," she said, slipping off my mother's robe, "I gotta take another shower." She went into the bathroom. "Why don't you go to your closet and get me the pink robe with the green top? Thanks."

When I came back with the costume, she was just coming out of the bathroom, her hair damp from steam and her face red with heat. She sat down at the dressing table that went with my mother's bedroom suite and started making up her face. As she saw me watching her, she told me to go get a kitchen chair and set it beside her. Ron carried it in for me, and as B.J. put on her makeup, she'd reach over and put the same stuff on me.

Ron had gone into the living room to wait. "He won't stand for me wearing any of this except for my act," she said, drawing on my eyes until they seemed dark, sunken pools. "He's jealous as a hornet," she whispered. "He thinks makeup causes me to get stared at, and he doesn't like it." She pancaked all my freckles away, and when she finished I looked as if I'd been tanned on a foreign beach. As she touched me, the easy way that she did seemed as wonderful a gift as waking up and looking like the *real* Elizabeth Taylor. B.J. never held back from anybody.

"What do you think of this?" She sprayed on my wrist the perfume my mother always wore.

"My mother uses that." I said. "Sam—I mean Mr. Best gave it to her." We looked at each other in the mirror. She whispered: "Sam," and watched me when she said it. I wasn't sure what I was doing, except maybe fishing. I certainly had no desire to hurt or upset her in any way. If I sounded a little accusing, as though I wanted to protect Sam's interest in my mother—for whatever reason, and even more, his interest in me—B.J. picked up on that.

"You're right," she said. "He gave it to both me and your mom. He likes me to use things she uses. He even has me dress like her sometimes, fix my hair like her." She stopped and put her hand to her face. "I shouldn't be telling you this."

"It doesn't matter," I said. "I know."

Her face moved, letting go, seemingly relieved and viewing me a little differently. "Sam's really hurt about Ellen and Julie moving out. He won't say it, but he is." Looking in the mirror she smiled slightly, running her tongue down the edge of her chipped tooth and watching me. "Your mother's really been a good friend to Sam. She must be wonderful. He talks about her all the time."

I knew that wasn't true. Sam might be in love with my mother, but my mother was a version of B.J. and I was a smaller version of both of them; and I didn't know why or how we went together.

She put her arm around me, and we looked at ourselves and each other in the mirror. Then B.J. began to cry. I didn't know what to do. We looked at each other in the reflection of the mirror while tears washed off the makeup B.J. had just put on, leaving her eyes like smeared holes. She reached for a towel and began wiping her face. "I had someone like you once." Her words caught in her throat. Then she pushed her hair away from her face and looked back at me. "I'd have her now, sitting here just like this. . . ." She bit her lip and laughed. "Shoot. Look at me. I got to do this whole stuff all over again. Get up."

She sat down as I stood and started drawing on her eyes and mouth again, then covering up the red under her eyes. Her voice found a steadiness, and she tried to sound even and in control. She began telling me about being in New Mexico, fourteen years before. She would glance in the mirror at me standing behind her. She must have seen me as someone who could understand. She turned her face away from mine and aimed her voice into the space of air between us.

"I was eighteen." There was a tilt to her smile. She glanced into the mirror to meet my eyes while telling me how she looked—in calf-length skirts with stockings drawn on her legs. "Because, you know, during the war no one could buy stockings. I made seams up the back of my legs with mascara." She laughed, showing me the back of her calves under my mother's robe and using her finger to trace a line. "I wore my hair in a pageboy like this." She rolled her hair under, watching me in the mirror. "And I worked in a munitions plant in Texas." She put one hand on her hip and slung a leg out. "I made great bullets." She grinned.

I laughed. B.J. couldn't stay away from a joke any more than my mother could drive without changing lanes.

"You see," she stood up and walked to the bed where the costume was laid out, "I came from a big family—farmers, Texas cotton farmers whose cotton got eaten up by boll weevils or worms or drought and. . . . Well, I picked so much cotton from the time I was four, my fingers started growing like this." She made a cone with her hand and sucked in her lips and laughed. Her laughter was so wonderful, so deep, so full, like the whoops a pot-bellied man would send up, yet they came out of a middle section that was so slight I thought of balsa-wood gliders covered by tissue-thin paper. And her guffaws could taper off like the light sound of spilled coins. She went into the bathroom to put on the bikini, the first layer of her costume, and began talking to me through the propped-open door. "I had six brothers and two sisters. We were Catholic." She stuck her head out, pulled at her hair, pointing at what she meant to be the color: "Red-headed Irish Catholic. And," she laughed again, "Italian. My grandmother fell for a dark-skinned, black-eyed cotton farmer from Rome. Who wouldn't?"

She came back into the bedroom, wearing a one-piece swimsuit in bright red satin, so shiny it looked like Christmas wrapping paper. And while she began telling me about how she had left home during the war, she began doing a very curious thing. She grabbed a lipstick brush and sat down on my parents' bed. Propping her legs up and carefully positioning my mother's old robe over the bedspread, she began to dip the brush into the mascara and paint fishnet stockings on her legs, with seemingly hundreds of stars and a line up each of her calves, like the seam she had just explained to me she had drawn during the war. Luckily her right hand wasn't the one with the cast on it, and she could draw well. B.J. must have used her past, comically blending it into an act she was both proud and ashamed of. She told me how she moved to Austin, had gotten a job in a factory near there and spent three years. She lived in an apartment with two other girls, going to the U.S.O. on weekends, learning that she wanted to dance from seeing a New York troupe who came to entertain the men stationed near there or passing through.

"And I started, you know,"—her voice hesitated a moment while she tested my face in the mirror; I sat so still. She looked away from me, talking fast, glancing at the bedspread, concentrating on painting the stockings, which now went all the way up her thighs to the edge of the red satin where her skin was tender and pale. "Well," she went on, "I started going with this boy from Wisconsin. He said he loved me. Shoot! Any sailor from Wisconsin's going to love a girl from Texas every chance he gets—to get warm if nothing else. And, well . . . I just hadn't been raised like that. I got to where I couldn't sleep, I kept seeing my mama's face." She laughed, then quickly stopped. "She would have killed me. And *it*, I knew, would have killed her. I went to confession. I told the priest what I was doing. He said repent, say so many Hail Mary's, and stop doing it. Well, I repented and said the Hail Mary's—but I didn't stop. And I knew I wouldn't." She laughed and looked at me. "You have to imagine what it was like! Every boy I went out with had a chance of being killed, of never living to have anything, not a wife, a child, . . . another year! They were going to die! I don't know if you can understand that."

She looked up. I guess her insistence embarrassed her. She giggled. "Shoot, that year the most popular song was"—she tilted her head and sang softly—"Give Me Something to Remember You By." She stood up. "Anyway, this boy said he'd marry me."

With listening to her own voice, maybe she felt she had to convince me; I sensed she wanted me to approve of her. She smiled in the mirror and then looked down. "He said if he lived he would come back and make me his wife. And that's when he started messing it up. Because then he told me about his family, how he had lived, how he wanted to and would, if he came out of the war alive." She laughed, sending the infectious sound into the room but with a bitter, sad tone to it as she rammed the brush into its case. "It turned out his father owned a whole damn cheese factory! Imagine me, wife of the

Big Cheese!" Her voice was so full-blown, so funny when she said it, her eyes wide and rolling, I laughed. She seemed relieved. "For a while I thought, why not? I know cows as well as anybody—probably more." She laughed again. "But if *I* could seriously think about it, he couldn't. When I found out I was pregnant, I hinted I might want to marry him before he left. I didn't tell him why. I just suggested it. The war was about over then, at least in Europe. He didn't think anything, by then, would happen to him. But after a day of thinking it over, he said he couldn't. He couldn't marry until *after* the war. And from his face when he was saying it, I knew that after the war wouldn't be any different than that second he was looking at me and seeing that no way could he and I go back to Wisconsin and make cheese together!"

She laughed softly. "I don't blame him. I didn't have the background, the . . . what you call breeding, the know-how. But none of it mattered anyway. He got blown up on a ship named the *Bunker Hill*. May 11. This kamikaze pilot flew into his aircraft carrier just off Okinawa. The war was over, at least for him."

From the living room we could hear the record player. Ron had turned it on and settled down with a beer and cigarettes which he tended to smoke about like I ate Tootsie Rolls, one practically linked to the other. "He knows I take a long time," B.J. said, looking behind her at her legs. "Are my seams straight?" She glanced at me, smiling.

Her legs were so perfectly curved; the thighs and calves were like two Coca-Cola bottles standing upside down. She had every ingredient of the thoroughbred ankles that my grandmother wanted for me.

But her story wasn't over. And though she'd told me a lot,

maybe easing her guilt while she did, she wasn't through. She put her hands on my shoulders, looking at me again in the mirror.

"I went back to that priest." She grinned. Her eyes danced, her tongue found the edge of her chipped tooth that was like a slash between two words. "I told that priest his Hail Marys didn't work." She tried to laugh but her voice was flat. "I had sinned. I was like foul stuff you try not to step in. I hated myself, and at the same time I didn't. I wanted a child; I didn't see anything wrong with having a child. I didn't see anything wrong with sex! How could what I had done been so terrible that I should wish I was dead or had never lived? With the feel of life inside me, I couldn't turn my back on that or on myself, or even the Big Cheese, if he had lived! I would have married him no matter if he thought I was only a country bumpkin with a warm little center he especially liked. I didn't care. I was going to live; and the life inside me was going to live! That's all I knew. That's all I cared about.

"So that priest gave me the name of this doctor in New Mexico who ran a home—a hospital really. I called it the Dude Ranch for Women Carrying Unborn Life and for Alcoholics Who Wanted to Do Better." She smiled. "I waitressed. Dr. Lissaro was a little man, sweet, an Italian like my grandfather. He'd once been a surgeon until his hands started to shake, and he couldn't operate anymore. Then he bought this camp in the mountains near a desert and took in well-known people who didn't want anybody to know where they were.

"I wrote my parents that I'd gotten a new job in another war factory. They didn't care, not really. I'd been gone since I was fifteen. They never knew I had a baby down there. She was born that next December. I gave her a name, even though I knew she wouldn't get to keep it. I had her for a few minutes;

they wouldn't let me hold her. Dr. Lissaro said it'd make giving her up worse, so he held her up for me to see, and I called her Sam—," she looked up from where she'd been staring at the top of my head, touching my hair slightly every once in a while, "—Samantha," she said, finishing the name, but also letting us both realize that, by mistake, she'd said more than she'd meant to.

"How Sam?" I said, sounding like an Indian in a Wild West movie—but making sense to us; and I couldn't not ask.

She went into the bathroom. She turned on the water in the sink and stayed there a long while, it seemed, leaving me sitting on the dressing table stool, looking at myself. By now I was so fond of her, I wouldn't have tried anything that might have upset her. But I had to know; I wanted to know the rest. I followed her, stopping at the door and knocking, pretending to know more than I did.

"Where do you think she ended up?" I said, knocking lightly on the bathroom door. "Would Sam know? He told me he'd gone to that place, that ranch, or hospital or whatever you call it."

She was standing in front of the medicine chest, staring at herself in the mirror where my father had shaved every day we'd lived in that house. She turned and looked at me. "He's told you about being in that place?"

The window was open and the night air was cool. I nodded. Lying silently wasn't nearly like out loud.

By now she'd wound her hair into a knot on top of her head and pinned it under a black bowler hat. She'd tied a ribbon around her thumb in the cast, and was holding a stick, with a silk bandanna tied on it, over her shoulder like a hobo. "I'll tell you later," she said. "Some other time." Which is what anybody with half a brain knows means whoever said it *won't*, not unless pestered half to death at least. After she rubbed her face against my hair, she stepped back and smiled and stuck up her broken thumb and put the other hand on her hip in a sexy hitchhiking pose. "How do I look?"

I laughed. To me, and to just about everybody I knew, she looked wonderful. But I didn't want to change the subject, and I was getting ready to start my pestering, when Ron walked down the hall and tapped on the bedroom door, calling for her.

"You're going to grow up beautiful," she said. "Just look at you."

We were standing with my head just beneath her chin, looking at ourselves in the medicine cabinet mirror where my mother had given me my first lesson in brushing my teeth, making me stand on a stool and lean over the sink. Now, thanks to B.J.'s handiwork, I did look pretty good.

She stepped back. "I shouldn't have told you all of this, but I got started and . . . sugar, I've got to go."

Ron came into the room as we walked out of the bathroom. "B.J., it's nearly ten." He looked at me. "You want me to watch you home?"

"That's okay," I said. "It's not far."

B.J. slipped her feet into high-heeled tap shoes. "I'm going to be late again and Ella Jenkins and the band'll kill me!"

Just inside the back door, B.J. stopped and turned to me. "Maybe you want to stay here a while alone?"

"No," I said. "I guess not."

They escorted me to the edge of the yard where my grandparents' property began. Ron waved to me. "Take it easy, little lady." His voice was soft and teasing. "Don't do nothing the Queen of England wouldn't." He laughed, backing the truck up, and he and B.J. drove off.

I sneaked back into my grandparents' house. It had been

dark and silent for hours. I lay down, thinking about the night, feeling love for Sam, and love for B.J., and a terrible hunger for knowing, and at the same time, a fear. I didn't want to know anything that might change us. Staring up at the dark ceiling I listened to the night bugs and fell asleep after deciding not to wash off the face B.J. had given me until morning.

14.

A Visit in My Grandfather's Office

The back entrance to my grandfather's office opened into a room he called his lab. Beyond this was the treatment room and then the waiting room. Even though a young doctor drove over from Searcy every other Tuesday to hold a clinic at the other end of Main Street, no one was willing to let my grandfather retire. No one who had started with him wanted to change, which was a compliment to my grandfather, since he didn't believe in much treatment. Yet that also meant he'd never killed anyone. His own medicines were, in a sense, a form of treatment. But his specialty was histories.

His files were the size of law books, each one with the patient's name on it sitting in a bookcase behind a glass door, and the number and size of them never dwindled. Often I had heard him say to patients that he thought it was time to take a new history. Then they would start again at day one. My grandfather would take notes, writing in a large black-bound book, throwing in questions. Often he would repeat what the patient had just said, starting with: "Now let me get this right." My grandfather was more than a just good listener; he was, in himself, an entire show, sort of like the one on TV called "This Is Your Life."

That's probably part of what Joel had meant when he claimed that my grandfather was a great actor. Joel's mother had once suffered from nasal blockage. My grandfather supposedly exploded it with a piece of cotton dipped in the Outside Medicine, which was taking a great risk, considering the Outside was poisonous to the inside. But Mrs. Weiss had been cured, even though she had the side effect of smelling Maulden's Outside Medicine for several days afterward. In fact, a direct clue that someone had been at the Maulden Clinic was the distinctive odor of the Outside Medicine. It was the best remedy for acne and common zits that anyone could buy. Even Mr. Barber recommended it at the drug store, because he knew he didn't have anything to match it. On many days a whiff of my grandfather's Outside Medicine could be detected in the halls of the high school and in the aisles of stores all over town.

I sat on a stool in the lab, because I could hear my grandfather talking with a patient. My grandmother had sent me to fetch him for supper. But I wasn't in a hurry to get back to the house, and I didn't want to bust in on anybody naked.

Mrs. Elizabeth Clayton was relating the activities of her gall bladder, and she was talking a lot. She had a list of foods that set it off. She was, she said, down to eating almost nothing. She had lost fifteen pounds, and there was no way the flesh was not going to stop falling off—which, considering how much she must weigh, was a blessing in disguise, I thought. I was fascinated with blessings in disguise. It seemed that so much of life was blessings in disguise.

Mrs. Clayton was sick to death over the fact that she could no longer purchase the Inside Medicine. Finally my grandfather said that the only course of treatment was for her to lose just as much weight as would make her happy, and then she should go to Little Rock and have her gall bladder taken out.

Mrs. Clayton cried. I could hear her putting on her shoes and snapping her purse shut.

While I waited for her to leave, I stared at the equipment. Here in my grandfather's lab were giant porcelain tubs for mixing his medicines. There were boxes of empty pint bottles into which he poured it, and funnel devices with rubber hoses and clamps. On the walls opposite me were posters. One had a picture of Hadacol, a medicine that had gotten real famous when I'd been in about the first grade, and under it was: IF YOU THINK THIS IS GOOD, YOU'RE HALF RIGHT. Beside it were the Maulden Medicines with a picture of a heart-shaped shield, an armed knight holding it, emblazoned <u>INVINCIBLE</u>. I suppose that was a painful poster for my grandfather to look at, considering that all those medicines had now fallen into ill repute.

There was another poster showing a bottle of Milltown Don't Give A Damn Pills. They were tranquilizers that had once been very popular. Underneath, in red print, was EITHER/OR, IF YOU WANT TO GIVE A DAMN, YOU STILL CAN. IF YOU DON'T, YOU WON'T. DILUTE WHAT POLLUTES, MAULDEN'S HAS IT ALL.

The last poster showed the two bottles of Maulden's Medicines: HAVE YOU THOUGHT ABOUT WHERE THE AIR GOES WHEN WE'VE SPRAYED IT, SMOKED IN IT, DROPPED BOMBS IN IT? IF YOU WANT TO LIVE WITH NO COMPLAINTS, REACH NINETY, FEEL FIT, YOUNG, VITAL, THEN . . .

That was the one he had put in every newspaper and magazine that would let him. He sent four cases of his medicines to Eisenhower, six bottles to Nixon, and one of each to the speaker of the house. My grandfather said he preferred voting Republicans out of office to having them die there. He sent Nixon and Eisenhower just enough to tide them over. But to Harry Truman my grandfather regularly sent both kinds of the

Maulden Medicines, and the older Truman got, the prouder my grandfather became.

Mrs. Clayton closed the front door of the office and my grandfather opened the back room door and looked at me. "I didn't hear you come in."

"I was sent to tell you supper's ready. But I didn't want to barge in."

He stood, drooping his shoulders, but looking excited. I'd played chess with him and seen that look on his face when he took my queen. "I don't feel like eating," he said. "Do you?"

I raised my shoulders and let them drop.

He called over to the house and told my grandmother he was helping me with homework. No one but me minded.

For the next hour, my grandfather taught me—or attempted to teach me—the beginning steps for making the Inside Medicine. He told me we were going to mix acetone and bromoacetate and zinc and let it bubble, turn brown, heat it, and then use its crystals as vitamin C.

I nodded.

Just short of seeming to be brain-damaged, I slowly measured vials of yellow stuff and splashed them into basins. But my approach was the only thing I had seen to speed up my grandfather. He was like a circus trainer getting a seal to blow the right horn for "Row, Row, Row Your Boat." He clapped, praising me to the skies for any slight movement in the right direction. At the end of an hour I caught him looking at me with a mixture of wonderment and what may have been hopelessness.

"We'll get to the next step some other time," he said. "We need to let this one soak in." He put my vitamin C crystals—stuck on the bottom of a basin like caramel gravel—in a Mason jar and locked up the office.

As we walked home, if it hadn't been for lights from the sun porch, we'd have been stumbling all over in the dark. A faint odor of decomposition floated from the direction of the outhouse across the alleyway.

My grandmother had already gone to bed, but had left our supper on the stove under pot tops. It was Louella's biscuits drowned in Brer Rabbit molasses, along with heated-up soup. After a piece of Louella's chocolate cake, I went into the hall toward my room. Behind me, my grandfather flopped down in a chair and stared at the TV, which he did not turn on. Through the back window came the frantic sound of dried-out, dying bugs. Katydids did most of the rubbing, and my grandmother had told me the male cicadas were the only ones with "stridulating organs." That sounded dirty to me. But when she said it, she didn't seem to notice. I imagined the male cicadas squeezing out of their shells to run off naked. And in the morning I— as well as their mates—could find their husks stuck to a tree or weed, like calling cards.

I lay in the Man-from-Shiloh's bed, staring at the ceiling, holding my breath and hoping to hear my grandfather turn on the TV, scrape around in the kitchen—do anything to seem normal and alive. I lay there thinking. Maybe I should change, join in, become the fascinating debutante my grandmother wanted me to be, and at the same time spend a lot of time in back rooms mixing medicines. I could peddle them at debutante balls. What could be a better way for rich contacts? And what, if I really thought about it, could be a greater compromise? Debutantes would live forever, and everybody but me would be happy—which, of course, would be all right, too.

I rolled over and looked at my old house. My future wasn't up for grabs. It wasn't for anybody but me and Sam to worry about. I was his.

15.

I Learn About B.J. and Sam

The nights were cool, and the leaves seemed dusted with red and yellow chalk. Cicadas and katydids gave up their songs. On homecoming night B.J. and I walked to the school to the far-away sound of the Coldwater Band's bass drum, bought after a townwide raffle.

"And so," B.J. began, after I'd pestered her, pretending I knew what I didn't know, and asking her *please, please* to go on and tell me about how it was during the last of the war in New Mexico where she and Sam were. B.J. would laugh, touch my hair and call me "Flea," since I'd become such a pest—jumping her whenever I could. I even pretended to be crazy about history, about New Mexico, anything, just to get to talk about what had happened, and about Sam. I mentioned his name every chance I got.

"And so, Flea," B.J. said, "you want to know what it was like?" Cars were passing us, splashing beams of light onto the sidewalk. "It was the funniest thing you ever saw—Dr. Lissaro drove a Stanley Steamer. He picked me up at the train station in it, a car puffing like a dragon. Because, you see, no car company had made a new car in years. They were allowed to make only so many, the rest were army trucks and stuff; and there in New Mexico people were riding bicycles, using buggies, anything that'd move—and Dr. Lissaro had bought this old Stanley Steamer, made the last year the company sent them out. It was twenty years old, older than I was, and about as fast."

I would try to imagine how it was in New Mexico that year, 1945—the mountains, the desert, one so close to the other. It was late that May when Sam and B.J. rode the train in different cars and got off at the same stop.

Sam had met Gill in a bar in Texas, where Gill was celebrating getting home from the war with nothing worse than losing a lung. Since Sam had been a graduate of West Point and trained for war, he had spent most of the past three years in Italy, tromping with his troops in brown mud like porridge. The first thing Sam did when he was discharged from active duty was drink. He checked into a hotel in Galveston and began— spending days alone, drinking until he could sleep, sleeping until dreams woke him, drinking again to forget the dreams.

He was supposed to marry Ellen Lipscomb that October. Before the war she had ridden the train to West Point from Little Rock for football weekends and dances, going with Sam's parents at their invitation; and she would invite Sam to escort her during her debutante parties when he was home.

"You know, Flea . . . ," B.J. walked on the sidewalk toward the lights of the football field, "the saddest thing about Sam is Ellen."

"Why?" I asked, not able to even imagine what she was talking about.

"Well, from everything I've heard, and from what I've put together, she loves him. I mean really loves him." B.J. turned and looked at me; we stopped on the sidewalk and stared at each other a minute. The Coldwater Band struck up the fight song and we could hear the cheerleaders yelling. If B.J. was trying to tell me that Ellen's loving Sam was supposed to make us back off from him, she could do what she wanted. I figured

Ellen had stepped out of the picture, even though she and Sam weren't divorced yet—and if I was on the road to committing adultery with a still-married man when I got a little older, and was already definitely coveting my neighbor, it couldn't be helped. Sam loved me, and that's all the sign I needed. I wasn't ever going to give him up.

"And the sad thing about Sam is . . . ," B.J. started walking again, "I just don't think he can stand anybody loving him. He's got so much anger. He won't let anybody get close—not really."

I didn't agree with that. "I don't know about that," I said.

"Flea, Sam hates things." B.J. ducked her head and touched her forehead where her hair was pulled back and fastened. "You see, there were things his father did that Sam was ashamed to even tell me. And he didn't like the way things were at home—here." She told me he hated what his father believed, things everybody around him thought, the way he was forced to be. I didn't know what in the world she was talking about, so I pestered. Finally she told me things that made me see Sam as a little boy, and the scenes she painted played through my mind like a film, over and over. Still, it was hard to understand.

"You see, Flea," B.J. said, "Sam was a grown man by the time he figured out what was wrong with what he'd watched his father do—and even then Sam says he didn't have the sense or guts to say anything—and that's why he needs to forgive himself."

"About what? What?" I kept asking.

B.J. glanced at me in the dark that was lit by the street lights on Main. "Well, you see, as Sam told me, he'd hear his father in the hall or in his office as his father would answer the phone or go to the door and it would be a Saturday night or early Sunday morning. Someone from the county sheriff's office would be telling him that some man—some buck, he'd call him—was in trouble, had cut somebody or gotten too loud, drunk, was being arrested and would Mr. Best pay the bail? Then that next day, that man who'd been in trouble would be working somewhere on Mr. Best's land, paying off the bail that Mr. Best paid, and when it was paid off, Mr. Best would pay that same man wages on Friday night that he knew would be spent at his liquor store. And then Mr. Best would arrange for a little trouble to break out on Saturday night that would land that same man right back in Mr. Best's debt. And one of these was Ella Jenkins' father."

I was quiet a minute, trying to picture that. I tried to see Cab Jenkins as something like a prisoner working around the house where Sam now lived. "Does she know?"

"No—not really, I don't think. She only knows Mr. Best helped her father a lot—helped—that's a funny way to look at it."

The night was cool, and we pulled on our sweaters but didn't walk any faster.

"Then when Sam came back from the army, he was bothered by things that had happened there."

War and killing, I thought and said something about that.

"Yes," B.J. said. "But other things too."

"Like what?" I asked, not able to ever stop being nosy now.

"The army, Flea, you know, had two kinds of blood."

"What kinds?"

"White and Negro. And he hates himself," B.J. went on. "He hates what he thinks he has inherited. You see—," she looked at me, straight-on, her eyes held on me as though saying hard things could make us both strong: "Sam *believes* he's an alcoholic. That year at Dr. Lissaro's he was ready to admit it—

maybe that means he's not. I mean, it's *so* complicated. The last thing anybody wants to do is admit it. That year at Dr. Lissaro's every man there was nearly twice Sam's age. And he was the only one who believed, *really* believed, he had to be there. Most everybody else was sent by someone. But Sam asked Gill to find out where he could go. Gill got Dr. Lissaro's name from a doctor he'd known in the hospital. But I don't think Sam *has* to drink. I don't think it's his center—you know what I mean? I just don't think he thinks about it every minute, plans everything around it. Or maybe it's just that I want so bad to believe that.

"Anyway, what Dr. Lissaro would do, you see, was taper them off. They'd appear at the main lodge, like a ranch house with a big dining room, every afternoon, for whiskey that Dr. Lissaro would figure out each one ought to have—to keep off tremors, you know, and seizures and stuff. Every day, the amount got smaller, until after a few weeks or so—sometimes quicker, sometimes longer—they wouldn't be needing any amount at all. Sam stayed almost two months, so worn out, and needing a place to rest. But shoot, some of them would have stayed the rest of their lives if Dr. Lisarro had let them! But he'd dry them out slow; and us girls—there was always about six or seven there—we'd be the ones to dole it out. We didn't do it like feeding dogs. God knows they looked so pitiful, strolling in, some trying not to trot, to the lodge, tongues practically hanging out, hands shaking like machinery about to break, holding onto the edge of the counter by the kitchen. It'd been easy to see it as something awful like that. But Dr. Lissaro wouldn't let it; he treated them like they ought to have better, even if they didn't think so themselves—or even wanted it. Shoot, we'd walk out, some of us . . . ," she giggled, "bellies like watermelons under our skirts, some of us so young we looked still wet, sashaying like French maids, balancing trays with shot glasses, clear clean glass with whiskey like dark honey, and hand them out with white napkins. That's what killed me: napkins! But it saved us. You know what I mean? Dr. Lissaro wouldn't let things get low. We were that already."

B.J. stopped. She looked embarrassed. "Lord, we were a sight." She whooped laughter. "Pregnant unwed girls serving liquor to alcoholics on silver trays in a place like a kid's camp."

I played out in my mind how one day, probably, B.J. had passed Sam in the dining room. In my mind, I heard them speak the first time, then more frequently. I felt them beginning to love each other just as Sam and I did now.

B.J. told me how Dr. Lissaro would lend his Stanley Steamer to some of those ready to be discharged, to let them drive into the nearest town to buy new clothes. But Sam would not go. He told B.J. he had had too many near wrecks from drinking.

"I drove him," B.J. said. "He asked me to."

I imagined them going out alone in that old car, stopping by the road and picnicking—and maybe more—in a field on the way. I was jealous and yet I was living through it at the same time. But that night, B.J. and I sat on the bleachers at the football field and cheered on the Coldwater Tigers, B.J. yelling beside me. And it didn't matter that on homecoming night I couldn't even twirl a baton, not even when Corinne Hamilton twirled fire, wearing a sequined suit that dripped fringe from her tits and boot tops. Everybody said Corinne would probably end up Miss America. But I was B.J.'s friend. And everything that had changed so far was enough for me. I wanted to stop. I wanted our lives to stay there, right where they were, souped-up, having fun, and stuck together. And, oh, how we were stuck together! Stuck as a strange, loony, wonderful team! I even began to see how we fit. My mother—a later version of

B.J. And me—an early version of both of them, as well as the daughter B.J. had not wanted to give away. I was something kin to the B.J. that Sam had first fallen in love with in New Mexico in 1945. I was not only B.J.'s youth, I was Sam's as well. I was a part of their past and their present. *I was their love!*

On the way home, B.J. told me the rest: "I didn't mean to," she said. She looked at me pitifully, sad and disappointed in herself, and then she laughed, rolling it out like beer-belly laughter from the golden goose: "But it was the only job I could get!

"You see, after I had Sam—I mean Samantha—I left Lissaro's and I was so dumb I headed for a place called Las Vegas. But stupid me." She rolled her eyes up and stuck her tongue out. "It wasn't in no Nevada. It was in New Mexico! I didn't know! Shoot, to me, Las Vegas was Las Vegas and all I knew was I wanted to dance. I wasn't going back to no factory! I'd had enough of that. I had to move. I mean *move*." She twirled, leapt, and landed on the sidewalk and slashed one leg out to the side with her arm over it and spun like a dervish with her hair flying out like the cheerleaders' pom-poms.

"This fellow in a club there said, 'You wanna get to the other Las Vegas?'" She did an imitation, putting a fat, wet imaginary cigar in her mouth, licking her lips around it, her fingers curved over its bulk, and lowering her voice like a fat movie sheriff: "'Then young lady, you gotta take your clothes off.'

"He told me no one on earth was going to sit around watching me dance. That was boring as hell. But if I could learn to strip off my clothes while I was doing it; well then, I might could shoot two birds. I mean, you see, I could get experience, get into the entertainment business. He told me I'd probably priss into a drugstore one day, sit on a stool at the soda fountain, and get signed up by some guy who was on the lookout for Hollywood stars. I believed him. Why not! But—well, I just didn't want to take my clothes off in public like that. My mother would kill me!" She laughed.

"But I had to have a job. And then I studied this woman, Gypsy Rose Lee. I decided I'd get me up an act like hers, comedy, some clothes off, but with a whole lot of dance."

She grabbed my arm, looking into my eyes and swallowing the laughter that snuck out the side of her mouth anyway: "I called myself the Anatomic Bomber!"

We whooped. We bent over and held our stomachs and beat our thighs and ran down the sidewalk, while a bunch of Coldwater High School boys passed us in a pack and looked at us as if we were crazy or high or wanting it. When one of them grabbed her arm and asked did she want to go with him, B.J. said, "Get on," low and not ugly, but obviously meaning it.

We crossed over to the street the Second Baptist Church was on and turned up the alley toward our houses. "How did Sam find you?" I asked. "How'd he get you to move here?"

"Flea." She stopped and looked at me. "I'm going to tell you a secret"—as though she hadn't already.

She looked down the alley. "I was visiting at Lissaro's. I liked to take old clothes and things. For the girls, you know. And nobody knows here, but you see, Sam still goes back to Lissaro's every once in a while, when he needs to. That's why he made up this story about having an orphanage in Peru." She laughed. "Haven't you ever heard what he tells people in Coldwater when he comes back and they ask him why he looks so peaked?"

I laughed. I *had* heard, and the answer was so typically Sam. I lowered my voice, trying to become him: "I reckon orphans and South American food can do that to you."

The wonderful crazy mood was there and we fell on it like

kids jumping into a pile of leaves. Up until then, if knowing all that stuff about Sam could have made me cool off and love him less, the chances of that now were about as good as Kate the mule's for having babies. Secrets seemed to only make my love more sure. It was as if I had lived all those years with him, and knowing what he was most afraid of and what got the best of him was about like feeling as close to him as to myself.

B.J. and I walked on down the alley until we were beside my grandparents' house, and there in the darkness in front of the outhouse she punched my shoulder and hooted. "Watch this." She twirled around. "I been thinking about crazy, hicky cheers we could make up." She grinned. The night lights from the newspaper office were shooting up past her knees, and she did this cute little finger click like the Coldwater cheerleaders warming up, and then she yelled out: "Squeeze that orange. Drain that juice. All 'gainst Coldwater, ain't no use!"

I hooted, my voice like my Elizabeth Taylor chicken, clucking with excitement at her roosters. "Chewin' tobacco, Chewin' tobacco," I yelled. "Spit on the wall. Come on Coldwater. Get that ball!"

"Flea," she said, holding my chin in her hand and grinning at me. "You're adorable."

And damn! if I didn't believe her.

16.

Elizabeth Taylor Goes to Church

Some of the things that B.J. told me in her story worried me. I just couldn't understand how two people who loved each other wouldn't do anything about how they felt. Maybe B.J. really did back off from Sam because of Ellen. Maybe she loved him enough to step away if she thought that was really best for him. I guessed B.J. thought about Sam like she told me she'd felt about the Big Cheese: that she wasn't good enough to fit into his life. The only time I had ever come close to understanding that was when I remembered moving into the junior high in Memphis and being afraid to talk to anybody, or the way my grandfather had acted when he came to give a talk at the Peabody Hotel about his medicines. He'd looked in the mirror and combed his hair for a half-hour, and wore a three-piece suit, and used a plantation owner's voice that had nothing to do with him. It was the craziest thing in the world. Growing up in Coldwater had made us feel known and special, and then when we got out into the world we found out that what had made us strong could also embarrass us and make us doubt our worth.

While I stared at the ribbed bedspread on the Man-from-Shiloh's bed, a terrible thought came to me. Neither Sam nor I had ever said anything about how we felt. Maybe that was how things got mixed up and never done. Maybe love, untalked about, could be shoved around and put away—like B.J. getting hooked up with Ron, and my mother and father getting miserable with me, and then each other, and coming apart.

I looked at the wood curls carved on the Man-from-Shiloh's bed. It seemed the easiest thing in the world to do: "I love you," I said. I went out and sat on the chicken house roof and dropped kernels of corn to the ground, and when Elizabeth Taylor and her roosters came close and looked up at me, I leaned down and whispered: "I love you. I love you. I love you." There was nothing hard about that. But it could, as I also knew, sound empty and mean nothing. When I said it, I'd have to find some special way to do it. Some way to make it stick.

Whenever I passed the trophy case in the main hall of the high school, I'd look at the picture on the wall of Julie Best in her homecoming queen gear. She'd probably never told Sam she loved him. And if his wife, Ellen, had, obviously she hadn't done it right—it hadn't lasted.

From now on, I resolved that every Saturday that I went to the dancing school with Sam, and every afternoon that I was with him after school, I would carefully watch for just the right moment to say straight-out that I loved him. I practiced in the air, reaching up and grabbing his neck and pulling him down to where I could get a good lip-lock on him.

The next weekend was Halloween. I stayed quietly in the house, past the age of costumes and candy collecting, and answered the doorbell for the generation below me. The next morning Miss Pankhurst was on the phone to my grandmother and to half the other citizens of Coldwater. Terrible things had happened. Since there weren't many opportunities to get excited in Coldwater, a holiday could become an excuse for doing things that were barely connected with it. For instance, a farmer named Thomas Haskins bought a gravestone and held his own funeral on the Fourth of July. He was saving his family time and expense, he said; and they all went to the cemetery at midnight and shot off fireworks.

Usually, on the afternoon before Halloween night people took their yard chairs inside or locked them up, for fear they would be moved across town to someone else's yard. We expected that by morning most of the windows on Main Street would be soaped. During the night all sorts of people—even grown men into their forties or beyond—drove into Coldwater to do some prank.

Except for the idea of witches, Halloween seemed a man's night, at least the dark after-midnight part of it. I guess some of this came from, or went into, the story of Cinderella. I sure had the idea that if I stayed out past twelve I would lose whatever magic I had, and my ride home as well.

But in Coldwater, the Halloween of 1959 had a lot to do with women. When we woke up the next morning, anybody who went out on the street found a bra hanging on a telephone pole or a pair of bikini panties slung over a bush. Girdles were strung along Main Street, and a red slip flew from the high school flagpole. "Disgusting," Miss Pankhurst said. "Decadent," my grandmother announced. They agreed the Missionary Society should consider doing something about the next Halloween.

That morning also, the weather turned cold and we heard that the Mexicans had been driven home, leaving silently in the night as they usually did.

Then next Tuesday the long-awaited Missionary Society meeting finally took place. I was at school—thank goodness! But in spirit I was sure there; I had polished so much silver for it that I suspected I had silver poisoning, if there was such a thing.

Despite the fact that Louella served Sunrise salad, Waldorf salad, and beautiful petit fours, the luncheon was a flop. By the time I got home from school, my grandmother had already taken paregoric and gone to bed. So it was Louella who told me what had happened. First of all, the outhouse had not been moved. Ezekiel had delivered a mound of dirt and set it right beside the outhouse, ready to fill in the hole underneath the minute it got exposed. My grandmother even gave Ezekiel money to buy lilies in coffee cans to transplant on the covered-up hole to beautify the alley. She had called Mr. Rankin every day the week before, but on meeting day the outhouse still sat, dry, gray, too close and faintly odoriferous. When my grandmother called Mr. Rankin early that morning, angry and frantic, Mr. Rankin said that the man he'd hired to haul off the outhouse was sick. There wasn't time to get somebody else, and Mr. Rankin was too busy to worry about an outhouse.

My grandmother was furious. She wondered if Mr. Rankin had failed her on purpose. Her only recourse was to buy lots of curtains, though anybody coming in the sun porch entrance couldn't help but see the outhouse. And how could she change the entrance to her home? So not only my grandmother but also those guests who sat at the luncheon tables in the sun porch had to look out onto the alley with the outhouse clearly in view.

Almost worse than that were my chickens. It seems that when roosters are learning to crow they don't care when they do it. They practice all day long. My roosters crowed through the whole meeting. Whenever the secretary called a name from the roll, a rooster, it seemed, answered. Every name had to be repeated at least twice and even those had to be wedged in between crows. My grandmother told Louella she had never been so embarrassed in her life.

Miss Pankhurst wore the pumpkin-colored cloche she had bought in Memphis and had shown me during our bus ride. She smiled and laughed at everything, even the discussion about Halloween and the Mexicans' unsanitary habits. When my grandmother pshawed at her behavior, Miss Pankhurst apologized and blamed her uncontrollable joy on the important announcement that she would make at the end of the meeting.

Waiting until the last minute, and with great drama, Miss Pankhurst pulled off her gloves and held up her hand. A diamond ring was on her finger. "This is my official announcement," she said. "Mr. Foster Collins and I shall be married on Thanksgiving Day in the First Methodist Church." And with that, all the ladies stood up clapping and smiling, while expressing their surprise and happiness. For once their reaction totally drowned out my roosters. Shortly after that, lunch was served; afterward my grandmother escorted everyone to the front door and went to bed.

"It was sure some meeting!" Louella glanced at me. She was washing dishes while I sat listening to her and eating leftover petit fours. "And then Miss Pankhurst come into the kitchen here and asked your grandmother would she mind if you was the flower girl?"

"And what'd she say?"

"Said fine." Louella smiled and poured a glass of milk for me. "They going to get you some real pretty dress made up by Miss Leona." Leona Sutton was the best seamstress in town.

I sat and thought about that. Being in a wedding would be exactly right. I would learn how my own and Sam's would be.

By the time Sam had divorced Ellen, I figured I'd be about

sixteen. Nobody but country girls or somebody who was pregnant got married that early, but I didn't care what anybody
would say about it. Nothing mattered but that I would be
with Sam forever. The only part that gave me trouble was the
thought of being the Coldwater Homecoming Queen's step-
mother. But I'd send Julie off to school and get her a job up
North. Lord! it was wonderful how you could get life to behave.
I didn't need friends at school or a normal family together in
one place. I was a tap dancer passing as a ballerina with a pet
chicken. I was loved and in love with someone who would keep
me and care for me, no matter what. I sat looking at Louella,
with a stack of little cakes in front of me, feeling that sweet
strong secret, stuck deep, setting me apart. I was like some
quiz show contestant who'd rehearsed the questions before I
went on the air. I knew how everything was going to come out.
When I married Sam we'd be happy and safe and together.
Nothing in the whole world would bother us.

The air turned cooler and the fall rains began. The sidewalks
and rooftops were washed free of dust. Milky tan puddles lay
in the gravel roads, splashing up on everybody's hubcaps. On
Thanksgiving Day at four o'clock, after a big turkey dinner, my
grandparents and I were going to the First Methodist Church.

For once, wool would have felt good. But I was dressed in a
taffeta getup with something called "cap sleeves." Leona Sutton had made it for me, and its skirt was full enough to hide
thieves. I was a little too old to be a flower girl, but Miss Pankhurst needed somebody. At her age there wasn't even anyone
to give her away. My grandmother had declined the offer to be
matron of honor; she didn't think she could get down the aisle
in cold weather without a cane. Mrs. Barber, the soda jerk, had
accepted the honor. And of course Sam was the best man.

Just as I'd gotten dressed, I remembered that I'd wanted to take a corn muffin from Thanksgiving dinner to Elizabeth Taylor. I figured being a healthy chicken on Thanksgiving was something she'd want to celebrate. When nobody was watching me, I hurried out to the chicken yard in my wedding gear and gave it to her.

We decided to walk to church to help digest our dinner. I was carrying a basket with rose petals in it that I was supposed to sprinkle down the church aisle. The basket was decorated with yellow mums tied onto it, with something called baby's breath mixed in with the mums. But the breath was dried out, and it shed all the way there.

We passed the front of the newspaper office and the jewelry store. The church doors were propped open to let in the wonderful cool air. The wedding party had rehearsed everything the night before. And as we drew closer, I heard Mrs. Emiloo Harris already at work on her second organ piece.

The church was full. While my grandparents found a seat on the fourth pew, I hurried into a Sunday school room. There Miss Pankhurst hugged me. "Oh, sweet thing," she said, crushing me and my basket, making a few more stems of baby's breath go bald. "You look gorgeous." She examined my dress, which was blue, supposedly the color of sky. Mrs. Barber had on something made out of the same material.

Miss Pankhurst nervously picked up her own bouquet and then looked at my flower basket. "It's got problems, doesn't it?" She was in an ivory-colored lace dress with a hat and veil she had designed to match. She pulled down her veil and said, "But nothing can bother me today, not even a flower basket with stale flowers." She smiled.

Mrs. Barber said I looked like a doll out of a storybook, and that not a soul in the whole church would notice that my flower decorations were half-dead. All three of us peeked out the Sunday school room door as Mrs. Harris started on the fifth organ piece.

Foster Collins came out of the preacher's study with Sam, and they stood at the altar, smiling, but both looking a little under the weather from the bachelor party that Sam had thrown the night before. Behind Foster's glasses, his eyes were red. Sam's face was a little pale, and his eyes looked blurry.

By then Mrs. Harris had turned the organ-pumping over to Mr. Harris, who sat closely beside her, and he blew the organ up so that a very loud "Wedding March" began coming out of it. Miss Pankhurst sucked in her breath. "Well, here goes," she said, pushing me out.

I walked down the aisle, smiling, strewing rose petals on the carpet, just as I'd rehearsed; and as I did, Sam kept his eyes on me and I looked back. All the love and certainty of our secret were spraying from me to him. For us, this was also a rehearsal. I let him see my love and our secret promise in the way that I walked, and in my eyes, and in the way that, when I got to the altar, I stood opposite him, looking over with so much feeling. He winked.

Looking back down the aisle I saw that along with all the rose petals, I'd also left a trail of baby's breath. Then, to a great swell on the organ, Miss Pankhurst began her entry.

Standing so that I faced the guests, I could see B.J. and Ron in the last pew. Miss Pankhurst hadn't wanted to invite them, but B.J. had been in charge of Miss Pankhurst's wedding gifts, and at the last minute Miss Pankhurst had included B.J.—and Ron. B.J. was craning her neck now around the people in front of her to smile at me, so tickled at seeing me dressed up—and she looked so proud. I could see her love for me floating over the heads of everybody like blown clear bubbles that I could reach up to, touch and pop. And still they'd keep coming.

The preacher, who didn't have a D.D., was looked down

upon by my grandmother. Still, he was good at things like marriages, communion, and funerals; it was his sermons that my grandmother said were flimsy and half-illiterate.

He had just started giving the vows to Miss Pankhurst and Foster Collins when, following the trail of my baby's breath, Elizabeth Taylor came pecking down the aisle. I heard her soft clucking around the hem of my enormous skirt. At first, no one laughed. I looked down and saw her and I felt sick.

I ignored her. Everyone ignored her. The whole congregation was holding its breath.

For a while Elizabeth pecked at the fallen baby's breath and seemed content. Miss Pankhurst gave her bouquet to me, while Foster Collins prepared to put the wedding ring on her. Then, just as Sam took the ring out of his pocket and handed it to Foster, Elizabeth Taylor flapped up to the banister of the altar and sat. Behind me, I distinctly heard my grandmother's famous pshaw, and then a spattering of giggles.

I had to get my hands on Elizabeth or else she would ruin Miss Pankhurst's wedding. I moved behind the preacher and grabbed for her, but she clucked and flapped to the top of the organ, where Mrs. Harris sucked in her breath at the keyboard below Elizabeth and tried her best to look dignified. Mr. Harris was looking down at his feet as though studying the foot pedals that he was going to pump, trying to pretend that Elizabeth Taylor wasn't even there.

I went back to my place while Mrs. Barber gave the ring to Miss Pankhurst to put on Foster Collins; and then, thank goodness, the whole thing was over! "You may kiss the bride now," the preacher said. Mrs. Barber lifted Miss Pankhurst's veil. Foster pecked Miss Pankhurst's cheek with his lips, which is what they'd rehearsed, since Miss Pankhurst said she wasn't about to make a public display of passion. Mr. Harris began pumping air into the organ, and as Mrs. Harris played the opening chords for our march out, Elizabeth Taylor squawked in terror and flew to the podium. In the most athletic maneuver I'd ever made, I scooped her up and regained my place in the march up the aisle. Everybody was laughing. I hurried out, terribly embarrassed, with Elizabeth tucked under my arm like a football. I covered her face with my flower basket to help hold her. I wasn't exactly sure where her dern ear was, but I chose a place and whispered into it about like a cheerleader with laryngitis: "Soon as I get you home, I'm gonna wring your damn neck."

We all stood outside on the church steps. "I'm sorry," I said to Miss Pankhurst.

She put her arm through Foster Collins's and said, "Sugar, you couldn't help it."

Foster reached over and patted Elizabeth Taylor's head. "Shoot," he said, "the whole town of Coldwater was invited."

Sam handed me a small package of rice which was meant to be thrown at Miss Pankhurst and Foster. "No harm done," he said, then poured the rice into my hand. "Bet your chicken'll like this."

I held my hand open for Elizabeth, and while she was pecking it, my grandparents came out.

"I told you the chickens were a bad idea!" My grandmother was blaming my grandfather.

"Of course they were." My grandfather looked at her and then laughed. "The girl needs a poodle."

"I'm sorry, Colleen." Looking mortified, my grandmother began apologizing to Miss Pankhurst. But the new Mrs. Foster Collins touched my grandmother's arm and told her what she'd told me earlier: nothing could spoil this day.

B.J. and Ron came out, and they offered to walk Elizabeth

Taylor home for me. "You got to stay for the reception," B.J. told me while Ron took Elizabeth out of my arms.

Ron laughed. "Bet this is the first chicken ever to go to a church wedding in Coldwater. Good thing you don't have a turkey for a pet!" Then he and B.J. walked quietly across the street and started home.

The rest of us went into the basement and drank punch in honor of the new Mr. and Mrs. Foster Collins. When they were ready to leave for their honeymoon in Hot Springs, we showered them with rice all the way to Miss Pankhurst's car. It was parked in front of the church, and all of its windows had been soaped with the words "Just Hitched." Some old shoes of Sam's and Gill's were tied onto the back bumper. Foster climbed in behind the wheel, started the engine and they drove off. We all stood on the church steps waving as both of them waved back, all the way down Main and over the railroad tracks.

17.

The Death of My Chickens and the Addition of Toulouse

I don't think any of us, not even my grandmother, felt that Elizabeth Taylor's days should be numbered. It was as unintentional as the dancing school windows smashing down on B.J.'s thumbs. We *had* all agreed that the roosters ought to be sold. I didn't especially want to get rid of them, but I didn't object. Their crowing really had made them pests.

My grandparents arranged for a chicken farmer to buy them. I thought of it as like taking a dog who tore up things at home and placing him out on a big piece of land where he could run. I pictured my chickens pecking around on a farm, crowing their lungs out and not bothering anybody.

On the day we knew the chicken farmer was to come, I put Elizabeth in the hen house by herself and shut the door. My grandmother was in charge of seeing that the roosters were taken off. I went to school, and didn't think much more about it until I came home and went out into the backyard to let Elizabeth out of the hen house. When I couldn't find her, my grandmother and Louella came to help me look.

"Lord, honey," Louella said. "Nobody meant for this to happen."

I stared at the empty hen house.

My grandmother went inside to her bedroom to telephone the farmer. Louella and I couldn't stand not knowing what was happening. I got on the phone in the hall and Louella got on the one in the kitchen.

"Where's the hen?"

"What hen?"

"The hen my granddaughter shut up in the hen house!"

"I didn't see no hen."

Either Elizabeth had somehow gotten out, or else one of the farmer's helpers had thought she belonged with the group. Probably my grandmother hadn't been too clear about the men taking only the roosters. "Well, we're coming out to look for my granddaughter's pet hen," she told the farmer.

When he told her the chickens were already sitting in a cooler down at Thompson's Grocery Store, marked Super Fresh, my grandmother let out a little cry. I sucked in a big breath, and I could hear Louella moaning into the phone in the kitchen. We all hung up. In a few minutes my grandmother came out of her bedroom and looked at me. She of course probably knew I'd been listening, but none of us wanted to talk about that. "Your chicken's just run off," she said. "I told that man not to take the hen, and he said as far as he knew, he didn't. She'll turn up. If she can get through the fence to walk around town and even attend church, then she's here somewhere. Maybe she's hiding."

Louella and I went into the back yard to look again for Elizabeth. "She was just a chicken," Louella said quietly. "That's not like a real pet—what you can get attached to. Chickens is food."

Later when I was on the sun porch trying to do homework, I heard Louella whispering to my grandmother: "I think that hen really did get in with the roosters."

"Why do you think that?"

"That hen ain't anywhere around and I got a feeling about it."

My grandmother looked at Louella in silence. "As long as we're not sure, let's not speculate."

My desire for chicken that was baked, barbecued, or made any other way from the recipes my grandmother handed Louella every week, died with Elizabeth Taylor. Louella always served chicken several times a week and every Sunday, but now I just pushed it around on my plate with a polished silver fork until it looked messy and unfit to eat. Every chicken served, no matter how, looked to me small, feminine, and familiar.

"She's not eating. Something's got to be the matter with her. Test her blood," my grandmother said to my grandfather.

"She's not anemic. She's depressed."

"So now you agree with me! This divorce business is ruining her."

"Probably not."

I was filling up on bread and Louella's homemade preserves.

My grandfather leaned back in his chair. "I think she's afraid she's eating her pet."

My grandmother pshawed. But then she got quiet.

Bless my grandfather. Most of the time he never seemed to see me, and yet when I had trouble he usually knew what the trouble was. No wonder his patients loved him.

But the seed had been planted, and if doubt can spur imagination, then my grandmother's was at least starting off at a slow trot. She lay down her fork. "I just don't think we can go on like this. We'll have to stop serving chicken."

My grandfather cut up a fried thigh. "Doesn't bother me," he said. "Just fix something else for her to eat."

"Well, it's starting to affect me!" Rolling up her napkin and stuffing it into its silver ring, my grandmother looked across the table at me. "I feel responsible. I didn't like the chicken. Chickens as pets are not normal. But. . . ." She pushed her plate away and drank some water, still looking at me. "I can't sit here day after day thinking you're not eating because of some mistake I allowed to happen. It's ruining my stomach. We'll just have to quit eating chickens. I don't ever want to even *see* another chicken!"

My grandfather reached across the table and chose a fat breast from the meat plate. Taking a bite, he studied her. "Economically that's not good—chickens are cheap. But overall I think you're right." He reached into the center of the table and took a cream pitcher that he'd filled with his Inside Medicine and poured a little into all of our tall crystal glasses. It was many months before chicken was served again.

Considering the guilt that my grandmother felt for having been indirectly responsible for Elizabeth Taylor's death, you would think that for Christmas she would have given me a dog. Not that I especially wanted a dog. But the thought that I might want one had long been a point of argument between my grandparents. But even if I had, I don't think that would have mattered, for I was always given what was thought to be good for me. And for the Christmas of 1959, what my grandmother decided would be good for both of us was a fat green parrot named Toulouse.

I think my grandmother had ideas of a refined bird sitting on a perch in her living room, similar to the peacocks strutting about plantations. He was purchased through a bird dealer in Little Rock who had connections in Texas, and no one was certain how long Toulouse had been out of the jungles of South America. But my grandmother had been told that he was already at least forty-five years old, which meant he was in my parents' generation, so he'd had a long time to learn a little from a lot of different people. Also, my grandmother was assured that he had a sweet disposition, was disease-free, and was already in command of fifteen words.

What she didn't know was that eight of the fifteen words Toulouse was in command of were the kind that were likely to be written on the walls of bathrooms in honky-tonks and bus stations. And even though Toulouse was capable of speaking them clearly, he wasn't particular about when he used them. So on Christmas morning, totally unprovoked, Toulouse let loose a string of filthy language under the Christmas tree in my grandmother's living room.

At once he was banished to the bathroom, and there he stayed while we had Christmas dinner. Frankly, I was tickled to death he was there and had spilled his filthy words exactly when he did, for my parents had driven over from Memphis for the day and it was right after they walked in that Toulouse had yelled his stuff. It seemed to fit the whole damn situation.

My parents behaved as if they were good friends the whole time. They talked to each other like royalty on television. Over the past few months whenever they'd called me on the telephone, I barely listened to what they said. I usually just watched television while I was on the phone. And I hadn't read any of their letters since that time I was afraid they were dying, and that was months ago. So during Christmas dinner if they mentioned anything to me about what I was supposed to know about, I acted politely surprised, as if what they did didn't matter to me, anyway. We followed all the rules set out by Emily Post. And while we ate country-smoked ham, which Louella served—turkey was too closely related to chickens— Toulouse yelled his fifteen words behind the closed bathroom door.

Poor grandmother. Without knowing it, she had swapped a yardful of crowing roosters for one foul-mouthed parrot who had never read Emily Post and probably wouldn't have changed his vocabulary even if he had.

My parents stayed there for Christmas night, my mother sleeping with me and my father staying on the couch in the living room. While Toulouse sat in the bathroom on his perch in his cage, his eyes half closed and glazed over, I kept mine half closed too, while my mother tried pillow talk and worked on my hair. She kept asking me about school and a bunch of other junk. When I answered her I wasn't thinking about either her or Toulouse. I was thinking about Sam—me and Sam. It was strange how my mother and I could both be in the Man-from-Shiloh's bed, no more than six inches from touching each other, and yet never get close.

It didn't matter to me what my mother and father decided to do. I wouldn't have to live with either one of them, or at least for very long. In two years I'd be sixteen, married, and living with Sam in the big old house at the Mill Pond. My mother and father would be driving over to spend holidays with me and Sam. What they did with their lives wouldn't have anything to do with me.

By early morning of the next day they were ready to go. I went outside to see them off. My mother walked down the sun porch steps beside me. "You're sure everything fit all right? You don't want me to take anything back?"

"No. It's all fine," I said. "Thanks." They'd each given me a bunch of loot for Christmas.

"Take care, Punkin." My mother reached to hug me, calling me a dumb childhood name that made me think of Miss Pankhurst's hat.

My father came over, too. They were each going to take turns coming over to reach and hug me. When they did they each whispered that they loved me and missed me. My mother's eyes filled up with thick tears that glued all of her eyelashes together. My father kissed my cheek and looked at me as if I were the unexpected prize at the bottom of a cereal box. They said they'd call again that night and every week as usual, and would write a lot.

"How about writing to me, once in a while?" My father held on to my shoulder.

"Well, school work's heavy. And now there's exams and all."

My mother: "Take care. And don't study too hard. You remember what they say: all work and no play. . . ." She tweaked my shoulder, expecting me to finish it for her, making it seem as if we were in cahoots.

"Yeah, makes Jack a dull guy . . ." I said, pleasing her. But she didn't know about all the stuff my grandmother insisted I learn in order to keep myself a fascinating woman.

They each got in different cars. We watched them drive off, my father politely letting my mother back out of the driveway first. My grandparents went inside. I turned and looked down the sidewalk in the direction of the Mill Pond. I half-ran to the corner, turning it and heading to Sam's, blowing misty smoke out of my mouth in the chilled air like a cigar-smoking gangster. Frost was on the grass, as though webs had been spun on the yards during the night to lie like pockets of snow with dew making them shine in the morning sun. I stood in front of Sam's house. The light was on in his study. I walked close, the grass cushioning my feet but getting them wet.

I stood on tiptoe and peeked in the window. He was sitting in a big easy chair. Beside him on a table were photographs. There were some framed snapshots and a big picture of Ellen. She was leaning against a tree. I'd never noticed before how much the shape of her shoulders and the way that she stood was so much like my mother's and B.J.'s. In Sam's hand was a glass of something that I knew had whiskey in it. He seemed to be just staring into space. It was a good thing I'd come to keep him company. I tapped on the window, grinning. He looked up; his glasses fell a little onto his nose, and he smiled and took them off. He came to the window and motioned for me to come to the back door. Then he let me in and offered me a cup of coffee. That made me laugh.

Coffee drinking was just another secret we had from my grandmother, since I'd taken it up with him and Gill in the afternoons on our jaunts. I told him about Toulouse, and we laughed till the coffee jiggled over into the saucers. Then I gave him the Christmas present I'd picked out in the jewelry store and asked B.J. to get engraved. It was a key ring with *Sam* written on it on one side, and on the other, *Sally*. I'd wanted to put *love* or *forever* or part of a poem by Elizabeth Barrett Browning, but there wasn't room. I watched him look at it, holding it in his big hand, rubbing his thumb across it, and this nice smile came over his face and he was looking at me.

I realized then I'd sort of embarrassed him. Maybe he hadn't gotten me anything. But surely he knew that didn't matter. He loved me; and I knew that. It didn't have to be shown how much by what something cost. He thanked me, whispering it almost, saying it low. Then, "Yours isn't quite ready yet," he said. "I had to order it, and B.J. said it'd be in soon. It'll be a New Year's present—if that's all right."

It didn't matter, I told him. The sun was coming in the windows of his study now. It was going to be a beautiful cold and clear day. I wanted to reach up and kiss him just as I'd seen B.J. do when I'd been hiding under the railroad trestle that day I'd fallen in the Mill Pond.

If lust was not supposed to get confused with love, it sure stumped me on how to keep them apart.

He stood there, grinning at me. I seemed to tickle him every second of his life. I felt disgusted because my hands were as good as paralyzed. I just couldn't figure out how to put my arms around his neck and bend him down to me. It was obvious I was going to have to find out things.

We stood in silence a minute. Neither of us could think of a thing to say, but it didn't matter. We were comfortable and antsy—both at the same time. "I guess I got to go feed Toulouse," I said. We both laughed at that. "My grandmother doesn't like to touch him," I said. "If I don't do it, I guess he'd starve."

Sam waved to me as I walked ladylike out the front door to the sidewalk. Then I sprinted down the side street home.

Short of washing Toulouse's mouth out, my grandmother was handling him the only way she knew how. There in the bathroom our showers gave Toulouse the humid air of the tropics. And he thrived. He seemed excited to see us whenever we popped in, and he chatted away the whole time we were there.

"I've been taken advantage of," my grandmother said. "Do you think those dealers did this to me on purpose?"

My grandfather pshawed. "How could they have done it on purpose? They don't know you. How would they know you wouldn't like a parrot who cusses? Some people'd pay extra."

"Ha!" She twisted up her mouth and bit the inside of her lip. "What am I going to do?"

"Give him away," my grandfather suggested. "Sell him. Get him a speech therapist."

My grandmother stared at him. "It's the child's present. I can't take back a present."

Then she asked me point-blank. "Do you like the bird? I know he's got a problem. But do you like him?"

"Yessum." I really did.

Whenever we went into the bathroom, Toulouse always greeted us with: "Up yours." And whenever we left, he always said, "See ya later, queer."

I taught him to say certain things about where he was. Now he said, often and with disgust, that the room smelled like a wet poodle. And when I noticed that he'd learned the jingles to my grandfather's advertisements for his medicines, a few weeks later he began adding: "You've ruined my life; you've ruined my life. Quack and Nincompoop, Nincompoop."

In some ways having Toulouse was hard on us, but I always thought of him as mostly educational.

18.

Writing For B.J.

Not long after Christmas B.J. came to the back window of my room and tapped on the glass, calling, "Flea." I would hate to think what my grandmother would have thought about B.J. if she'd seen her. But B.J. had ways of carrying off everything.

I went outside to meet her and we walked into the yard of my old house, where B.J. asked me to sit down in a glider swing under the pecan tree. "I want you to help me write this," she said. She laughed and smiled, and looked excited as she spread out a paper on her lap. She had written, or tried to write, an engagement announcement. It was for her and Ron, and half the words were misspelled or placed wrong.

"I'd be embarrassed to show this to anybody else." She looked at me. "But you know how to do this, don't you? Doesn't your grandmother teach you how?"

I looked at the paper. I could fix the spelling. But she was asking me for more. And, strangely, what she wanted was the sort of stuff that my family wanted me to know, but that I didn't especially want to use. In my opinion, if manners were supposed to help people get along, I didn't see them working. They covered up what was important. I could see nothing worthwhile in knowing which fork to use, except that by knowing it I might not be talked about after I left a party. Even my grandmother, with all the rules she knew and judged others by, lacked what I thought was probably called tact. Her pshaw certainly wasn't outlawed—or even mentioned—in any of her etiquette books, but it wasn't exactly nice. And even if B.J. and Ron's engagement was announced in just the right words, that was still no guarantee it would come out right.

But I did know that the rules mattered a lot to Coldwater and to people like my grandmother, and that with the proper announcement B.J. would become more proper. Besides, I was just as glad to have B.J. get married, so there wouldn't be a chance that Sam might leave me for her. I went inside and got the copy of the etiquette book that my grandmother had given me.

The afternoon was mild, a warm late December day with leaves on the ground and the grass the color of tea. In the kitchen of my parents' house B.J. and I worked out an announcement. We wrote cover letters to the *Arkansas Gazette* and the *Coldwater Gazette*, and along with them we put in beautiful photographs of B.J., her face hopeful and open on a background of swirling mist.

We hand-delivered one envelope to Mr. Rankin at the newspaper office, mailed the other, and then walked slowly up the alley to the back of my parents' house. As we passed the outhouse we stopped to examine the lilies Ezekiel had left in cans beside the dirt mound. B.J. turned on the hose at my grandfather's clinic to water them.

In my parents' kitchen B.J. fixed us hot chocolate and said she had a surprise for me. But she got sidetracked while she thought again about what we'd just done: sending out her engagement notices. While we stirred the hot liquid, dunking marshmallows with spoons, she warmed her hands on the cup and lifted her fingers while she talked. I watched the edge of her finger tap the rim of her cup, then lie quiet for a second.

The level of her voice changed, as though signaling the sharing of something only she and I would have.

As she talked she looked at me directly, never moving her eyes, the green of them rimmed in a thin line of gray and flecked with yellow. "It's funny, you know. I wanted to be a famous dancer everybody would know about. But the truth is, I'm not really suited for that." She rubbed the back of her neck and laughed lightly. "What I need is a house full of kids." She stood up and pulled my head against her, hugging me in a funny way. "Shoot, Flea, you know, I'm going to be happy. I really am."

She walked to the stove and began pouring another cup of chocolate. "I told Sam today that I'm marrying Ron." She stared out the window. She came back to the table. Her eyes moved toward the door and she bit her lip. "I thought I saw Sam walking from the cotton office to the Weiss's pool hall. Did he go there—do you know?" I shook my head and said I didn't know. Then she touched my shoulder. "Good Lord, Flea, I almost forgot what I wanted to tell you."

She did a quick little pirouette on the linoleum and held a dish towel across her face except for her eyes. "Guess where you're going New Year's Eve?" She laughed. "The Silver Moon! Sam's going to take you."

I turned the empty cup in my hand. "But won't I have trouble getting in, especially on a night like that?"

B.J. shook her head, handing me a cookie. "No one cares who Sam takes where. As long as you're with him, age won't matter." She grinned at me. "Besides, the place will be so crowded no one will notice you." Then she sat down and told me about the dance she'd made up, and how Ella Jenkins had taught her to sing one certain part low in her throat and say some of the words.

She took me into my old room and opened the familiar closet, thumbing through the costumes hanging there to show me the new one she would wear. Laughing, she pulled it out and held it up. The whole skirt of it could unwind like a cocoon in reverse. As she slid it over my fingers, it reminded me of the color of a new leaf—tender, yellow-green. It seemed I had touched something as thin and fragile as an insect's wing. I was thinking of seeing B.J. in it at the Silver Moon. Then in my mind came pictures, my whole head filling up with me and Sam watching B.J. and being together on New Year's Eve. And what is it that everybody does at midnight, unless they're dead or blacked-out or too strange to even mention? Kiss. Kiss! We'd sure enough now just have to get on with it.

B.J. sat down on my old bed and patted a place for me beside her. "I don't guess your grandparents have said anything about what I told them yesterday?"

I looked at her steadily. I hadn't even known she'd come to our house yesterday.

"Ron wants to leave. He wants to go right away. He had me settle the lease on this house."

I stared at her a minute; and then, as though naming what she had said would help me understand it, I said like a little kid pointing to something in a book: "Moving?"

She nodded. "He's got a job in Oklahoma starting in two weeks. We're getting married out there." She smiled and touched my arm. "You can come visit. I'll write and you can come out and see me. Maybe this summer, after school."

"Why?" I said, not meaning anything about visiting or me, but why she had to leave. She knew what I meant, and I knew that she wouldn't answer, but I had to ask her anyway. Ron didn't want to stay where Sam was. I had seen him look at B.J. and Sam when he had come to the dancing school to pick up

B.J. on Saturday afternoons. I had seen the jealousy in the way he watched them. But I hadn't thought that he would want to leave.

B.J. was talking about some job, telling me about it like she was a commercial coming on right in the middle of some program so fine that you could have shot the damn man selling Campbell's Soup or whatever.

The thought of B.J. leaving was like a hard and heavy weight I would have to pick up and take out the door with me. She would write me letters, yes. She might even call me. I could even ride the bus, going for days and nights through flat dry land to visit her. Maybe once. Maybe twice. The letters could pile up and sit under the Man-from-Shiloh's bed with the unopened ones from my mother and from my father. And like them, too, B.J. would not be there. She would not be there for me to mess around with, to fix my hair or tell me I was going to turn out beautiful. She would exist only on flat, dead paper, with words she couldn't spell or think up going back and forth between us. Pretty soon I wouldn't open her letters, either. We would die. B.J. and I—the two of us together like we were now —would no longer be in the world. We would change.

I got up to go. If she loved me, it wasn't love enough for her to make Ron stay in Coldwater. I was someone who could be thrown away. I could be left and written to and called. I was like those chickens who got ordered and were sent and then were forgotten to be picked up. Sam was the only person in the whole world I could count on.

The backyard of my grandparents' house was empty except for leafless branches and sticks lying on the ground as I walked home. I went in the back door and lay down on the Man-from-Shiloh's bed. I hadn't yet gotten used to the long silence in the chicken yard.

I would still have Sam. I would have him now all to myself.

I pulled the suitcase out from under the Man-from-Shiloh's bed and took out the tight skirt I'd bought at the Mercantile. I put it on and stood on a chair in front of the dresser mirror so I could see my middle. I thought about how I would appear with Sam at the Silver Moon. I rolled up my collar and padded the hips of the tight green tube. It was terrible. I looked awful.

How could what I had once thought looked grand seem so ridiculous now? It was crazy—thinking one thing one minute, then changing my mind the next. I didn't care about looking bad, sloppy, or wrong. But I couldn't stand the thought of appearing ridiculous.

I could buy something else to wear. Money wasn't an object; I'd come out of Christmas loaded. But what could I buy that could make me grow ten years, or look like something besides a fourteen-year-old girl Sam Best was going to get special permission for?

19.

The New Year and the Silver Moon

Two days before my debut at the Silver Moon, Louella saved me. She was cooking black-eyed peas with hog jowls and making cornbread. Along with turnip greens, this would be served on New Year's Day. Since she was going to have the day off, she was cooking all this special stuff to store in the refrigerator, and anybody who didn't eat it would have bad luck through the whole new year. This wasn't just a belief of Louella's. Everybody I knew believed it.

She broke an egg into the cornbread batter, and while I stood beside her greasing the muffin tins, she said: "If you ask me, luck's in the Lord and the Devil's in the people. But eating this don't hurt." She broke another egg into the mixing bowl. "But I sure going to need luck at the Baptists' tomorrow. I got to get up early to make sure I get me something."

For a minute I didn't know what she was talking about. She offered me a taste of the pot-liquor on a wooden spoon and said: "Every year them Baptists just about fix me and my mama up for a whole year."

Then I remembered about the New Year's rummage sale at the Second Baptist Church. It was an annual event that I used to watch from one of the windows in my old house. Tables of goods were set up all over the church yard and sidewalks. The sale, though, could be ticklish, because often people unloaded what they'd been given for Christmas and didn't want, and even if you held onto the gifts for several years before you donated them, sometimes the giver's memory outlasted the receiver's.

"What time does it start?" I asked.

"You going to go?"

"Maybe. Maybe not. I just wondered."

"Eight. But you got to get there way 'fore that if you want anything good."

I was there at seven. My grandparents thought I was outside cleaning Toulouse's cage. No one could be sure how long it might take to clean a forty-five-year-old parrot's cage, so I set Toulouse in the garage and went to the Second Baptist Rummage Sale.

Louella didn't see me right away. But when she did, I would need a plan. I bought a stuffed bear for a quarter and asked for a shopping bag to carry him in. When Louella examined it, she assured me the Baptists were getting the best part of that deal. Half the bear's ear was missing, and it was a putrid lavender. He had probably been a prize for knocking down wooden milk bottles at a carnival. In Louella's opinion I shouldn't have paid more than a dime for him. She snorted and criticized the Baptists' greed.

After Louella left I picked through the clothes tables. Nothing seemed right. I examined every piece of clothing donated to the Baptists, and was almost ready to accept the fact that nothing would help me, when I caught sight of an army fatigue jacket. Soldiers got to go anywhere. I'd seen them on street corners late at night. They traveled all over the world. Even as young as some of them were, they got to see everything. I bought the whole uniform.

After I hid it under my bear, I walked up the alley. Overnight, in the mound of dirt that Ezekiel had set beside the outhouse, some kids had made a cross out of some sticks and set it in the ground to look like a grave.

Toulouse squawked at the sight of my bear. I hid my uniform in the hen house and took Toulouse and the bear inside in time for breakfast. Then when Louella said something about seeing me at the rummage sale, I held up the bear for my grandparents to admire.

The wrinkles in my grandmother's face moved and her eyes watered. No doubt the sight of me holding that purple Baptist bear got to her. "Oh, well . . . if it makes you feel better," she said. So the bear ended up on the Man-from-Shiloh's bed, propped against the pillows.

The next day, the last of the year, was dry, cold, the afternoon sunny and quiet. After supper I watched a TV special about the changing of a decade and waited for my grandparents to leave. They were going to Colleen and Foster Collins's to play bridge. Sam had told them he was taking me to a party, and they were pleased to have me out of the way and occupied.

With Sam I didn't worry about what he'd say when he saw me in uniform. I didn't even think it would look strange doing the midnight kiss with me dressed in fatigues. I thought it would look reckless and exciting. I'd read that sex thrived on the unexpected. Everything I did seemed fine to Sam. But with my grandparents I took special precautions, and waited until after they left for Miss Pankhurst's house. Then I went into the bathroom to change.

"Up yours," Toulouse said, greeting me as usual as soon as I opened the door. I hung my fatigue jacket on the shower rod. While everyone else my age might have been fooling around with friends, my peer group was Sam, B.J., Louella, Gill, my grandparents, and a middle-aged parrot. The only pressure I got to drink anything was aimed at the Inside Medicine. And the only person to make fun of how I looked was Toulouse.

"Strange. Strange," he kept saying as I dressed carefully. "Everything in here is very strange." He clucked his tongue at the end of it.

"Go suck a worm," I said.

The waist of my army pants had to be drawn up with a belt. Behind me, Toulouse was watching, his beady eyes and insulting beak reflected in the mirror beside me. The trouble was that the bird had no feelings. Whatever insults I gave him he only gave me back, using them even better.

Fortunately the soldier whose clothes I'd bought had been scrawny and short. Probably it was Mrs. Hobbs's son, who'd fought in Korea. He sold insurance now in Searcy and had a wife. I rolled up the tops of the pants. I only had loafers to wear, and I put a white shirt on under the green jacket. My hair I stuffed under the triangle-shaped hat, and I used some of my grandfather's Brylcreem to mold sideburns. In the mirror, I thought I looked about nineteen. My uniform wasn't exactly right, but obviously I was a soldier on leave. I was slight and short, but so had been Mrs. Hobbs's son. And my calves looked as if they'd marched plenty.

"Pew," Toulouse said. "Who's been sleeping in your mouth?"

But in spite of his comment, which had really been mine, I thought I was ready. I liked the way I looked. Dressed like this, I could walk down Beale Street or into Times Square by myself. I could see and taste everything about the world and no one would bother me or make me stop.

Turning around, I got ready to go out the bathroom door into the hall. And as soon as I did, Toulouse said, as he usually did: "See ya later, queer."

I knew that his words were only a habit. But they hit me

with sickening clarity. I sucked in my breath. Did I really look like that?

While my stomach rolled up into a knot, my arms started to itch. I could put on one of those Tara dresses. I could even wear the flower girl dress left over from Miss Pankhurst's wedding. But that idea made me a little sick, too. If I did, I'd get stuck in a corner and everyone would treat me like a little girl. Sam would probably never kiss me. But at least I'd look normal.

Gill rang the doorbell. Leaning against the glass, he saw me in the hall. For a moment we stared at each other.

Opening the unlocked door, he came in, wearing a fancy cowboy-type suit and his boots squeaking on my grandmother's tacky rug. He looked sour; at least he wasn't smiling. Halfway down the hall he squinted at me. Then he stopped, staring.

"Good God." His voice was a whisper. He came close. "You get the idea we was going in costume?"

The look on his face told me that Toulouse had been right. I shook my head *no*, while my mouth opened with *yes*. "I thought B.J. told me that."

"Well, it's not true." Gill blew out air, whistling over his teeth. "Not like that, anyway." He cocked his head and looked at my sideburns. My whole head felt greasy.

Sam had come to the porch. "What's the trouble?"

Gill took me by the arm and led me outside. Sam smelled like whiskey. His face looked swollen. I'd never seen him like that—not that bad. He seemed rushed.

Gill pointed to me on the front stoop. "She thought we were supposed to go in costume."

Sam smiled at me. His mouth wouldn't stay in shape, and he bit his lip and rubbed his hands. "So what? She can if she wants to." He walked back to the Land Rover.

"But this?" Gill was leading me down the steps.

"I don't see anything wrong with it." Sam opened the door to the Land Rover. "Come on. Get in."

I turned around. "I think I'll go change," I said.

Sam reached toward me. "No, honey. We don't have time. They're holding a table for us. And besides, you look fine. I like the idea of a costume."

Sam sat down in the Land Rover. He leaned back, looking tired. He took a handkerchief and wiped his face. Gill was still leaning on the hood of the Land Rover, studying Sam. "Oh for Christ sake, Gill, just get in and let's go."

Something popped in Gill. He opened the Land Rover's door and leaned in, his voice hoarse, rising, trying to whisper, but instead rasping: "I see what you're up to! I've lived with you long enough to see how you do it! You don't think I know. But I found the empty bottle in the garbage this morning. You sat up all night—called it an allergy attack, couldn't breathe. Well, it was an attack all right. And you think you can blame it on that girl. You think you're miserable because she's getting married. But you'll use anything as an excuse: me, B.J., this girl here! It doesn't matter. At any time, anybody can give you a reason. It only means you're ready. You've gotta go. You're on your way out right now. You'll drink yourself into a stupor and be sick for weeks. That's why you hired me. You think I'll do anything to see you're taken care of. Well, I won't, not this time. I can see what you're doing!"

Gill was talking so fast that my mind couldn't catch hold of his words. But Sam pushed him. "Get in the Rover, Gill. Get in and drive or I'll get somebody else."

Gill looked at Sam and then turned quickly and started walking down the sidewalk toward the Mill Pond street.

"Oh, Christ!" Sam said, and opened the jeep door. But instead of going after Gill, he came to me. "Come on, sweetheart, let's go."

He put one hand at my back to push me along and then opened the Land Rover's door. I sat down, scared, but obedient as usual; and I saw Gill standing in front of my parents' house, watching us.

Sam thumped the Rover's hood as he walked around and got into the driver's seat. "Now," he said as he turned the key in the ignition and let the motor grind a minute. He slowly drove off with the Land Rover seeming to just float away from the sidewalk beside my grandparents' lawn and into the middle of the street.

At first I didn't know what the sound was; I thought the Land Rover had been hit by a fallen tree, but then I realized that Gill had jumped onto the back of it and was standing on the bumper, mashed up against the rear window.

Sam drove on for a second, then stopped. He smiled. Gill slid off and came to the front of the Land Rover. Silently Sam got out and Gill sat down in the driver's seat and then Sam came around and opened the door beside me. "Let's get in back," he said.

We drove down the street and turned the corner and headed for the highway. Gill was still angry, driving fast, turning corners so quickly that Sam and I fell against each other and had to grab the seams on the upholstery.

"You're going to like this," Sam said, meaning the night; and while he said it, he buttoned his coat and wiped his hands on his knees. He smelled strongly of whiskey and shaving lotion. "B.J. keeps getting better. I think Ella Jenkins has taught her a lot."

In the dark, with only the car lights behind us, I could sense Sam staring at me. He reached up and patted the hat over my hair. "You always look so much like your mama."

I sat quiet, still, and then he touched my hand. "Pretty soon you'll leave." He wiped the window glass where his breath had left a circle. "I talked to your mother today. I called her. She says things'll be settled by spring."

My arm itched and I felt a line of small bumps growing. Whenever B.J. got farther away from Sam, I'd figured out, that's when he called my mother. I'd put memories together and figured out that he'd met us at the bus station in Memphis after B.J. had started going with Ron. And he'd first told my mother he loved her that summer day when I hid in the pantry, way before he'd found B.J. in New Mexico. So, in a sense, his love for my mother was like a spare tire riding in his mind that he probably knew he would never pull out and use. My mother's unhappiness was like a yardstick for all of us. I think we sensed that if she ever became happy, she'd pull all of us along with her. But I didn't say anything and instead stared at the back of Gill's neck, which, in the dark, looked like a thin stalk a long way from us.

Reaching in his coat pocket, Sam gave me a box. Inside was a necklace, a gold chain with a ballet slipper. And on the toe of the shoe was a red stone. Sam laughed. "The jewelry store didn't have tap shoes." He laughed again. "What your grandmother doesn't know's not going to kill her. But we don't want to take a chance." He helped me fasten the clasp.

"Thank you," I whispered while the Land Rover turned onto the highway.

Gill was still driving like the getaway man from a holdup. We sped past the truckstop and plowed-under fields. In the dark quiet, I sensed Gill's anger at both of us, and it put Sam and me together even tighter into a stubborn team. Quietly I reached up to take off my hat and pull the pins out of my hair. Stuffing the hat in my pocket, I let my hair hang loose, wild. I knew it was ugly. But at least now I wouldn't look as if I was trying to be anything I wasn't. I'd just appear strange and tacky, tough and mean. But I couldn't go on not looking like what I'd intended. And if there was a chance that the way I looked would embarrass Sam or Gill, I didn't want to do it.

Sam watched me. Briefly he stroked my hair. His touch was soft, then he looked away.

He loved me—maybe more than anyone, more maybe than I could even care about myself—and at that moment I could feel something about both of us that made me know Sam better than I'd known anyone. It was a feeling that I'd been having ever since I was very small. It came in the dark, sometimes even the dark behind my eyelids in the middle of the day, or even sometimes when I had been laid on a bed during an afternoon to nap. I saw myself: a small bubble that with a slight gasp, popped and leaked into the air, invisible. Loose in the world like that, I was so small I didn't count. And giving myself up that way made me think I knew a terrifying and very real thing. For I could feel my smallness, and yet in the middle there was a very hard tiny center that was me, no matter what. To bring myself back I had to concentrate on something close up: a loose thread in a bedspread, or someone's face talking to me, or the sounds of bugs, outside, rubbing their wings together, signaling, until pretty soon I could put myself back together, layer on layer, so I was this freckled-faced kid lying on a bed somewhere, or this sort of stupid girl who'd tried to dress like a soldier but had only ended up looking queer, riding down the highway in a silver Land Rover beside a man she loved. And what I knew about Sam that one certain second was that somewhere in the middle of him, almost as certainly as if I could put my hand on it, the center of his life was shifting, moving, going someplace where maybe none of us could bring it back. Maybe his doing so was because of me.

I turned and looked at his face in the dark. The dim lights

from the dashboard and from the moon outside let me see his profile like a silhouette pasted against the window. I knew every turn of his face better than I knew my own. More than anything, what I wanted was to move things around in all our lives. I knew what Sam had taught me about love: that it was to go into someone's world and become part of their scheme of things. In his mind I was not a picture of something he wanted me to be. I simply was and would always be worthy of his love. But now he was moving out of my world where I couldn't go —shutting me out—and it seemed that somehow it was my fault. I didn't know how or why. Just as always, I'd ruined it.

Suddenly I grabbed his hand and began saying crazy, wild things, whispering faster than a jazz horn could blow, telling him all sorts of things that probably Gill was too far away to hear, because of the distance between the seats. But even if he could hear, I didn't care. Anyone, I'm sure, could have heard the frantic sound of me trying to reach into Sam and arrange things, change his mind, his direction, the course he was on. Over and over I told him that I wasn't going to leave. I was going to stay with him forever. I would be good and I would always love him. I was going to marry him. "We'll be together forever," I said, my voice low but so full it was shaking. I hugged his arm and put my hand in his. "You and me." But Sam, though he kissed the top of my head and patted my hand, wouldn't look back at me. He only stared far into the dark fields on the side of the road with his eyes blurred and closing, and his head falling back against the seat, too heavy to move.

We pulled into the gravel parking lot. The tires crunched and the lights on the roof of the nightclub outlined a crescent moon. The building was of painted blocks of concrete and the windows were high slits where no one could see in or out. Cars

were parked in the gravel lot in front. When the door opened
to let people in, the sound of music came out.

"Dark as a hellhole in Africa," Gill said as he opened the
Land Rover's door and promptly stepped in a hole. Rubbing
his ankle, he opened the door for me.

A man as big as Frankenstein's monster stood at the entrance, but sure enough, with a few words from Sam I got to go
in. Nobody knew what I was supposed to be, anyway. With my
hair down it was evident that I was a girl, but in an army getup
and my hair greasy I looked either low-class or harebrained.
Even the woman at the coat-check stared at me, then looked
away embarrassed when I caught her studying my face.

The piano was turned with its raw wood back facing the
empty circle of floor, and with tables surrounding it. A delicious low moaning came out of it and blended with the dark
voice of the woman playing it. Ella Jenkins sat behind the
high top of the piano, her face as much in harmony with the
color of the wood as her voice was with the notes coming from
under her hands. Her eyes were closed as she rolled back, her
waist curving backward while her throat let slide out the final
notes of a blues song. Behind her a man playing a saxophone
aimed the bell of his horn toward the ceiling and whined over
the dying note of Ella's voice. Brushes on a drum swirled and
stopped.

Opening her eyes, Ella saw us being led to a table near her,
and as Sam leaned to sit down Ella let a roll of chords move
over the piano. She threw her head back and laughed. Her
teeth shone like a sudden burst of someone throwing confetti
on a parade. Without stopping, she turned the chuckles in her
throat into the first notes of a song about somebody so rich
that he could hire men to plant trees when he wanted shade.
Everyone around us laughed, looking at Sam. He sat down,

grinning, placing his arm around me and leaning against the table.

Gill eased back in his chair, his face less angry now as Ella joked with her voice and used the notes under her fingers to play with the words, too. "Life is sweet for those who live on Easy Street," she sang, while glancing at Sam. Then she moaned and spoke: "Tell us about it, Mr. Best."

Ella's voice was like a deep jar that she swirled the words around in and then poured out over a teasing edge.

While Gill brought us all something to drink, Ella started a new song. Sam sent Gill to the bar to get me a cherry to put in my Coke, and then reached into his coat pocket and took out his flask. He filled his glass and leaned over it, propping his elbows on the table. Ella sang something fast. The beat was solid and monotonous but the words were clear and funny. The saxophone came out loud behind her.

Gill came back and sat down. B.J. got up from a table near the bar. Until then I hadn't seen her. She was sitting with Ron, and she came toward us wearing a coat over her costume.

Leaning over us she smiled, taller in her high heels than I was used to seeing her. She said several things to Sam, but he didn't answer. If B.J. was trying to reach him, she didn't do a damn bit better than I had, because after a minute he pushed away from her and took his drink and went to the piano and sat beside Ella, who moved over, smiling, making room for him.

While her fingers found chords with no particular melody, Ella said that it was time to sing her most requested number. She laughed once, a loud quick sound that she lowered into her opening note. Then the saxophone moaned and Sam sang along with Ella, and everyone in the whole room seemed to laugh.

B.J. stood behind me and put her hands on my shoulders.

Sam's voice was deep, off-key a little, but nice and scratchy under Ella's. And every note she sang seemed wrapped in a thick honey tone, just on the verge of a laugh. Everyone in the whole room was smiling. Then the claps and whistles filled the room and the laughter eased out.

"Come on, Flea," B.J. said, touching my back.

She led me into a long hall and then a dressing room. In the mirror I watched her pull up my collar and ask me what in the heck I had on, and at the same time hug me so I couldn't answer, while she told me that I was the cutest thing in the world. She was laughing that deep-coated laugh that reminded me of warm honey. She was brushing my hair when two women came in, dressed in costumes similar to B.J.'s. While they put on makeup, B.J. chatted with them and told them I was her kid sister just out of the army from Texas.

One of them, whose name B.J. told me was Sue, looked at me and laughed. "Oh, yeah," she said. "A wack."

The other one laughed. "No. A wax."

B.J. and I laughed. Our eyes met in the mirror. For the first time I saw how funny I really did look.

While B.J. kept kidding them about what kind of gun I could shoot and how I could drive tanks, she'd grin at me in the mirror. She put makeup on both of us, so that when she was done she looked wonderful and I looked like something the U.S. Army would dishonorably discharge.

"Cute kid," the woman named Sue said, turning to examine me more closely. She was dressed in an orange costume that I could tell would come off with one touch on a certain string, and her mouth was colored to match it. She held her lips out sort of pouted, and a scarf was tied around her hair so it trailed over one shoulder. "Look what I got from Mr. Easy Street," she said, opening a box of candy and passing it around.

"Nice Christmas present, wouldn't you say?" When she smiled she didn't look so tough. In the mirror I could see how her teeth were too small for her face, and wrinkles dug half circles around her mouth.

"No, thanks," B.J. said, waving the candy away. She walked behind me to the other side of the room where she had left her makeup case and started rummaging around in it.

"What'd you get?" Sue said, following B.J. while lighting a cigarette.

"Same thing. Sam gave us all the same thing." B.J. was hunting around in the bag, pulling up things and putting them back.

"You're blowing it," Sue said, saying it low as if she didn't want me to hear. She got closer to B.J., but I could still hear what she said, since I could halfway read her lips by watching her in the mirror. Sue leaned close to the back of B.J. and tried to whisper: "Marrying Tillman's going to cut you off with Sam."

B.J. shrugged her shoulders, yet I could tell she was having a hard time meaning it. "Oh well, can't have everything. Right, Sue?"

"Ought not. But I got a feeling it's different with you and Sam. You all got something else going. That's why I don't see why you're messing it up by getting married. You could probably end up the next Mrs. Best if you played your cards right." She looked around. "Now wouldn't that be swell?" She hummed a few bars of "Easy Street" and laughed. The other woman watched and laughed, too.

"Yeah, well, Sam's too old for me." B.J. tried to sound light.

Sue laughed. "Just about right to leave you a rich widow."

"Okay, Sue." B.J. came back to me, carrying a lipstick she'd found in the bag. She tipped my face up and put it on. Her fingers were shaking a little. Then she brushed my hair all over again, pulling my head like crazy.

Sue put a coat on over her costume and walked out. The other one poked at her hair with her hands a little and then left too.

B.J. stared at me in the mirror. She looked ready to cry and forced the bristles of the brush into her palm. "I can't let you think of me like that. I guess you might already, but not like that. . . ." She sat down and touched my hand, then moved back. "I know I shouldn't do this. But I'm going to tell you how things are, because I can't stand being something to you I'm not. It'd hurt too much for you to think of me that way. And even though my telling you's going to be selfish on my part, I can't help it. You just got to know the truth."

Sitting down beside me, she looked into her lap and pretended to study her hands. "You have to understand something about Sam, Flea. I don't know how to say this. . . . But the truth is, sometime soon after Sam was married he got too afraid of having more children. You see, he's scared of what he thinks he is and what he thinks he has inherited and what he thinks he might pass on." She looked at me, letting her words find meaning in the way that I looked back at her. "That's what ruined his marriage more than anything. And sometimes . . ." she walked across the room. "Well, there are rumors he goes out with women here, or other places around the state. And some people even say that he goes with Ella Jenkins, but I don't believe that. They're friends, and that's all. But people will say anything; you know that, and Sam's the kind of person stories naturally grow up around."

She wrapped a scarf around her neck and straightened the dresser, talking fast. "I know some people think I broke up Sam's marriage, but that's not true. He talked me into leaving

New Mexico and come be with him. And then . . . well, I met Ron, and Sam . . . oh, Flea. You know, I've always told Sam I'd never marry him. There's no way I'd ever mess up things for him like that." She smiled, then looked at me. "And the thing I've got to make him see is that what he needs to do is go back to Ellen. She's the one who loves him. But Sam just can't seem to accept that. He's always got to go after somebody he knows he can't have. And I've got to straighten him out about me marrying Ron or he's going to end up at Lissaro's the rest of the month."

She looked at me in the mirror, meeting my eyes. "I'm awful. I'll burn in Hell. I told you all this because I wanted me to look good to you. To save myself." She sat down with her back to me, looking through stuff on the dressing table. "You need to go on now. I've got to get ready to sing." I saw her watching me in the mirror just as I was about to walk out. "I can't sing worth a damn and that's what's wrong with my act. Nobody past a dink town in Arkansas hires a woman who can't do anything but dance."

I walked slowly down the hall, thinking about all she'd told me.

She was wrong. *I* loved Sam. He could have *me*.

20.

I Am an Object of Desire

"Where's Sam?" I asked, sitting down beside Gill.

Gill looked sour. He didn't say anything to me. He helped me scoot my chair up under the table and pulled it close to him. I could tell he and Sam had argued.

B.J. came onto the dance floor. I glanced around me but I didn't see Sam. Anybody can make it back in time for a midnight kiss—when they want to. And I knew that Sam would.

B.J. had a bittersweet voice slanting a little off-key, which she knew about and even admitted. It was no voice for making a living with. But always there was that wonderful way of strumming her words out, Southern but wiry, coated with a tease and followed by her laugh, that sounded delicious to me. But mainly, there was her way of moving—fluid, not tied-down like the rest of us. She seemed made of something that wasn't skin, bone, muscle, or anything with limits. She could move like someone breaking through some invisible web, and yet at other times as easily and quietly as if her body were supported by air that no one else could feel. I sat beside Gill and we watched and laughed, then sat quietly, almost hypnotized, as B.J., with Ella playing and singing behind her, moved us through moods.

Wearing her scarf like a cape—a cover of huge wings—twirling a red-striped beach umbrella and carrying a basket, B.J.

came trotting onto the center of the floor. While Ella beat loud quick chords, B.J. set down her basket and spread out a beach towel the size of a wash cloth. Then she leaned back on her heels, and, in a second, moved forward, her face now as though inviting the whole room to share a secret while she sang. She and Ella traded verses: "Got off the train here at two-o-five. Caught the beat here 'bout quarter to five. . . ."

B.J.'s feet followed the rhythm along with Ella's hands. And while Ella sang, B.J. tapped out the words and everyone laughed: "I got two left feet, but when we meet. . . ."

They worked the room up into a hand-clapping love of motion with that honey-coated teasing that Ella and B.J. poured out together. They belted out the final chorus with such joy and fun that everyone seemed to be moving something: hands, feet, fingers, glasses on tabletops, each other.

"Come on now. Just watch her. Move your feet. What's that, sir?" B.J. teasingly cupped her ear with her hand while Ella pointed to B.J. and said, as everyone laughed, "T'ain't her sister." Then together: "Sweet rhythm of mine."

B.J. was the center. She was the star—at least at the Silver Moon. And for a while I had this nervous, dreading knot in my middle, waiting for her to do what I knew she would. But when she let her scarf fall, dancing in the fancy top of an imitation 1900s bathing suit with the insect-wing skirt still on, winding in the air as she moved, like the airborne tail of a child's kite, I was hypnotized.

She turned and lifted away the edge of her skirt and let it fall on the floor beside the piano. There were whistles and applause. While Ella's fingers began running over the piano keys in a soft tune that settled into chords, B.J. reached into her basket and pulled out a huge bottle of suntan lotion and began oiling herself. A trumpet moaned up toward the ceiling in the long note of "Summertime," and B.J.'s voice began, saying salty and straight the words she'd written herself:

"The livin' here ain't easy. But I'm doin' fine." She winked.

"Stayin' down by the river in the hot summertime.

"Fryin' fish for supper, after I drop my line." She pulled a midget-sized fishing pole out of her basket, dropped one sleeve off her shoulder as she cast her over-sized line close to the audience.

"And if what I pull in, ain't cookin' size,

"I don't throw 'em back,

"And I don't criticize.

"And if I get hot . . ." She twirled around. "I improvise." She slipped out of the bloomers and gave a comic heave to the top of the strapless one-piece green suit she wore underneath. When the audience got quiet again, she said low:

"I have a reputation for being . . . wise."

She danced some more, pretending to be sunning herself, rubbing on more oil and checking her fishing line. She turned her back, unzipped the bathing suit, and said over her shoulder:

"And when I don't get no bite.

"I just spend the night.

" 'Cause when I fish, I do it right." And untying the lacing that held the suit together so she could slip out of it easily, she picked up the umbrella, twirled it and twirled herself, showing the last and least of her costumes. Then she put the umbrella on her shoulder, slung out one hip and winked. "Now if you think I've been talkin' about fishin', I'd say, there's a whole lot you've been missin'." The trumpet blew up loud toward the ceiling and Ella began the final chorus of "Sweet Rhythm of

Mine" again. B.J. danced and sang out the last words behind the twirling umbrella with her feet going wild beneath it and the place going crazy with applause and laughter.

I turned around in my chair to look again for Sam. I saw Ron standing by the wall. He was watching B.J., and he didn't look pleased. I could tell he was just about to explode with feeling so jealous; he was having to share her with everybody there. When I looked back at B.J., she was standing, wearing just about nothing, eating up the applause, loving it.

No wonder Ron wanted her to leave Coldwater with him.

The act was over when Ella beat out a few last chords and the trumpet sent out two golden notes like an apostrophe. Then B.J., surrounded with applause, smiled and reached out her arms—as I would always remember her.

After a few minutes, B.J. ran off the dance floor into the hall. I pushed past everybody crowded around the door, intending to find B.J. and tell her how great I'd thought she'd been, but when I finally got past everybody, B.J. was gone. I looked in the dressing room and a few other places, but she must have hurried off somewhere with Ron. When I started back to Gill, the hall was empty. Ella was singing again and everybody had gone in to hear her. I was about halfway down the hall when two men came out of the men's room in front of me and started strutting in my direction. They were sucking in their breaths and blowing them out and sort of chirping at me like all those roosters had done around my Elizabeth. Before I could move, one man put both arms over my shoulders beside my head and loosely pinned me to the wall. "What we got here?" he breathed.

They were both drunk, smelling of liquor and blowing it all over me when they talked. "Off on a pass?" The other one laughed. I couldn't tell if they were teasing, or if they really believed I was in the army. Ella's voice sang in the opening at the end of the hall. The other man started running his hands around my chest and body and then the first one kissed me. All I could think about were the waxy lips made out of bubblegum that kids could buy at the dime store.

I tried to step away but they were blocking me. "Easy, guys," I said, fluffing my hair and wiping my mouth. Half of B.J.'s handiwork on my lips came off in my palm. I was breathing like a mule in the middle of a heat stroke. "I got to go in there a minute," I said, smiling and nodding toward the door marked Dames.

"Oh."

"Oh, yeah," the other one said.

They stepped back to let me move.

Inside, I locked the door and dry-heaved into the toilet. Words I'd already heard from Toulouse were written all over the walls. I sat down on the closed toilet seat and tried to think. I could wait them out. After a while they'd leave, wouldn't they? I ran over in my mind the way cowboys at the Ritz had avoided ambushes.

After a few minutes one of the guys banged on the door. "Come on, hon. We're waitin'."

"I got a problem," I yelled.

"What?"

"Can't say. It's personal."

"Oh, hell."

"She's fooling us," the other one said. His voice was dark and thick.

"I need a drink," I yelled. "Can you bring me one from the bar?"

"She's stalling," one said.

They worked at the door latch. It was only a hook like the one on my grandparents' screen door. I heard one of them walk around and go down the hall. In a few minutes a straightened-out coathanger came into the crack of the door and picked at the latch. My skin itched all over and I jumped up and stood on top of the commode. There was a small window high up on the wall.

I could hear the faint sound of someone singing, her voice as high-pitched as a police siren. I knew it was Sue. I could hear catcalls and whistles, and I felt that in the next few seconds I would go crazy or stiff or never be found alive. I must have climbed the wall like a tree frog with suckers on his feet. I threw my legs out the high narrow window over the john and landed on the ground outside.

I could hear the two men still calling for me. They were too drunk even to guide the coathanger right. They were pounding on the door, yelling. "We're gonna wait," one of them said. "Sure as hell are," the other one yelled. "I like a good tease—but don't get ridiculous!"

I ran around to the front of the Silver Moon and with my heart beating like a gone-crazy drummer, I calmly walked past the man who was the bouncer and past the woman who checked hats. I nodded to both of them. They didn't say a word about whether I had paid or anything. I guess there were advantages to looking like I did, for afterwards nobody forgot me. I walked into the main room just in time to hear Sue's dying note and see her final twirl that left her wearing close to nothing. I stood at the back near the bar. There were lots of people standing up. I looked again for Sam. The smoke was thick, and the lights on Sue came through it in long white rays. I'd never felt so strong and slick. I was proud of myself. Those two men were probably still trying to pick the lock in the back of the Silver Moon and bust in on me. I stood waiting until the end of Sue's act when I could walk back through the crowd to where I knew Gill was sitting.

My mind then played a strange trick on me—the kind that happens when you look at something and you say to yourself, "No, I don't know that." And then when you look away, another part of your mind says, "Oh, but yes." I looked back at what I did not think I knew.

In the corner near the hall, at a big table with a lot of men sitting around him, was Sam. He was leaning back in his chair, his neck as though it had no strength in it, his head seemingly loose. His eyes were half-closed. He was drunker than the men I'd gotten away from in the back hall. That Sam was not anyone I knew.

I looked at Gill. He was looking around the room. Looking for me. Ella was playing the piano. People were beginning to move around, now that all the acts were over.

"Come on, sweet pea." Gill came up to me and took me by the elbow. "You and me need to head on home."

It took us a good ten minutes just to walk to the door, because even though I could tell Gill was just putting on a fake good mood, he was stopping to collect pre-midnight kisses from anybody worth kissing. I kept glancing back at Sam. He had his arm against the shoulder of some man and it looked as if they were arguing. By midnight he probably wouldn't even know me. By then I'd probably even be wishing I wasn't there.

We drove home in silence—me and Gill. The Land Rover's heater didn't help much with the night air. It was cold. The fields were so dark that we couldn't see the ground as we rode past. When we pulled up in front of my grandparents' house, Gill opened the jeep door and walked me to the front steps. My grandparents had given me a key and I put it in the lock. I turned sideways to face Gill and I said, in almost a whisper: "You're going back for him, aren't you?"

Gill smiled at me. "Of course."

21.

The Joys of Stretch

That whole winter and early spring was like looking in the mirror in the funhouse at the state fair. All the lines of what was familiar were stretched and pulled, twisted into what I barely recognized and didn't want to. I lay on the Man-from-Shiloh's bed one Saturday morning and watched B.J. and Ron load all their things from my parents' house into a truck. B.J. came to say goodbye to me.

I stood on the front porch steps until she and Ron got in the truck. Then I went inside and didn't watch them as they drove off. She could wave until her arms fell off. She could look back to where I'd been standing and see only air.

Sometimes I spent the afternoon with Sam, but it was as if he was somewhere other than beside me. Each day he started with a tablespoon of salty, red-hot pepper sauce. It not only helped him wake up, it was the only way he could taste anything. He would drink gallons of coffee, sometimes with me sitting beside him chattering on about school and anything I could think of. He frequently called out, "Come in," when no one was at the door. He talked to the refrigerator as if it were someone alive expecting terrific manners. He seemed really lonely. I knew he had to be. I was. Sometimes he clutched at his chest as though in pain. And no matter how Gill tried to hide liquor from him, he always had some from somewhere. He bought morning-glory seeds at the Mercantile and ground them up and drank them, hulls and all, with a glass of wine. They caused him to see pictures, and he would leave us while sitting in his bedroom just as certainly as if he had joined the foreign legion. In his mind, I guess he had.

When he shaved he took pills so his hands would stop shaking. Gill begged him to stop drinking. Sam said he would as soon as he could stop smoking.

It was the strangest thing in the world, how I could be so lonely I felt that I might die. And nobody knew it. Or at least if they ever did they wouldn't know why or how much. And if I told them why it'd seem crazy and small, compared to all the awful things that could happen in the world. I probably couldn't put a name on my loneliness anyway. I couldn't make it sound alive or real or as big as it was.

On Valentine's Day a light snow fell but melted before supper. Sometimes sheets of ice kept people off the sidewalks. By the beginning of March, the whole town smelled of old, scorched wool and damp socks.

I called up a tried-and-true method for at least getting the blood to move. I shoplifted a switchblade right in front of Mr. Weiss's eyes. And if he saw me, he looked away, either impressed by my gall or embarrassed to do anything because of the sorry state of my family and who I was. Later I learned, with relief, that he had driven to Little Rock for glasses, so I guess he just couldn't see me or else didn't believe his eyes. Because it was a big beautiful black-handled switchblade like some people had cut each other with a few years before in an argument at the pool hall. On the sign outside the pool hall, the Weisses had painted, "The Lucky Lion." But because of the bad fight that had been there, and others that still happened near there, its nickname was "The Bloody Bucket."

I took my knife and after school I stood behind the garage,

with Toulouse in his cage on the ground beside me, and practiced knife-throwing into the side of the dried-out hen house. Just for the heck of it, I drew a picture of a boy with an apple on his head. I aimed for the apple but didn't flinch when I hit him between the eyes. Toulouse happily urged me on. Between the two of us we called that penciled, apple-wearing bugger every name in the universe.

Pictures of what I had thought would be—Sam and me married, living together, having fun every damn minute of the day, he and me as the family I so much wanted and now still couldn't have—flew by in my head like moths beating at whatever light I had accidentally left on in my mind. Because most of everything I had once known and counted on I pushed into a rotten darkness and refused to look at. I didn't want to remember B.J. whispering, touching my chin, calling me Flea. I didn't want to think about Sam reaching over and stirring sugar into my afternoon coffee in a café he owned, smiling and telling me a joke.

One night Miss Pankhurst—her married name really never caught on—came to my grandparents' house, nervous and crying. It was raining hard, one of those rains that if we had lived farther north would have been a spring blizzard. She shook her raincoat outside the sun porch and slipped off her galoshes. Miss Pankhurst was the only person I knew who would never forget rubber boots even in the middle of a personal crisis.

"I've never been so miserable!" She blew her nose. "He's left me." She set her boots in front of the heater.

I was told to go into my room and read.

"Foster? Why?" My grandfather made Miss Pankhurst a cup of hot tea heavily laced with the Inside Medicine.

The sun porch began to smell like rubber boots burning.

"What'd he do to you?" My grandmother wiped off Miss Pankhurst's galoshes and set them farther away from the heater's vent.

I listened from the hall and moved Toulouse's cage outside the bathroom door.

"He's just downright miserable with me." Miss Pankhurst broke down and after a minute blew her nose into my grandfather's handkerchief.

My grandmother gently prodded her and then she finally leaned over and pinched Miss Pankhurst's chin in her hand and forced her to look up. "All right, Colleen, just what is it? Cut out this sobbing and tell us."

Miss Pankhurst sucked in her breath. "He think's I'm too rich for him." Her voice quivered. "We all know I married beneath me—but I don't care! It doesn't mean a hill of beans to me that I'm married to a bus driver!" She sobbed again, then breathed and went on. "Daddy's dead. So who else alive should care—except me! But it's driving him crazy. All he can think about is that he's living in *my* house, and he's eating *my* food, taking baths in *my* tubs, and he's sleeping in *my* bed." She threw up her hands. "Oh, I know I tell him all the time that it's not true. He gets a little check for helping out in the library, and of course he drives the bus route to Memphis. But frankly, Emily, just between you and me, he doesn't make enough to count." She put her face in her hands and cried. "Oh, what am I going to do? I can't help myself. I love him."

"Damn the male ego!" My grandmother slapped the arm of the chair Miss Pankhurst was sitting in and pshawed very loudly.

My grandfather cleared his throat. "Nobody likes to feel he's being kept."

"But what am I going to do?" Miss Pankhurst raised her head and looked at both my grandparents. Crying had made her cheeks swell, and her hair was wet from the rain and her permanent wave was loose and wild. She wiped her mouth. "I know it's silly and stupid. I'm forty-nine years old; I didn't think I'd ever get married. I sound like somebody in a soap opera. But I didn't think anything like this could happen to me! I didn't think I'd let it—something as messy as this, I mean. But I can't stop it. It's just as true as they say in those stupid movies!" She made her voice unreal and grating: "I don't think I can live without him." Then her voice grew steady and she firmly said: "I'm not sure I want to go on living without him."

She put her head down and silently cried a moment, then laughed and reached for my grandmother's hand. "Oh, Emily, love makes us all act so common. I can forgive everybody everything now. I'm just as base as any woman who walked down the street and thought about nothing else."

While the rain beat against the windows and the rubber boots baked and Toulouse and I hid at the end of the hall, Miss Pankhurst squeezed my grandmother's hands and cried.

I lay on the Man-from-Shiloh's bed, looking up at the ceiling, listening to the sounds of nothing outside—cicadas and crickets, frogs and peepers asleep with winter. I thought about marriages and people and men and women getting along. Nothing about it seemed simple. Even being unmarried but intended, like me and Sam, wasn't easy. It could get out-of-whack and in trouble—like now. Living was, after all, mostly a lonely business.

That next week Foster Collins moved into my parents' old house. My grandfather gave it to him at half the usual rent. Foster said that while he was living there, he was going to think up something to do with his life. Something big. He checked out a lot of books on business at the library.

The late March sun was warm, and daffodils moved around in the breeze, nodding their two-toned yellow heads like bowing Chinese, reminding me of my own too-polite self. On Saturday, since the dancing school had closed down after B.J. moved, I was at my usual black, angry wits' end. I polished my switchblade, took Toulouse out of his cage, stroked his head and neck —which he loved—and with Toulouse's feet curving over a towel I threw over my shoulder to protect my skin from his sharp toes, I headed for the Mill Pond.

I sugar-footed it across a plank in the shallow part behind Miss Pankhurst's sad, almost empty house and walked into the woods on one side of the pasture. "Strange, strange," Toulouse squawked, looking up at the trees that must have jogged some primeval memory of where he or his ancestors had once been. He clung to my shoulder like something stapled. "Lordy!" he screamed when I threw my switchblade into a tree trunk. Then "Ah," when I wiggled it loose and stepped back to throw again.

I looked up and walked to the edge of the open field to look for the cow I'd had that misunderstanding with so many months ago, or the snake I was armed against now. I didn't see either, but I saw Joel Weiss standing on the railroad track looking across the field at me. He must have been messing around at the Bloody Bucket and was walking the track home, which was a shortcut to Main Street since it paralleled the highway. He slid down the track's bank and walked toward me.

When he got close, Toulouse screamed out: "Up yours!"

Joel busted out laughing and inspected Toulouse, who'd never been out of my grandmother's bathroom for long. Not many people even knew about him.

"That's the greatest bird I've ever seen." Joel reached to pat Toulouse's head. Toulouse spit out insults while lowering his head and neck to be scratched. Joel couldn't stop laughing.

"Ah," Toulouse kept saying. Then louder: "Lordy!" It was his signal that he missed the switchblade, I thought. But Joel had taken one out of his pocket and was holding it, which Toulouse had seen before I did.

"Wanna play Stretch?" Joel pressed the button on the knife handle that sent the blade out with a little pop that made Toulouse's feathers shake.

We stood face to face and, since I was a girl and his guest in a sense, I threw first. My knife blade stuck up and trembled in the black mud like a shocked cat's tail. Joel moved his foot to where the blade was, and I took my knife out of the mud. Then he threw his knife and I stretched my foot to where it landed. Pretty soon, he'd stretched me out until I couldn't stand up anymore.

We played over and over, hours it seemed. Toulouse held on like someone struggling on a reeling bus. He flapped his wings for balance and cussed the whole time. I loved the way the knife blade would thunk into the mud and then go softly "fuuut" when I pulled it out to throw again.

And then, strangely, it seemed that kissing got on both our minds. I say this because I saw a crazy, dewy look in Joel's eye; and he kept staring at my lips. I know it was on my mind. It seemed like something I was supposed to do because I hadn't done it yet, unless you counted those creeps at the Silver Moon. But Joel had probably kissed a lot, if the way he strutted was any sign of his previous experience.

On our seventh game of Stretch, we lined up, face to face, closer than usual. And as I leaned forward, trying to watch my knife blade as though carefully aiming it, Joel grabbed both my shoulders, accidentally knocked Toulouse off, and kissed me quickly and squarely, like the soft smack of a midget boxing glove.

"Mercy!" Toulouse screamed, his tail feathers trailing in the mud of our game. Then he yelled, "Shit." He looked like a drunk majorette; he was lifting his feet so high to keep his toes out of the mud. He flapped his wings a lot.

"Here," Joel said, grabbing Toulouse and holding him while I wiped Toulouse's feet with the towel. All the while Toulouse kept cussing, which thankfully broke the ice after Joel's and my kiss. I had heard that conversation after sex was the hardest part. And after our kiss it sure seemed true, except that Toulouse saved us.

The tin roof of the Bloody Bucket glinted in the sun on the other side of the railroad track, and Toulouse seemed to be attracted by it. Then he simply flapped himself out and became exhausted and settled down on the towel of my shoulder like a warm lump.

Joel offered to walk me home, but I said I had some errands to run, which was an outright lie. I wanted to hang around Sam's house. I watched Joel walk toward Main Street, and then I walked back to the shallow end of the Mill Pond, tiptoed over the plank, and walked behind Miss Pankhurst's house toward Sam's.

What was pushing me to snoop around to see if Sam was home was a gnawing feeling left over from *the kiss*. Maybe he'd seen me. Maybe he would think I'd gotten interested in boys my own age. He might think I'd deserted him, had given up, and would not wait. I felt, deep down, that if I could just find out what it was about me that had made him change and leave me, I could fix it.

Toulouse and I passed by Miss Pankhurst's back porch and

her azalea bed, which was unkempt but blooming. Purple flowers hung in place or else lay strewn on the ground like old cherry tomatoes. The dogwoods were in bloom, and their white petals lit up the whole neighborhood and the pasture where the cows grazed, making the field look like a white-dappled quilt.

I knew that Miss Pankhurst was at the library. She and Foster still saw each other, and one night I heard her come to the door of my parents' house and beg Foster to let her do his laundry. But Foster wouldn't give her anything to wash. He said he wouldn't live with her until he could settle himself into some business that could support a wife.

The garage door at Sam's house was open and the Land Rover was parked in the drive. There was some luggage and stuff in the side yard. I saw Gill coming out of the house, carrying things.

"You going somewhere?" I asked, my voice low and sudden. I stood at the end of the drive near an azalea bush.

I had startled him. Gill stopped to look at me. "Hey." He smiled. By then I was standing close to him, helping him load things into the backseat of the Land Rover. He laughed and talked to Toulouse and me.

"So where you going?" I asked again, since he hadn't answered the first time.

He closed the car door. "A little drive on down through Texas. Sam's got some business there."

I knew what he meant. He was taking Sam to Lissaro's. I knew he'd tried to get Sam well without taking him before now.

"Come on in," Gill said. "We're having lunch before we leave. There's enough for you."

Toulouse dozed on my shoulder and made sounds like an old person sucking his teeth.

I followed Gill into the kitchen and helped him ladle soup into bowls and set the table. I heard boots clumping in the hall, and then Sam's voice: "I told you I don't want any lunch. Let's just go." I recognized his voice in spite of the fact that it had grown hoarse, as though he kept a constant cold. His breathing could be heard all the way into the kitchen. He seemed to always be short of breath, especially when he was mad.

Sam stood in the doorway, and his mouth slid shakily into a half-grin. "Well, girl. I didn't know you were here. How're you?" he said, his voice low, hoarse and whispery.

Toulouse screamed and hopped on my shoulder. Sam sat down at the table beside me.

Gill washed his hands at the sink, then glanced back at Toulouse. "I sure wish I had a bird like that," he said.

I looked at Sam, saying nothing, only smiling a little. He looked so unhappy that I wanted to reach out and touch him. His face was wide and puffy, as if he were obese, and his eyes looked at me with the vacant stare of a mounted deer-head. His skin was broken out in patches of red, and because I'd heard my grandfather talk about the conditions he'd had to treat on old Mr. Best, I knew it meant that Sam was starving. He was drinking his calories and letting his skin thin out in places like tissue paper. Nothing about him looked lovable. The lines in his face were dug like trenches around his mouth; his hair seemed more gray and dry. His hands trembled a little. He moved them off the table and hid them in his lap. I just simply had not been good enough. It was all my fault.

There was silence between us. Even if I had reached out and tried to touch his hand and keep it from trembling while he picked up the spoon and tried to eat the soup, he wouldn't have felt me touching him. Sam was gone.

He spilled a little of the soup onto the front of his shirt because his hand trembled so much that he couldn't guide it, and his eyes glazed over with a wetness that would not fall and would not dry. He put his head in his hands and would not look at me. I got up. Even Toulouse was quiet, so tired from his day out in the world that he had nothing to say but "Ah," when I set him down on the back of a chair. I walked around the table. I picked up silverware. I turned on the water full force and began washing dishes. I ran my hand up and down my hair, and locked my knees and unlocked them a million times, waiting for Gill to leave the room. When he finally picked up a stack of books by the back door and headed out to the Land Rover with them, it didn't take me longer than a second to grab Sam from the back, and put my arms around his shoulders and yell out: "What is it? I know it's me. I know it's my fault. But just tell me. What is it about me that ruins things?" My voice sounded crazy, jerking and half-sobbing. And Sam turned around and got up and looked down at me as though he didn't know who I was. "I love you," I screamed. "I love you. But I've done something to lose you. Tell me! Please tell me!"

He quickly touched my cheek and covered it with the whole length of his warm palm and left it there. He didn't really seem to see me or understand any of my words. His eyes were glazed over with dullness. I had butted my head against a barrier I could not see but that was definitely there. It was like thick glass, hard, cold, invisible. Sam reached into his pocket and pulled out a dollar bill and placed it in my hand. "Go have a good time," he said.

When he turned around I saw Gill standing in the kitchen doorway behind him, watching us.

Gill walked to Sam and put his arm on his shoulder. "Come

on, champ," he said. "I want you to sit a minute out on the porch. I got a little bit more business to see about, and then we'll head off."

Going out the kitchen door Gill leaned back and looked at me. "Stay there."

He must have read my mind. I had no intention of standing in that sour, dead kitchen, smelling warmed-up soup and remembering my own screaming voice that had hit dead air and now lay in my head like a sick echo. In two seconds I was out the kitchen door and running down to the Mill Pond, heading for the exact spot where months before I'd fallen in. I had in mind just to run out my anger, to let fly at the bank of the stream until my feet, sucking in and out of the muck, would finally give out and I'd be done. Or the mother cow would gore me for good this time. Or I'd just slap jump in the damn water, get bit by a moccasin, and end it all. Anything was possible; I didn't have any definite plan.

I ran up one side of the bank, then splashed through the shallow part to head up the other side. I ran through a bunch of those dumb cows huddled up under a tree together and got them so riled they bellowed and loped off in all directions like a marble shot into the main bunch in a drawn circle. I climbed up the train trestle, walked over the pond on it and came down on the other side. And when I was coming back-ass-ward off the incline, holding onto bitterweed so as not to slip, someone grabbed me at the waist and made me stand still. "Whoa, Cisco. You're going to burn dern holes in your shoes."

Gill put a hand on my shoulder and kept it there while we walked to the patio on the lawn, where he'd set a pitcher of iced tea. Half a glass was already gone. He must have been sitting in that chair, watching me run like a bee-stung mule all over the damn place. He poured me some tea in a glass and told me to sit down.

"That's okay," I said. "I don't want anything. I got to go home."

"Okay." He sat down and looked at me. "Sam and me got to hit the road anyway. But if you want to hear what I got to say about what I heard in there, it'll take about as long as somebody like you can drink a glass of tea." He pushed the glass toward me. "Anyway, you done forgot that poor bird. He's still setting in there in the kitchen wondering if he's been left for good."

"Lord," I said. "Toulouse."

"You're just such a rotten, awful person. Here you've done left your bird, and you think you sent Sam into a tailspin and got him drinking so much he's close to bottom."

He was looking at me with a hint of teasing, but serious in the slight smile and steady way that he was keeping his eyes on my face. I was still standing up. He sat back and propped one leg on the edge of another chair. "I'll tell you a little secret. Sam makes everybody feel like that."

The sun was overhead, crossing over the railroad track and there was a breeze; the long fringed leaves of a willow tree blew like unkempt hair. Gill looked away from me and stared across the pasture where the cows were grazing calmly again. "I been watching Sam for years now. Every time he gets on one of these binges, it seems it's because of something I've done. I rack my mind, wondering. But the dern truth of the matter is, he heads off because of something in *him*. He can blame it on any number of things. I could, too. But the simple reason is, nothing in the whole world causes it. What does is inside him."

My voice came out like someone else spoke it. "It's not me?"

"No." Gill squinted, looking into the sun behind me. He threaded his fingers together. "And it's not me, either. And it's not Ellen, or Julie, or B.J., or anybody in the whole dern United States. Sometimes we might get to feeling so guilty that we make it worse. But it's never outright just one person, or thing."

He handed me a lemon. "You want a squirt?"

"No."

"Well, if you ain't going to drink that tea, I am."

I pushed the glass over to him.

"You think just like I used to, that it was something you did that caused him to get sick like this. But you just got to know that there's some things we can't do nothing about. Sam's drinking is about like your mama and daddy setting off in separate directions. It's just one of those things we have no say over."

I sat down and stared at him. "We don't?"

He looked at me. For a minute he didn't say anything. He was studying my face. I showed no more understanding of what he was saying than Sam's face had when I had yelled at him in the kitchen. But unlike Sam I could hear and listen. The words would stay in my head. I leaned forward in the chair, as though almost daring him to say something that would make sense.

His voice was calm and low and I held on to it like it was something I could almost feel with my hands.

"Now," he said, "I can't tell you anything that somebody'd want to write down as the gospel. But over a good number of years I have found out some things that seem to make sense. A lot of it come to me when I was flying bombers in the war, and nothing about that was a game. For the first time, things was real—and could cost. I was just twenty-two, but the idea that come to me's been good ever since. It seemed to me I had to divide things that happen in the world into two parts. There was the ones I could do something about—like the direction I flew in, and whether or not my plane was fit, and maybe even who was going with me to help. And then there was this other part—like the gun down in the brush on the mountain that might have got aimed in my direction just that morning, or the storm that might hit, or the fact that whoever was with me might get sick or not do his job when he should for some good reason. Those were not things I could have a say over or do anything about. And I got to admit, it was a hard idea to let inside myself. For being the hotshot that I was and thought of myself as being, it meant I had to say there was some things I just wasn't equal to. There was some things I just didn't have any power over."

For a minute we sat quiet. "And you think that's like Sam?" I said.

"Yep."

"And my parents?"

He nodded. "But of course I can make Sam go get help. I'm good for that. And you're good for letting your parents know you're still part of them. They might have trouble getting along with each other, but that don't have nothing to do with how they get along with you."

Gill went inside the house and brought Toulouse out, carrying him on his forearm. We sat down and let Toulouse yell out a few cuss words toward the Mill Pond. Gill told me that if I ever wanted to get rid of Toulouse, he'd be happy to buy him. We sat a few minutes, looking into the pasture on the other side of the Mill Pond, watching the cows graze. Sam dozed in a chair on the side porch beside the Land Rover.

A little later Toulouse and I stood watching as Gill walked

Sam to the backseat and helped him slide in. Seeing Sam so helpless and sick like that was a sharp and terrible pain. I couldn't stand still and watch it. But his being that way was not because of me. I saw that now. I also knew that I loved him. And I would wait for him to come back. As Sam and Gill drove off, I turned around to hurry back to my grandparents' house. There was so much more I wanted to find out.

After supper I took Toulouse out of the bathroom and put him on the footboard of the Man-from-Shiloh's bed. He clicked his feet against the wood like somebody tap-dancing. I pulled out the suitcase under the Man-from-Shiloh's bed and took out all my parents' letters. I opened them and stayed up half the night reading what my mother and father had written—covering so much time. What I knew now was as clear as the addresses on the front of the envelopes—each coming from different places but to the same place. To me. A light came on in the window of my parents' old house and I heard Foster Collins come out the side door. I watched him walk across the yard and pick up the newspaper.

The new thought I was now sure of was steady and hard, as unmovable as the earth under all that dust in Coldwater. If my parents had trouble loving each other, that didn't also mean they had trouble loving me.

PART III

22.

The Return of the Mexicans and the Outhouse Maneuver

I spent the spring waiting. Separation was, to my mother, exciting, I think. She kept putting off making things definite. But I didn't want to leave Coldwater until Sam came back. I didn't plan to leave for very long, anyway. As soon as Sam was well, we'd get on with our plans to marry. I would never leave Coldwater for good.

I'd talk on the phone in the hall:

"How's school?" My father would say.

"Fine."

"How's the weather?"

"Already getting hot."

I told my mother about working at the Missionary Society's Spring Fling:

"Was it fun?"

I said they'd made tons of money.

On the sidewalk in front of the Methodist Church I'd put a sign up saying "Tarts 25¢," and dozens of people had walked down the sidewalk out of curiosity if nothing else.

Sam stayed gone that whole summer. Gill told everybody that he was developing some business interests in South America. But I also found out that several times when Gill drove down for him, Sam would ask to stop at a restaurant no more than a few miles from Lissaro's, and then he would go in and buy beer. Gill would turn right around and take Sam back.

I walked down the Main Street of Coldwater, looking into the windows of the Mercantile, seeing the reflection of my own face, alone, thrown against the colors of prom dresses, dog-food bags, and salt licks. It was comforting, but scary—knowing that there were things about living you could do nothing about.

I threw the knife blade into the side of the hen house. People who loved each other shouldn't go off and leave each other. They ought to do better.

Summer was like that snake that had been attracted to me in the Mill Pond. It crawled up around me, causing sweat and nightmares. The nights were sweltering all through that summer. In the Man-from-Shiloh's bed I tossed like a load of clothes in my grandmother's dryer.

I watched news on the TV with my grandfather. That summer we began to hear: K-E-Double-N-E-D-Y, Jack's the Nation's Favorite Guy, and Come and Click with Dick, the One that None Can Lick. Four colored kids went into a dime store in North Carolina and sat down at the lunch counter. They called it a sit-in and started trying it out all over town. The store managers raised their coffee prices to a dollar a cup and unscrewed the seats. Mrs. Barber worried about the stools in the Rexall's.

Then in late August the migrant workers came. I stood on the sidewalk, watching them being driven down Main Street in the backs of trucks. Most of the Mexicans went to Hersham's Farm. Again the sidewalks of Coldwater were crowded. The Missionary Society talked about what a problem it was—the cotton pickers' unsanitary habits. Since the Society had been so successful with the Spring Fling, they felt powerful. They decided that before they tackled the Mexicans, they would first tackle Halloween. They would cure the town of hanging underwear all over the place.

And so, in the autumn of that year, exactly thirteen months after my return to Coldwater, the days were much the same, yet with almost everything changed. In a few weeks I would turn fifteen. I felt old. The season was dry; dust hung on like veils. I'd heard people in Coldwater say they'd seen Sam in Little Rock, doing business. When I asked Gill, he said that Sam was indeed doing fine. He would be home soon.

I would go down to the woods by the Mill Pond and meet Joel. Of course, I was practicing kissing him to be ready for Sam. This was a secret from Joel, but he didn't seem to mind.

Joel looked at me; then he glanced down at the mud: "Wanna do that contest bit?"

I pulled my knife blade out of the ground. It was the Missionary Society's plan he was talking about. I didn't want to take too long to answer Joel, but I couldn't lead him on, either; I was Sam's.

I looked out into the pasture and cleaned off my knife blade with my finger. Joel was asking me to be in the Missionary Society's king and queen contest. Anyone in the whole town could enter, as long as they were male and female. The winner was to be the couple who got the most votes, and votes were to be pennies. It was supposed to be a sweet reverse on trick-or-treat. You could knock on doors, offer some sort of sweet for sale, and ask for a vote. At midnight Miss Pankhurst would crown the Coldwater King and Queen of October at a townwide dance. The whole business was supposed to keep everybody so busy that the idea of doing a crude prank wouldn't cross anyone's mind.

I thought about being in the contest with Joel and threw my head back and flipped my switchblade to land a good two feet from his shoe. He couldn't stretch much after that. "I don't know why not," I said. "I mean, it's all the same to me."

But it wasn't to my grandmother.

I was sitting in the sun porch peeling eggs for some exotic aspic that would be served at my grandmother's annual Missionary Society luncheon. She had gotten her hands on a fancy recipe which would harden eggs and tomatoes together in a jell. And we were trying it out, two weeks before the meeting —which Louella and I called the Aspic Rehearsal. Never again during modern times would the Missionary Society be so fêted. And as I dug my fingers into the eggshells, my grandmother leaned over me, asking if I couldn't peel faster. She had no idea of the agony of the thing. Eggshells under fingernails are akin to Chinese water torture.

"I don't mean to rush you, dear," she said. "But we have to help Louella with all those baked goods—the things for you and that *Weiss* boy."

I didn't peel any faster and I didn't even consider peeling faster.

"Why, if I had only known that you were interested in being the October Queen—I could have arranged it with someone like . . . Mrs. Ramsey's son."

I held up an egg. I told her I thought that one was rotten.

"Oh, good heavens!" She took a whiff.

There was a knock at the door and Louella let Ezekiel in. A few days before, my grandmother had called Mr. Rankin because once again the outhouse was on her mind. She was determined to have it moved and had written letters to the editor all winter and spring about how it was compromising Coldwater's entrance into the modern age. But Mr. Rankin had made no moves to move it. He had other things on his mind. In his office, he hung up pictures of Franklin Roosevelt and Abraham Lincoln and martyred newspaper editors who'd fought duels with their readers. He wrote editorials saying that he himself had always believed that the Negro in the South was entitled to the same opportunities that a white man was entitled to. It was time, he said, for Coldwater and the rest of the South to join with people like him. He told my grandfather he expected his house would be bombed. He propped a rifle in the back of his office beside the printing press.

The whole Missionary Society would have canceled their subscriptions to the *Coldwater Gazette*, except that no one wanted to miss out on the local news. So when my grandmother called Mr. Rankin, she swallowed her pride and suggested they reverse the arrangements of the year before: *she* would have the outhouse moved, and *he* could fill in the hole underneath. Otherwise the agreement was the same: Mr. Rankin wanted the outhouse burned, and my grandmother wanted it taken care of before the Missionary Society meeting. So again Ezekiel was hired.

He stood before my egg-peeling table looking at my grandmother. "Miz Maulden?" His voice was soft. "There's trouble on the outhouse."

My grandmother was still looking for bad eggs, rolling them over and sniffing the area. "What do you mean, Ezekiel?"

He looked down, then up. "Well, Miz Maulden, don't nobody want to go to the trouble to burn it."

She looked from the eggs to him. "What are you going to do?"

"Don't know." He shifted his weight and traded the hat to his other hand. "That's what I come to talk about."

"Well, *what*?"

"Might take more. I was wondering if you was willing to back up the cost?"

She looked again at the eggs.

"No. Now, what we agreed on should be plenty. I can't see why you. . . ."

"Miz Maulden." He took a step closer. "I ain't taking you. You don't see." He watched her rolling the eggs around. "You know, it going to take about two men to shift that toilet up onto a truck. Hard lifting. Take about two dollars apiece. That's four dollars. Now, it going to take a lot of gas to get that truck all the way to where we can burn it. Cost of that truck be about eight dollars. When they get out there, they going have to lift it down again. Course that's easier. Be about three dollars. Now, wait a minute, Miz Maulden. I promises you—just let me show, okay? We figures it take about a hour for the toilet to burn. Dollar an hour for each of them men makes two dollars. Whole thing take about half a day. All of it adds up to twenty dollars . . . only way you can do it."

I couldn't keep up with Ezekiel's arithmetic, but my grandmother pshawed loudly and said it was ridiculous.

"Well, you think on it." He put on his hat. "And I'll see if I can do better."

He went out through the sun porch door and Louella trotted in to give him something to eat, wrapped in a section of newspaper.

My grandmother was angry now. She was pushing the eggs around roughly and staring at them. She said she'd always known that underneath Ezekiel was a crafty low-down . . . then she stopped and held up an egg. In despair she swept a half dozen or so into the sling she made of her skirt and carried them like that, bent over, to Louella in the kitchen.

After Louella returned from Thompsons' Grocery with new eggs, my grandmother and I went into the sun porch for an early supper. Louella brought it there. She put a plate of Waldorf salad and sliced ham on the table along with a small portion of the aspic for a test. But I was still reluctant to eat anything connected with chickens.

Halfway through, Ezekiel knocked on the sun porch door again. He came in quickly and took off his hat. He grinned. "I done better," he said. "You'll like this."

My grandmother squeezed another lemon into her tea and said she seriously doubted it.

Ezekiel shifted his weight. He looked up, then down. "You know," he said, "how the Mexican pickers is a problem about. . . ." He cleared his throat and looked at our plates. "I don't want to mention it with you here in front of food. . . . But Mr. Jimmy Hersham is willing to have his foreman, that English-speaking one—Pedro, I think he's called—have that toilet taken to his field. Good idea, I think."

My grandmother put down her fork. The fact of what he'd said, and the perfect fit of it, moved her face into a look I'd rarely seen. "Oh, Ezekiel!" she said. "That's excellent!"

He traded his hat to his other hand. "That'll end our problems. Take off that fire-watching fee, too." He smiled. "Course you know, Mr. Hersham expected me to get the truck for them Mexicans to use. But I won't be supervising then, neither—that Pedro will. And Mr. Hersham might would pay you back. But I needs that money to get the boys that'll help. I can use my own truck, but them boys won't move until they sees I got something green in my pocket. I got to have chains and a rope, too. That's a heavy toilet. Comes to fifteen dollars."

My grandmother got up and paced a minute. She stopped and looked at him. "Ezekiel. . . . That's way too much and we both know it."

But she got her purse. Digging out the bills, she went on and told him it wrenched every fiber of her body to pay him that, but she guessed he deserved some of it. Then she handed over the money and she added: "When is the outhouse going to be moved?"

Ezekiel didn't hesitate. It would be in the next few days, he told her.

"It has to be," she said. "The luncheon is a week from Monday. Mr. Rankin has to have time to fill in the hole."

"Yessum. Yessum." Ezekiel said he hadn't thought about that. He put on his hat, said his goodbyes and left. Louella gave him a drink of water on the way out.

I went through the sun porch door, and I stood in the alley for a moment. The outhouse was fully in view. The lilies Ezekiel had brought in cans were still there, straining at the metal, hanging over the sides. They'd get planted now. The outhouse would get moved. I thought about the afternoon when B.J. had watered the lilies, and the slow, dawdling way we'd walked home from Mr. Rankin's office after delivering her engagement announcement. She had written me two letters, but I knew not many more would come.

I walked to the end of the street and, in the early dark, I stood in front of Sam's house. He was somewhere near. He would be home soon. We would be together.

The shadows of trees were being swallowed by a solid darkness. Clouds like dark rocks hung in a gray sky. And like a crazy person, I whispered aloud to no one, "Yes." Then I laughed. Joel's face flirted in my mind, and my grandmother's comments about my being the Missionary Society's October Queen with him rolled in my memory like well-aimed marbles. If I won, my picture with him would be on the front page of the *Coldwater Gazette*. Sam could see it; my grandmother would be embarrassed by it; and best of all, I'd dress up in some Halloween getup that'd make me look like B.J. I'd jolt Sam's memories with ideas of what could be. It'd be just like we were getting B.J. back and making everything as it had been. We'd all be reminded of the time being wasted. My parents could even see me in the paper, too, and know they shouldn't be tearing themselves apart.

My grandfather had still not come home for supper, and my grandmother sent me to fetch him. I dreaded going over there and getting pulled into another whole evening of medicine-making. I walked slowly through his lab, then stood at the door to his office, examining the bones, skulls, and stuff in his glass cases. I could see him in his chair at his desk, rared back, not moving, still and big. My grandmother said he was half-deaf. His ears had white hair growing out of them, and even though most times I thought he seemed to hear fine, they looked defunct. He turned around and saw me, and his voice was so quick and ready, it startled me: "You're just who I need to see."

"I came to tell you supper was ready," I said.

"I'm not hungry." He stared up at the ceiling with cobwebs in the corners. Then he held out to me a typed letter and whispered, "I'm in a bind." He glanced at me once to see if I was reading the letter. I didn't want to. I had other things on my mind. But the look on his face was asking me my opinion. I hadn't had anybody wanting to know what I thought in a long time. Not since Sam had gone away.

The letter was from the state medical licensing board, and it said that they were sending an inspector to go over my grandfather's books to make certain he was not selling any of his medicines.

Suddenly his chair snapped down and his feet hit the floor. "Here they go sending some guy from the state board to visit me, and I'm not doing anything wrong! I'm not selling it, and I'm not giving it to anyone who's not in my family. I'll admit I'm finding a lot of cousins I didn't know I had." He laughed a little but then quickly stopped. I wasn't used to seeing him worried. He leaned back, but in only a few minutes the chair snapped forward again. "I ought to do something to help myself."

He motioned me to follow him into the lab and when we got to the storeroom door, he opened it. There were shelves all the way to the ceiling filled with medicines. They weren't labeled but I knew what they were. The Outside Medicine was yolk-colored; the Inside a shade lighter.

He picked up a bottle and held it to the light. "If I told you I intended to take all of this myself, what would you say?" He looked at me. I didn't say anything. I returned his gaze with the eyes of a good hunting dog. "You're right," he said. "No one in his right mind would believe me."

He asked me to help clear a path to the sink. We pushed things out of the way, and then he filled one of the vats with soapy water. After we poured out the medicine he said we'd have to wash and dry all the bottles and hide them.

There had to be a better way of getting rid of the medicine than just pouring it out. I'd made some of it, and I guess I felt a little maternal about that, just as I had on the night that Foster Collins and my grandfather had been examining my baby chicks. Yet I didn't want to have to hide the bottles any more than I wanted to pour them out. But I also didn't want to see my grandfather lose his license, or be embarrassed publicly anymore.

He handed me the first bottle, the cap already loosened. The

liquid came out in gulps and the drain swallowed it with a
slight burp. He handed me another bottle. It would have made
so much more sense for me to be the one to trot back and
forth to the storeroom for the bottles. I was so much faster.
But of the two of us, I was the only one who could pour. To
him it was just too painful. The sound of the stuff going down
the drain was awful. I tried to think of ways I could distract
us. The room smelled like lemons and something oily. I said
that Grandmother had arranged for the migrants at Hersham's
Farm to inherit the outhouse.

"Well, I'll swannie!" he said. He whooped and hollered a
minute over that. "How'd she'd come up with a brilliant idea
like that one?"

"I don't know," I said. I wasn't about to tell him it was Ezekiel's idea. If somebody happened to be admiring the person
he was married to, you shouldn't mess with it.

He kept handing me bottles. There were at least a hundred
more. I had made up my mind that after number twelve I would
suggest that we stop and think; there had to be a better way.
But despite my decision my hands didn't stop.

"Sally?" My grandfather stood at the storeroom door. "I think
we ought to stop."

I stood still and didn't say a word.

His voice was loud. "I'm going to tell the truth. I made every
one of these bottles for myself and for those I care about, and
if those government men don't believe me, to hell with them!
I'm not going to act like some hillbilly with a revenuer coming
up the road." Then he walked around flapping his arms. "If
those government men don't believe me and think I'm a crook,
it'll be my hard luck—because it'll be the truth."

What he said didn't make sense, but I knew the sense he
meant to make.

I also knew he should save himself, and that I ought to help him. We could hide the stuff and sell it to anyone who could claim kinship. Using the Bible as our guide, we could cover all of Coldwater. The only way we would be found out was if all the people in this part of Arkansas lived to be over a hundred. We'd be on the news then, with those centenarian Russians who ate yogurt. And when one of us held up his little yellow bottle—even if we'd all agreed not to, there's always someone hellbent on telling the truth—we'd have to build an airstrip in Coldwater to handle the jets. My grandfather would go down in history along with Rudolph, Harry Truman, and Robin Hood.

"I really think we ought to hide it," I said.

He didn't even look at me. He went to the back door and with his hand on the light switch, he turned toward me and then cut off the light. "I like the truth best," he said.

He locked the office door. For a minute we just stood there and looked up at the sky. I could have socked him. Here he'd asked my opinion but wouldn't take it.

It was a cloudy night, black, hopeless. As if the dark mood were catching, I looked into the end of the alley and knew that I could never become the Coldwater October Queen. Corinne Hamilton was running. She was paired up with Benjamin Levy. If she wore one of her twirling costumes or something similar and sold nothing but stale raisins, she'd win. I had never won anything. All I was doing was playing a joke on myself. I couldn't become like B.J. I couldn't get my parents back as a family. I couldn't make Sam stronger. My memories of all of them seemed trumped up, too sweet, unreal.

Only the lights from my grandmother's sun porch kept my grandfather and me from stumbling in the dark. The outhouse looked desolate, condemned, haunted. I thought of how it would be when my grandfather lost his license to practice medicine and was written up in all the papers for violating the court's rules. He ought to do better.

He put his hand on my shoulder. "It feels good to know that what I'm doing is right!" He started then. I saw it in his eyes. What little light there was bounced off them like foxfire. It was a look a cat gets when it's lying flat, twitching, watching a bird in the grass, ready to pounce. He talked about the determined resolve of Patrick Henry, the Duke of Wellington, Jefferson Davis, General Patton, and above all, Harry Truman. He talked of moon travel, Davy Crockett, Custer, and the I.R.S. I knew it wouldn't be likely that he'd go back to the pouring-out idea.

Inside the sun porch he hung up his holey lab coat on a hook by the door. My grandmother was in her bedroom on the phone, and we could hear her telling somebody about the arrangements for the outhouse. She'd probably already called all the members of the Missionary Society.

My grandfather and I got a snack in the kitchen. The refrigerator was stuffed with eggs and aspic, and then we settled down together on the couch opposite the TV to watch the debate between Kennedy and Nixon. Kennedy was tanned; and Nixon looked like my grandmother's aspic—thin and pasty.

Just before bed my grandfather and I went into the kitchen to put our dishes up. He took a bottle of the Inside Medicine and poured us each a glass of it, calling it a nightcap.

The darkness of a night without stars and a moon no bigger than the sliver of a fingernail made the kitchen windows seem gone, blown-out. I put the glass of the Inside Medicine to my lips and drank, but it tasted so terrible that for a second I thought my grandfather had poured us Mr. Clean by mistake.

I'd been so mean and mad all night. If we had just drunk Mr. Clean, it might only prove to be my first real blessing in disguise. I think we both felt doomed.

23.

My Grandmother and Charles Rankin Are in Cahoots

My grandfather didn't tell my grandmother her life was about to change. I knew that *I* should tell her about the licensing inspector. But just like my grandfather, I didn't get around to it. She was so wrapped up in having the outhouse moved to Hersham's Farm that, strangely, she was the most cheerful of any of us. I think that's the main reason my grandfather and I didn't want to mess with her.

I put Toulouse on the bedpost and sat in front of the Man-from-Shiloh's dresser while blowing out my cheeks and sticking out my tongue and planning my Halloween costume. I was going as a Lady of the Evening. I would sell tarts and dress like one, and my grandmother would have a stroke; and I'd be sent to prison for manslaughter. My grandfather would probably already be there.

My grandmother took me to Leona Sutton's to be measured for a costume, since she was determined for me to win the contest, using beauty and refinement as weapons. If I didn't, then at least I'd look nice while strolling around Coldwater with a Jew.

We crossed the street near the Second Baptist Church and walked to a small frame house on the edge of a field. Across from it was the row of houses where Louella lived. A tractor was parked in the field, which was planted with turnip greens.

In the sun, I could smell them, the faint odor of the plants' leaves. It seemed as though they were cooking slightly. Pale yellow butterflies lit on them, flitting across the field like blown paper. I stood still a minute. My grandmother walked on ahead of me. There seemed to be hundreds of those butterflies, dancing across the rich green turnip field. I didn't tend to think of butterflies coming out in October. They seemed out of place. They lay so lightly all across the field, they were like a yellow dancing blanket—moving and at the same time still.

A pair of tall skinny bird dogs came out from under Leona's house to greet us, licking my hands, jumping up. In her dining room, fat, widened-out Leona Sutton, who reminded me of fresh dough rising in warm air, smiled around the pins she put in her mouth. While using her mouth and bosom as places to keep pins, she twirled me around on her dining room table and stuck together a costume that none of us was certain about. My grandmother studied my face. I turned on Leona's dining room table like a wound-up doll set to a broken rhythm. "I know," my grandmother said suddenly. "Leona, make a wand and a tall pointed hat. She can be the Good Witch of the North in the *Wizard of Oz*. How's that?"

Leona and my grandmother designed my outfit, and I didn't give a damn.

Later that day after we'd gotten home Louella came through the back door with a handful of greens that she'd gone to pick for supper. She tied on her apron, after putting the greens in the sink. "And now . . ." she came over and hugged me. "Honey, you going to be the October Queen for sure. Cause I'm going to make the sweetest, best candy any soul ever set his teeth into! I'm going to make you chocolate drops, pecan chips, green and pink mints and. . . ." She stopped and held her breath. "You and that Weiss boy's gonna be crowned for sure. . . . I'm. . . ."

My grandmother thumped in from her room. She looked pleased and informed me that she had told Louella yesterday that since I was running I might as well win. Therefore Louella had been ordered to make divinity.

My grandfather, who was sitting in the den, roared, clapping and yelling like a man at a ball game. "Oh you'll win with divinity!" he said. "Louella's is heaven itself."

Louella was crowding my face. "What you think?"

"Fine."

That afternoon my grandmother wrote her final letter to the editor. She addressed it to the Citizens of Coldwater, and in it she explained how she and Mr. Rankin were cooperating for the betterment of the community. She said that she had taken it upon herself to have the outhouse from behind Charles Rankin's newspaper office moved to James Hersham's farm for the use of the migrants. And then she sent me off with the sealed letter to the newspaper office.

Mr. Rankin was walking around between the machines yelling at a typesetter. He wore a gray-green apron and reminded me of a grasshopper, bent-over, thin, freckled and pale, ready to spit. He took my grandmother's letter from me, scanned it and smiled. "Your grandmother has a way with words." Then he looked at me and smiled again. "I hope you don't inherit it."

When I got back, the divinity-making was going on. Louella had lined trays up on the counters, the tables, the pantry shelves, on stools. I didn't see how in the world I could carry all of it, much less sell it. She and my grandmother sure seemed hellbent on making me the queen.

My grandfather was at his office, hiding the medicines, I hoped—but also knew that he wasn't. I looked out the window at my parents' house. The light was on in my old bedroom. The idea about becoming like B.J. and getting my picture in the paper was still there. Even though once it'd been thrown away and half-buried, it was now back and growing to full-force. Old ideas seem to be like that, tough as weeds and hard to get rid of, especially when they get mixed in with something like love or hope. I didn't have much more of an idea of what I was doing than a coot in hell, but somebody had to do something about the sorry state of Sam and me.

I slipped out the back door and walked over the short drive-way to knock at the kitchen door of my old house. When Foster Collins saw me, he looked surprised but pleased. He wore horned-rimmed glasses now, and his cheeks were sunken a little more than usual. His hair, sticking up as though he had been plowing his hands through it, was more gray than a year ago; and his shirt was unbuttoned, hanging loosely over a T-shirt.

He thought of me as a kid and, because I made him feel uncertain and a little nervous, he offered me hot chocolate and asked me to sit down. The cup he set in front of me was one of B.J.'s pink flowered china cups. I remembered her and Ron driving off in his pickup. Probably she couldn't fit everything in.

Foster Collins and I sat a while, talking about the weather and bus trips and school. Then he smiled slightly and asked me if I'd mind looking at something he was writing.

He showed me two versions of an article named "The Ozarks by Bus." When I told him that I liked the first one best, he smiled and said he did, too. And as I got up to go I asked him if he'd mind if I looked around a little.

"Make yourself at home," he said. We laughed a little at that, seeing as how it was my home to begin with. Then Foster went to sit down at the desk in my old bedroom and look through some papers.

I went around the house, looking in closets and the drawers of old chests. Out on the back porch where the washing machine was kept was one of those twirly skirts that B.J. used to strip off. It had a little hole in the skirt and she'd probably left it for somebody to use as a dust cloth. Behind the drier I found an old bikini top that must have gotten lost in the wash.

Hearing me in the doorway, Foster turned around. "I'm going to go on home now," I said. I'd wadded up the costume parts and stuffed them in my pockets. I tried to stand so that it wouldn't look like I had swollen hips.

When I got back to my grandparents', Louella was getting ready to go on home. She took her purse out of the pantry where she kept it, covered all the trays of divinity with wax paper, and set out a Roach Hotel.

As my grandmother passed the kitchen, she suddenly stopped. "Louella, I almost forgot. Can you find Ezekiel?"

Louella rested her pocketbook on the top of a kitchen chair and thought a minute. "Seems he's patching Mr. Tyler's porch."

"Well, run over there and remind him that he's supposed to move that outhouse before Tuesday. And not to forget it."

"Yessum."

While she was gone my grandparents and I moved to the front porch, where we settled in the swing to cool off and watch down the street for anything that moved.

My grandmother was content. The air was warm, but filled with the smell of fall leaves and Louella's cooking. My grandfather didn't eat anything off the plate of divinity and chocolate drops that Louella had left us to try out.

The chimes started. We sat back in the swing to listen to them. The light was becoming gray. It would last only a few minutes, it seemed, before dark would come, sudden and thick. The short days were one of the first signs that summer was over. The chains on the swing squeaked a little and my grand-mother hummed along with "A Church in the Wildwood," which was being broadcast out of the Methodist steeple.

Most of the screens on the porch were blocked with dirt. The gray siltlike dust, which was always eager to move with whatever breeze came, had settled into some of the small wire holes of the screening. My grandfather was staring into the yard, and probably into all eternity, trying to get himself ready for what he thought would be the biggest change in his life. It was my grandmother's legs that were setting the slow safe rhythm of the swing that she wanted us all to sit to.

Suddenly the record being chimed out of the church steeple got stuck. Leaning forward slightly as the same refrain was played over and over, I strained along with the record, until, as I was holding my breath and bending forward to urge the record on, someone scratchily lifted off the needle.

The tune hung in my mind unfinished, driving me crazy. I kept finishing the notes in my head.

Then another record came on. In a few minutes I eased back in the swing again, letting my feet push it back and forth along with my grandmother's. The old, interrupted notes were remembered, but no longer mattered.

Out on the street, a big new car that I didn't recognize slowed down, and somebody honked the horn and leaned out. For a second I thought it was B.J., or my mother—something about the set of her shoulders and the color of her hair made me think that. But it was Ellen Best. She waved at my grand-mother and called out that she'd just been over visiting for the day. She asked my grandmother how she was, and called hello to my grandfather and me. Then she drove on.

Out of the dusk I saw Louella walking fast down the side-walk. She came in the screen porch door. She was a little out of breath, and she straightened her scarf. The front of her uniform was dotted with chocolate stains and misaimed butter. She stared at us.

"Miz Maulden. Ezekiel said it's not him moving that outhouse. It's that Pedro. He said you'd remember that. He said Pedro'd do it before Monday. You're not to worry. Ezekiel said that Pedro's going to do it."

24.

The Outhouse Is Moved

Halloween night came mild, clear, with the air slightly chilled so that my grandmother said I had a choice—to wear a sweater or two pairs of underwear. But she didn't know about B.J.'s costume.

I drew fishnet stockings on my legs, then put on the organdy dress and walked into the living room.

My grandmother looked me over as royalty does the troops. Leona Sutton's handiwork had given me a long skirt in blue organdy with gossamer puffed sleeves that looked like swollen butterflies. I had a pointed hat with a veil, a wand, and silver shoes. I was a princess, beautiful—at a distance.

She clipped a few stray threads and let me wear lipstick that she put on like a Clara Bow bow and that outside I immediately smeared into a fat, sexy mouth. But first Joel arrived and stood on the front steps, where we could see his shape through the glass in the door as he rang the bell.

When my grandmother opened the door, she gasped a little. Joel stood grinning, his eyes black, his teeth white, his skin the color of olive, wearing a devil suit. The red cotton of it had been starched so that it shined a little. I half-expected my grandmother to say he was appropriately dressed. But Joel grinned and said, "It's sheets, Rit-ed."

His mother had made it in one day and he himself had sewn

on the tail: sheet-casing stuffed with newspapers. When he moved, he crackled a little.

My grandmother sent me off with a huge red hatbox stuffed full of Louella's treats. Joel carried a sack of gum that his father had donated from the dime store. It had just turned dark.

"Where you want to start?" I said.

"I'm not much on this door-to-door thing." He lifted the top of the hat box. "Your grandmother must be serious about you winning." He ate a piece.

"Those aren't for you!" I said, so loud that I scared myself.

He backed up to a tree next to the sidewalk and lit a cigarette. "So why don't you start over there on that street and I'll sit here."

"I thought you were serious about this." I said.

"I am. I'm just not much of a door knocker."

I started walking toward the Mill Pond street. Joel followed me, carrying his tail like a wine steward would carry a napkin. The sidewalks were filling up with other couples now. I knocked on a few doors while Joel stood in the background. Several people dug into their pockets to put something in my Mason jar.

After I'd done a few houses, I had thirty-two pennies, four dimes, a nickel and a paperclip stuck to a scummy Cloret. "Blazing start," Joel said.

I headed for Miss Pankhurst's. When she came to the door, I could see into the living room behind her where, set up on a card table with his writing materials, was Foster Collins. Miss Pankhurst wore a fancy dress with a low-cut back. She was the new president of the Missionary Society, and obviously she was ready to go to the high school at midnight to do the crowning. "Why Sally Maulden!" She came out onto the porch. "I heard about this dress Leona was making. Turn around, dear. I want to get the full effect."

She lifted the hem and studied Leona's seams. "Your grandmother was afraid it wouldn't turn out. Leona's not much good with organdy. She tends to snag it."

Joel went to the bushes and lit another cigarette. I could see the red tip of his Winston through the azalea leaves.

Miss Pankhurst and Foster Collins bought a half-row of divinity and dropped nickels, dimes, and quarters into my fruit jar, and while they did Miss Pankhurst told me that she and Foster were collaborating on a project called "America by Bus." She grinned so wide that her mouth looked smashed. She said they were going to spend that whole next year riding buses all over everywhere.

Joel was waiting for me at the bottom of the steps. As we started to the sidewalk, next door at the Levys' house, there was the sound of voices. We watched Benjamin, tall and hook-nosed, his glasses the only thing wrong about an otherwise perfect Palladin getup, walk to the driveway and get into a white Cadillac. He wore silver guns, black boots, shirt . . . everything. No doubt he had printed cards with "Have Gun Will Travel" to hand out all over town. He backed the Cadillac out of the driveway and drove around the corner.

"Damn!" Joel said. He grabbed the hatbox, as though that would allow me to run better, and took off.

The Cadillac was parked in front of Corinne Hamilton's, and Joel and I hunkered in some bushes. He handed me back the hatbox and I checked to see if the divinity was all right.

Corinne came out wearing a Wonder Woman suit. I had the feeling that it was made-over twirling gear. She even wore boots. Her lips were so shined up that I could see them like red flares in the porch light. The top of her costume was two huge hearts like they were barely covering ocean buoys. And when she walked, the buoys nodded to everyone in the ocean. If she were padded, she'd done it right. From every angle she looked real.

"Hell!" Joel raised up a little. "They're going to drive all over town. How can we compete with that?"

We sat in our bushes and watched.

Corinne said that her uncle lived on the next street and she'd promised to show him her getup when she got it on. Benjamin opened the Cadillac door and twirled a gun. Corinne giggled. I guess he was nervous. He dropped the gun and a cap went off.

Corinne's mother opened the door. The giant eye of her TV was lit behind her.

"Just fooling around," Corinne yelled. Then she laughed. "Benji's gun went off."

"His best shot," Joel said.

The Cadillac took off and suddenly Joel broke out of the bushes. "Leave that there," he yelled, meaning my hatbox. But I was too nervous to part with it. I didn't have the slightest idea why Joel was so worked up over Benjamin Levy, unless he was running after another view of Corinne. Or, maybe it was something between Jews I didn't understand. But I was quiet and didn't ask questions, and we stopped at the set of bushes that Joel pointed to, just outside Corinne's uncle's house.

The white Cadillac was parked in front. "Hot damn!" Joel said, and told me to stay there. He skulked out and hunched down beside the car. With one sudden jerk from underneath, he pulled out a red-plastic-coated wire and brought it to me. I hid it under the tissue paper in the hatbox. We watched as Corinne and Benjamin came out. Corinne was good at small talk. She was carrying a tray of brownies that her aunt had made her to sell. She sat down in the front seat of the car and twirled her legs in, pointing the toes of her boots. Benjamin shut the door. He got in beside her and ground the engine half a dozen times. When it wouldn't start he got out and looked under the hood. Corinne's uncle came out with a flashlight and looked around down in the motor, and said he thought it must be the distributor cap.

Benjamin adjusted his glasses. Already he'd gotten a habit of resting his palms on his gun handles. He looked at Corinne. "No sweat," he said. He had another Fleetwood at home and they'd just go get that.

"Damn!" Joel hissed.

Corinne fancy-pantsed it down the walk and Benjamin escorted her, his hands on his guns. Joel looked depressed.

"If we didn't waste so much time," I said, "we'd be better off." I left Joel sitting there and went up the walk to Corinne's relatives and knocked.

Corinne's uncle opened the door. He was overweight and slightly red all over. He looked at me. "Well . . . I been wondering how you are. You hear much from your folks? You know who gets you yet?"

Corinne's aunt stuck her head out and pinched his bicep. "Mind your own business." Then to me: "Ain't that right, darlin'?" She opened her mouth and sucked in a breath. "Why, don't you look grand!" She had a mustache of red fuzz. "Your grandfather can't sell any more of that medicine, can he?"

"No'm." I held out my divinity.

"Oh, Bill! Don't this look good! I reckon it's been a coon's age since I had a piece of divinity. Buy us some, Bill."

The uncle reached into his pocket and forked over a handful of change. The aunt elbowed him and he threw in a whole dollar. I got the idea that even though they had a sweet tooth —they were both real fat—they were giving me money more out of sympathy than anything else.

The aunt reached into my hatbox and pulled out the divinity by the handfuls. She accidentally brought up the red wire, but like somebody at a dinner party noticing a hair, she politely put it back. "I don't know anybody who deserves to be queen more than you do, except maybe Corinne," she said. "I think you ought to get runner-up. Don't you, Bill?"

"I reckon," he said, and ate a piece. "Beer might cut this sweet," he said and left.

Corinne's aunt smiled at me and closed the door.

I went back to the bushes. Joel was smoking another Winston. It was so dark that we couldn't see each other. "We're getting nowhere fast," I said.

Joel must have been leaning against a tree. I couldn't see him in the dark. There was a sucking noise that I couldn't place. "We don't stand a chance anyway," I said. "What's the use? We might as well eat this stuff and forget it."

I knew that wasn't the truth, though. I could walk down Main Street and everyone who saw me would put something in my fruit jar just because of who I was and the pitiful state of my family. I hated that.

There was silence except for that odd sucking noise. Then, strangely, words started coming out of my mouth so fast that Joel was probably staring toward me in the dark, wondering if in the last few minutes I'd lost my mind and was now a certified loony. I finished with marriage and family and people who could twirl fire, and started on my grandfather and how it would be when the government inspector came and took away his license to practice medicine. My grandfather would get written up in the newspaper as an outlaw, and for all I knew he might could end up in prison. Probably I was even an accomplice for helping make so much of the medicine. At least the Inside kind. I never had gotten far enough along to learn how to make the Outside Medicine. Then when Joel asked me why my grandfather didn't just hide the stuff and I told him that he didn't want to act like a crook, and Joel laughed—that's when I realized something important about family.

"You know," Joel said, "your grandfather's a real strange bird."

I might feel murderous about my family not doing things better, but not just anybody could run them down. You had to belong. "I don't like your saying that," I said, my voice right huffy, and I could feel my mouth pinching up mean.

Joel laughed and told me that I was getting feisty.

I reached for the hatbox where I'd set it down. Only one piece of divinity was left. Joel had been sitting over it in the dark, eating. That was the sucking sound I couldn't put my finger on. "Now what are we going to do?" I said.

When he took a deep drag on his cigarette, it lit Joel's face and he was grinning, puffing and grinning. He was looking at me. "You really want to be that queen bad, don't you?"

The whole idea of being the Coldwater October Queen now seemed silly and stupid. But getting my picture in the paper as sort of a present to Sam wasn't. And in my B.J. costume, I'd probably look so raunchy that my parents would get back together out of guilt, if nothing else.

"Fifty dollars is nothing to sneeze at," I said.

"You're damn right." Joel reached into the hatbox and ate the last piece. He wiped his hands on his devil suit. "We just need to go on down to the pool hall and get my dad to run a few games for us."

I didn't have the slightest idea what he was talking about,

but I wasn't going to admit that. As Joel started walking, I followed him. We could have cut through the backyard of Sam's house and gotten on the train trestle and walked it all the way to the pool hall, but Joel said that we needed to be seen on Main Street.

I let him go on ahead of me. He crossed over to the other sidewalk, but I kept straight so as to go by Sam's house. There was a light on in the back. I knew that was Gill. But the whole second story was lit up, too. As I got close and passed on the other side where the driveway was, I saw that the garage door was slightly open and that a car was inside. It was too dark to see if it was the Land Rover.

Joel stopped and watched me. "Come on. We got to hurry up and do this if we're going to get it done."

Farther down the sidewalk I could hear children talking. "I'll be there in a minute," I said to Joel.

He stood, still watching me in the dim light of only street lights and the porch light at Sam's house. I wanted to go up and knock on the door. It seemed I could almost feel that he was there. Then Joel called to me again, and I was sure he was going to disturb the whole damn neighborhood.

I couldn't go up to Sam's door, anyway, and trick or treat like a little kid—even if I was only in the contest. Sam wouldn't necessarily know that. I didn't want him to see me dressed up in that stupid dress. The B.J. costume underneath was meant for him.

"Sally! We got to go."

Joel was just about having a conniption fit on the other sidewalk.

A group of little kids came along and went up to the door on Sam's porch. I stood and watched them—all five dressed like monsters and cowboys, or fairy queens.

My breath sucked in as the door opened and Sam stood there. He was tan and thin—looking wonderful. He was grinning and buying treats, handing out votes and offering candy.

I watched him bend down. "Now, just who do we have here? Buffalo Bill—maybe?" He was sitting on the back of his heels so he could be the same height as those kids. I was about to bust, silently crying out: "I'm here. I'm here, too." I could hear him laugh. The sound of it was like something I was starving for and had been made to do without. He kept on saying silly stupid stuff that I could have listened to forever. His voice came straight to me and I could feel it spreading out inside me, moving around and playing in my head over and over. It was all I could do to not run up and put my arms around him and tell him that I was there, too.

Joel touched my hand, reaching for the hatbox. "I'll take this. Now, come on; we got to go! It's a long way down the highway."

As I walked across the street with Joel I glanced back. Sam closed the door and the little kids headed for the next house.

Joel and I walked fast around the corner and ended up in front of Thompson's Grocery. There were a lot of kids in costumes going into stores with their fruit jars. Being Saturday night, it was a good idea. Everything was open. The street was filled with farmers and Mexicans and town people. I tried to keep my mind on the contest and where we were going, but all I could think about was Sam.

Just as I suspected, almost everybody on the whole damn street stopped to put something in my fruit jar just because of who I was and the pitiful state of my family. There was Turly Caine, who came to my grandfather for arthritis. And Mrs. Kincaid, who had kidney stones. They all made a big fuss over my stupid-looking dress and asked what I'd heard lately from my parents. It was just about enough to make me throw up. I was glad that Joel had the idea of going to the pool hall. I couldn't have taken a whole lot more of that sympathy junk.

A line of trucks was parked along the street. Mexicans were climbing in and sitting down. Some wore ponchos in the cool night air. On a Saturday night it seemed early to be taking them back to the farms. But they'd arranged themselves in bunches for the different farms that they worked on. Their wonderful staccato of words sounded to me half like a love song and half a cry of murder.

When Joel and I reached the highway the moon was shining, and the pavement stretched away like a dark ribbon. Tall weeds grew at the sides with ditches behind them. We walked on the gravel shoulder of the road, saying nothing. My fruit jar jangled and the empty hatbox thumped. Every once in a while a car or truck would come along, spraying us with its lights, then pass, leaving us watching the small red circles of its rear lights as it disappeared in the distance. Joel and I stepped toward the darkness, and the moon lit it just as we reached it, so that the trip seemed endless and blind.

"We're going to spend all night walking this stupid highway," Joel said. "We've got to do something." He looked toward the train trestle as though now considering that. Behind us was the whine of an approaching car. Joel turned and held out his thumb, but the car didn't stop.

The next did, though. It was a banged-up truck with wood sides for carrying cattle. The door to the cab swung open and we ran and jumped in, Joel first.

When we got settled, what I could see in the light before I closed the door was Joel squashed up against about a three-hundred-pound man with four teeth. "What you kids up to?" He glanced at Joel's tail which was curled around his foot on the accelerator. He had on a baseball cap, and it looked greasy.

Joel told him that we were headed for the pool hall, not quite a mile down the road. I sat by the door, listening to the rattles, being aware that at any minute the door could fly open and I might be sucked onto hard pavement.

"We're running for Queen and King of October," I said, always volunteering answers when I was nervous. I held up the fruit jar to the dashboard light. "Would you like to vote?"

"What you get if you win?" he asked.

"Our picture in the newspaper," I said.

"And fifty dollars." Joel said. "Each." He pointed to where the man should stop. The pool hall was lit up like a skating rink. It was a square tin building with cars and trucks parked in front.

The man turned into the driveway and stopped. He put one fat arm over the steering wheel and flashed his teeth. The truck idled so rough his stomach vibrated. "Don't hurry off now," he said as we climbed out. "I want to give you a vote."

I held out the jar. Joel had already started across the parking lot to the pool hall. I could hear him walking on the gravel.

The man slid across the seat and dropped a dime in the jar. Then he reached toward me and ran his hand down my cheek. He put his open palm on the back of my neck and pulled me toward him, flashing all four teeth. "You're right pretty, Queen a October." He laughed. He forced my head back and his face came close.

"You're supposed to buy chocolate drops," I said, pressing the hatbox up under his chin. "And you might just want to know, I'm Dr. Maulden's granddaughter."

He let go of my neck and put the truck in gear. "Good for you," he said and drove off.

I hurried to catch up with Joel, feeling tough. And famous. Everybody had heard of my grandfather. As we walked near the door of the Lucky Lion, I said to Joel: "I know I'm not sup-posed to go in. I'll wait out here." Women were banned from the pool hall.

"It's too cold." He led me to the back of the building. "You can wait in the kitchen."

We went in through the door there. The only windows were small rectangular slits near the ceiling. In summer it must have been hot enough to cook without the stove. Joel showed me a stool and I sat on it, holding the fruit jar while he went through the swinging doors into the other room. I could hear the tap of the cue sticks and then the clacking of the balls as they rolled on the tables. I looked around the kitchen and saw the big refrigerators that I thought Mrs. Weiss probably kept her foreign foods in. There were cases of beer stacked almost to the ceiling.

Joel came through the swinging door, and Mr. Weiss was with him. He looked good in his new glasses. His stomach was wide and soft like a sponge ball. Looking at me, he took the Mason jar out of my hand. "How's your grandfather?"

"Fine," I said.

"Your grandma get that outhouse moved?"

"Not yet."

He shook the jar. "We'll see what we can do about filling this up."

He brought me a Pepsi. "Make yourself at home. It's best you stay back here. It shouldn't take long." He picked up the jar, and he and Joel went into the other room.

I pulled the stool close to the swinging doors where, through the space between them, I could see into the other room. It was smoky and dark and loud with men and a constant clack of billiard sounds.

Mr. Weiss waited until the bets had been made and then he

rapped a cue stick on one of the tables and held up the fruit jar. The men stopped playing and looked at him. Mr. Weiss put his other hand on Joel's shoulder. "My boy here's running for the King of October." Joel coolly whipped his tail like the whole thing was a joke. I guess it was.

"Long live the king!" someone yelled.

There was laughter, and a few beer caps popped. When they settled down, Mr. Weiss said in a voice that sounded a little hoarse. "I'll give five free games to the winner of this game if he'll put his win in this jar." He shook the fruit jar and the coins inside it jangled.

There were a couple of cheers and the balls clacked again as they were made ready for a new game.

Joel stood in front of the room, holding the jar. Mr. Weiss sat down in a big easy chair in one corner and read a magazine. The games seemed to take a long time. I finished my Pepsi and set the bottle on the table.

The games at the tables each ended with a round of cheers. One man from each of the tables picked up the dollars that had been waiting all that time on the beer cooler and took them to Joel. Joel quickly stuffed them into the fruit jar, and Mr. Weiss wrote out the passes for the free games.

I pushed back from the door just as Joel walked into the kitchen. He unscrewed the jar and spilled out the money onto the table. We bent over it, counting.

Then we busted out laughing. "How's that for a winner?" Joel said. We had forty-one dollars and twenty-two cents.

Out on the highway, Joel flagged down a farmer's pickup with a load of Mexicans in it. The farmer had forgotten to pick up a prescription at the drug store and had to drive back to town for it. The moonlight and the truck lights on the highway made the pavement look like the silver scales of a fish. Cushioned by the net petticoats, the Mason jar bumped on my lap. I straightened my hat, pulled at my sleeves, and felt the eyes of the Mexicans in the back of the truck looking in the window at us. But, if anything, it was Joel's getup they were fascinated with.

We pulled up to the drugstore. Joel and I slid across the seat and got out where the farmer parked. For a minute the Mexicans studied us in the artificial street light. Most of them smiled.

The clock inside the drugstore said nine o'clock. We'd finished so early that we'd have a long wait before heading to the school gym. With as much money as we had we couldn't trot up there until the last minute, or it would seem suspicious.

I looked at Joel. The lights from Main Street made him seem older. The shape of his face was so fine. He leaned against the wall of the drugstore. He glanced at me. "We got a long time. What you want to do?"

I made myself look straight at him. I smiled. My voice was low but it wasn't anywhere near a whisper. "Bust into my grandfather's office," I said.

I didn't have to convince Joel about what I had in mind. We took off at a fast walk to the alley between my grandfather's office and my grandparents' house. Everything was quiet and dark, except for the light in the sun porch and the one in the kitchen, which were meant for me. My grandmother had on her reading light in her bedroom.

Joel pointed to some bushes, then saw a better hideout—the outhouse. All afternoon my grandmother had watched it nervously because it had not been moved. Then she decided that she shouldn't get too worried until Sunday and instead had poured all her energy into getting me ready to be the Coldwater October Queen.

From the side of the outhouse, Joel peeked around it to make certain that everything was quiet. Then he skulked to a back window of my grandfather's office, carrying a brick he'd found in the alley, and broke it. The glass tinkled to the ground. When he got the window unlocked and open we climbed through. Joel helped me get my dress through the window. The petticoats got stuck on the windowsill, and he lost his temper and cussed a little. It was like stuffing cotton into a medicine bottle. When we got me through, Joel stared at me a few seconds. Until then I don't think he'd looked at my costume, even with all the fuss that everyone had been making over it.

Joel had plenty of matches for his Winstons and he lit our way through the lab as I led the way to the storeroom. "Holy Christ!" he said after striking two matches and catching a glimpse of the bottles shelved all the way to the ceiling. "Anything likely to blow up if I keep using these?" He held the match close to my face and waited for my answer.

"I don't know," I said.

When the match burned down to his fingers and nothing had blown up, he lit another. "You going to pour it out?"

"No." I had several possibilities in mind. And when I told them to Joel, he added to them. Finally we settled on the idea of selling the medicines and mixing in the proceeds with our pool hall donations. For a minute I had a touch of bad conscience thinking about breaking the Missionary Society's rules. I was afraid of turning in so much money to Miss Pankhurst at the high school gym that it would look suspicious—as if we hadn't sold just candy. But Joel said that he thought the Missionary Society rules meant you could sell anything fit for human consumption and that didn't rule out a little yellow liquid. And as far as the pool games went, he assured me that we hadn't broken any rules at all. Pool was essential to the mental health of the whole community. Without it, Joel said, some men would go mad. Without those free games his father had just given out, some of those men wouldn't have gotten back to the pool hall for a game for weeks. Then Joel added that no one would ever suspect us of doing anything wrong, because who in the whole town of Coldwater would ever think that Dr. Maulden's granddaughter wasn't doing things exactly right?

For a minute, we were both quiet. He lit another match and, in the sudden flare of that small lighted circle, we looked at each other. We were both grinning. I led our way to where my grandfather kept his files. We got Mrs. Clayton's phone number and Joel called her and said that he was a friend of Dr. Maulden's. He said he was sorry that he didn't know anything new about her galdbladder, but he *did* know that for some time she'd been wanting some of Dr. Maulden's medicines. And then Joel told her that tonight only there would be an unlimited quantity available. It was not for sale, she had to understand. But for the next twenty minutes she could pick up whatever amount she wanted. She could not come to the office to pick it up, because of how it might look. But she could come to the front of the outhouse in the alley behind Dr. Maulden's office. Yes, the same outhouse that Mrs. Maulden had been writing so much about in the newspaper. And from there she could take whatever amount of the medicine she wanted. And too, she could leave a small donation, if she wanted to. In fact, it would be very nice.

I couldn't believe the sound of Joel's voice. It was deep and foreign and I figured that he must be calling on some hidden hormones. When he hung up, we rolled around on the floor for a while with our hands on our mouths trying to laugh without making any sounds. We had to hurry and get the medicine set up on the ground in front of the outhouse where it faced the newspaper office, so that no one nor the medicines could be seen from the alley. We took as many bottles as we could. The brick we'd used to break into the office we put on the ground and then put our fruit jar on top of it for donations. We watched from the dark of the office while Mrs. Clayton quietly came down the alley and slipped in front of the outhouse. I called Turly Caine and talked to him about his arthritis. I used a voice straight out of Hollywood. I sounded like Kate Smith with a cold, and when I hung up I delivered two dozen bottles of the Outside Medicine to the ground in front of the outhouse. It kept going on like that until we decided we had to slow up the traffic or we might be noticed. We told the next patient to stock up by bringing a suitcase to carry it away in. We found an empty galvanized tub with handles on it and filled it full of bottles as though we were icing beer. We carried it then, carefully, slowly, to the outhouse.

"No," Joel said, "put the Outside kind on *that* side of the brick."

"How about this?" I stacked the bottles up in a pyramid.

"This ain't no art show."

"Shhh," I said. "Listen."

We froze, bottles in mid-air. There was a clanking like chains being moved. I imagined someone dressed up like a ghost walking down the alley. Suddenly we heard talking—men's voices, mumbled. We were hunched over, squatting on the ground with the bottles of medicine around us. Then someone walked up to the back wall of the outhouse and began rocking

it slowly. I saw a big shoe come around one side of the outhouse and then stop, as though whoever was wearing it had
seen us.

"Oh-my-God!" Joel whispered. "They've found us and are
going to tip this over on us!" He put one hand against the front
of the outhouse to try to hold it off if it came smashing down
on us and the medicines. But the outhouse now seemed stuck,
leaning slightly as though whoever was messing with it had
stopped, at least for a moment.

I was terrified. My legs shook.

"Make a run for it." Joel looked at me. "Get a bottle by the
neck and if someone grabs you, bust it over his head."

We each grabbed a bottle. I got the Outside kind because I
knew that when it touched newly cut flesh, it burned. Joel took
the fruit jar with all our money in it. And we took off around
the side of the outhouse, aiming for the bushes behind the post
office, because we didn't want to head back to my grandfather's
office for fear of incriminating ourselves.

But as we ran nothing happened. No one tried to stop us.
I heard "Oh-my-God" again, but it was not in Joel's voice. It
came from a dark, startled, liquid voice, male and old. On the
way I ran into someone in a poncho. He immediately bowed
and said: "Commo talley voo, amigos."

When Joel and I made it to the bushes, we lay flat and looked
through the bottom of the leaves. The Mexican I had bumped
into was Ezekiel.

There were three men, all dressed like Mexicans. And the
one that I knew to be Ezekiel looked in front of the outhouse
at Joel's and my display of bottles and exhaled a comment in
the name of the Lord. He looked around, searching for where
we were. But we were so frozen to the ground beneath the
covering of leaves in the darkness that there was no way to see

us without coming close. And he wasn't about to do that. No Mexican would have a good reason. He seemed just as eager to pretend to be a good Mexican as we were to be innocent. So we each ignored what had happened in the previous few minutes.

The counterfeit Mexicans started whispering and then formed an assembly line to the truck, putting all of my grandfather's medicines into it and moving with great speed.

For the next few minutes, with the detached sense of sitting in the Ritz, I watched the men in ponchos rock the outhouse free from its base and lift it. They edged it onto the truck-bed and then scooted it all the way in so that they could wrap a chain around the bottom part to keep it from falling out. The outhouse was lying on its side in the truck and, without getting close, no one could tell what it was.

Two men pushed the truck down the alley, making only a soft padding sound of tires and feet on layers of dust, which, if the Good Lord had put everything on earth for a reason, as people in Coldwater believed, the dust had now found its.

Joel stood up. "What in hell was that all about?"

"I don't know," I said. But I told him that some Mexican called Pedro was supposed to move that outhouse to Jimmy Hersham's farm.

Joel looked at me and smiled. "God, I love nights like this."

We decided we might as well head for the school. We had gotten rid of enough medicine. The rest could be samples.

While I waited in the bushes, Joel carefully went back inside my grandfather's office to make sure that we hadn't left any evidence. He locked the door, and we walked to the high school.

Cars were parked all around it and even on the playground. The gym was decorated with streamers overhead and butcher paper on the floor for the king and queen to walk down. Almost everybody from the Missionary Society had already gone to bed. Miss Pankhurst was counting the money in the fruit jars while Foster and a bunch of teachers helped her.

Kids were dancing in their socks on the varnished wood floor. Joel and I set our Mason jar on the table in front of Miss Pankhurst and the teachers and waited.

The principal was keeping the final tabulations of the counting and as Miss Pankhurst and the teachers got down to the last few pennies, he was grinning and shaking his head in a combination of disbelief and pleasure. He walked to the microphone, and the Home Ec. teacher took the record off the turntable and the principal said—after the microphone made one ear-splitting squawk: "And now, we're going to do what we all came here for."

I never had any doubt. To the sound of my own name, I walked to the stage, stood there beside Joel and felt the glittering crown mashed onto my head. A record plopped onto the turntable, and Joel and I started off the next dance.

Everybody crowded around, watching and clapping, and Joel took my hand, pulled me up to him so as to wind up the beginning steps of The Bop. The music seemed to come up through the floor and into our feet and Joel threw me out and we danced connected by curved fingers. The sound of applause was all around me. One side of the ceiling lights went off, and the voice of Johnny Mathis came on with "Chances Are."

Joel and I danced silently. Pulling my hand behind his back, he guided me with his other, and I buried my head in the curve of his neck.

After a while, Miss Pankhurst tapped on my shoulder and told us that it was time for the picture. She led Joel and me into a locker room where an out-of-town photographer was going to take it. He posed us against a solid-colored wall. Then he stuck his head under a black cloth and said, "Say 'Peaches'."

But just as the flash on the camera came on, Joel squeezed my hand, turned toward me and whispered, "Say 'Pool.'"

It wasn't until after I walked back out onto the dance floor with everybody watching me—and there was this little ripple of applause again, and the dancers opened up the middle of the floor for me and Joel, and after Joel walked me home and we stopped and messed around a little and kissed a pretty big long one in the shadows of the magnolia tree—that I felt the skirt of the B.J. costume stuck with sweat to the inside of my legs. All night it'd been on me. But since that moment when Joel pulled me away from Sam's house—totally forgotten.

25.

The Morning After

I lay in the Man-from-Shiloh's bed only long enough to see the pink light hit the back of the chicken house. Then I was out the door with Toulouse's cage—as if going to clean it. I left the cage, with Toulouse in it, behind the garage and headed to Sam's.

I knew that he might not be awake yet. But I could wait. I had to see him and let him know that I was there, ready for him. I went around to the back of his house where I could look in the kitchen windows.

The room was quiet and still dark. I sat on a chair on the back porch and looked out across the dark water of the Mill Pond, watching the sun light up the pasture, watching the shapes of cows come into sight under the trees.

It must have been nearly an hour before I heard someone come into the kitchen and a light come on. I stood up and, through the window, I saw Sam in his pajama bottoms only, measuring out coffee into the coffeepot, looking so sexy that I could barely keep from opening the door and busting in on him. I stood at the window, planting myself on the porch, waiting for him to turn around and see me.

He let the water run and then leaned into the pantry and pulled out sugar. He unwrapped a loaf of bread and put two slices in the toaster. He was thin and wonderful, well and just as I remembered him when we were all together—me and him and B.J. He was going to see me in a minute, and we would grab and hug each other, and he would probably ask me if I was in that Halloween contest that the whole town had gone crazy over. I would tell him yes, laughing. He would ask me how I did. And then, teasingly, he would probably say that if I hadn't won was there any way that he could fix it?

I'd laugh. I'd go so damn crazy with a case of giggles that he'd probably look at me, half worried and half tickled, and ask had I gone loony without him knowing it? Then I'd tell him that I'd already fixed it.

He'd think I was kidding. But it was a known fact to everyone: I was the Coldwater October Queen. And now I was two inches away from being with Sam.

How can mornings be so good you want to lick them? How can a day start out so right you want *it* instead of pancakes floating in syrup or crowns that glitter and pictures in newspapers?

Sam opened the refrigerator door and took out jelly and milk. He turned toward the hall as if someone had called him. I stood with my face aimed toward the window, the wood like a frame I was looking through at something that I had never thought of seeing. Julie walked into the room and poured herself a glass of juice and drank it. She stood for a minute, looking at Sam and asking him had he gone out to the porch for the newspaper yet. And then she left and in walked Ellen. She had on this negligee under a flimsy robe, and she reached out and grabbed Sam and kissed him. He sat down and pulled her onto his lap and put his face against her neck, and they stayed there like that while I stepped back from the window and bent down so that there was no chance, now, I would be seen.

I crept off the side of the porch and walked behind Miss Pankhurst's house.

I stared at the pasture and the cows and the ribbonlike current of the Mill Pond. I would die, I thought. There was no room inside me for what I felt.

I ran down to the end of the street where the turnip greens field spread out near Leona Sutton's house. I ran through the field, kicking out at butterflies already touching down on the plants in the new early light.

It was definitely a world that I could not get to behave, or even do much about. I had belonged with Sam. All through that long year, I had believed that he loved me. It seemed I could stand anything but thinking he had not meant that. I remembered the early part of that year when I'd thought that my parents' love had been counterfeit, that it had just been a put-on, and lost. Nothing in the whole world seemed worse than feeling that.

I remembered Sam's face the many times that he had looked at me, so affectionately, and sometimes when he didn't think that I even knew he was watching me. There were all those long, hot afternoons when he had sat, watching for me walking home from school.

I remembered him touching my hair; and in my mind, I saw again the way that he had sometimes put the warm palm of his hand against my face.

Fatherly.

I realized the truth then. The night I'd told Sam I loved him and that I was going to marry him and that I would never leave was the night we'd gone to see B.J. dance. Sam had been drinking so much. Probably he had not even heard me. Probably he didn't even remember that night.

They were a family now—he, Julie, and Ellen. I couldn't mess with that.

I turned at the end of the field and ran up the alley. Loneliness would, I knew, be once again inside me like ice moving across a sore tooth.

I stopped a minute and looked at the place where the outhouse had been. The hole beneath it was open and deep. From behind the garage, I picked up Toulouse and carried him into the house. Louella was grinning, bustling around in the kitchen, stirring blueberries into batter. She looked at me. "I knew my divinity would do it."

I put Toulouse in the bathroom and my grandmother handed me the Sunday juice in a silver goblet. "Well, Leona's dress certainly didn't hurt." She was delighted I was the queen.

I sat down at the kitchen table to eat pancakes with my grandfather. He winked and said that I sure made a fine October Queen. He said my mother and father had called while I was out and that they were so pleased! They wanted us to send them the picture in the newspaper.

I remembered then that my grandfather hadn't been to his office yet.

My grandparents and Louella kept going on like that—making such a to-do about me winning. I sat at the kitchen table, eating pancakes with my grandfather, one side of my heart dying over Sam and the other being swelled out with the pride of my secrets. I would be so lonely without Sam; the thought of him as my future had been a part of me for so long. But the longer I sat, the more it seemed that the hole of losing Sam was filling up with the strength of who I was and what I could do and what I could gain for myself. That would always be mine. Like Sam's love, it might, at times, get misplaced. But it would never leave.

And what Sam had taught me about love would always be mine, too. I might not want to have to settle for just that. But I had to.

The phone rang. "Hello," Louella said. "This here's the Maulden's residence."

Louella didn't say any more because obviously my grandmother had picked up the phone in her bedroom. But Louella, her eyes growing wide, and her mouth opening like a kid blowing a bubble bigger and bigger, kept listening. And then she covered her mouth to keep it from busting out with laughter.

My grandfather and I sat over our pancakes, stalled, watching Louella hang up, softly, obviously guilty that she hadn't put the phone back on its handle before then. She looked at me and my grandfather. "Oh Miz Maulden's in awful trouble." She wiped her hands on her apron.

My grandfather looked at her, his brow wrinkled.

Louella's eyes got big. "That outhouse she was moving for Mr. Rankin . . . it's settin' in the middle of Main Street!" She nodded. "And Mr. Rankin thinks she did it on purpose. That's him on the phone. He thinks she's using him for a joke."

Suddenly I laughed.

My grandmother came thumping down the hall, her hair wild, her eyes wild, her face wild: "Good Lord in Heaven," she breathed. Then she told us about the outhouse just as Louella had.

"Calmly, Emily." My grandfather poured some Inside Medicine into her prune juice.

"How can I be calm, Horace! I'm under attack! He thinks I'm a criminal."

"It can't be that bad."

"Well, it *is* sitting right there on Main Street and with his newspaper's name on it. Everybody knows I was in charge of moving it!"

But then the moment hung in silence a moment. And my grandmother breathed: "Ezekiel."

It wasn't a matter of more than ten minutes before my grandmother had ordered my grandfather to warm up his Chrysler, had combed her hair—halfway—put on a dress and was getting in to sit beside him, while I sat in the back. I wasn't about to miss out on anything if I could help it. And whereas I could have easily reminded her that Pedro had moved the outhouse, I also knew he hadn't.

She told my grandfather to go around the back way. "I can't stand to ride down Main Street; I don't even want to see it."

"You're right," my grandfather said, looking out the Chrysler's back window as he backed up. And he winked at me. "It'll probably raise your blood pressure."

From the backseat I could see only the side of her face. But I could tell that it was a pinched severe look she gave my grandfather. "You needn't take this lightly," she said. "It's humiliating. You should have heard Mr. Rankin on the phone!"

My grandfather hunched his shoulders. I guess with this bad news, on top of what he thought was going to be *his* bad news, my grandfather was being careful. There sure were a lot of things I wanted to see happen.

"I merely find a little humor in this, that's all," he said. "But it is bad—if Ezekiel disobeyed you. He shouldn't cause you embarrassment."

We pulled up to Ezekiel's house, a gray-board dog-trot cabin set on concrete blocks. Three little children were playing with a puppy, running and shrieking up to and then under the porch, the puppy chasing, panting. They stopped and began staring at us. Soon four older children joined them, three coming from behind the house and one coming from under it. They sat on the edge of the porch and joined in the staring. A second later Ezekiel came through the door. He was smiling; he had on a pair of overalls but there weren't any tools hanging from them. "Morning, Dr. Maulden. Pretty Sunday, ain't it?"

"I've come to talk about something that happened last night, Ezekiel." My grandfather was standing in the yard, using his plantation voice and he looked straight at Ezekiel. "Miz Maulden thinks you played a dirty trick on her."

Ezekiel looked at the car and my grandmother sitting in it. His mouth dropped open, and he tilted his head. "What you talking about, Dr. Maulden?"

"That outhouse that's sitting on Main Street."

"You mean that outhouse is on *Main Street?*"

I could see Ezekiel's neck jump forward in his collar, leaning his head toward my grandmother. He saw me in the backseat and nodded, his eyes meeting mine. I didn't say a word or move.

He looked at my grandfather. "You mean that Pedro done gone and done that?"

Then he walked over to the car and tapped on the glass beside my grandmother. "Miz Maulden. Miz Maulden."

She rolled down her window. She looked out at him with her face still pinched in anger.

"I do give you my sympathy. That was a awful thing for that Pedro to go and do."

My grandfather came up beside him. "You mean you didn't have anything to do with it?"

Ezekiel was standing beside the car looking down at my grandmother. "You 'members, Miz Maulden; I was only getting the truck to use. That Pedro was in charge of the moving. Why, I wouldn't have known where exactly them Mexican pickers was wanting to put that toilet—to get the most use out of it, that is." Then he looked at my grandfather beside him. "I ain't had no business about that toilet since I let Pedro use my truck." He pointed to the black pickup parked under a tree. "It was right back here, bright and early."

While my grandfather started the engine, Ezekiel looked in the back window at me and said, his face nervous, "Lo there. How you this morning?"

"Fine," I said.

I knew he was worried I was going to give him away. I guess I *was* having to choose between my grandmother and Ezekiel. But if I told on Ezekiel, I might also get close to telling on myself. And I wasn't about to give up being the Coldwater October Queen. It was just too much damn fun—being special.

We went to Mr. Hersham's farm, and even before he told us, we could tell from the silence and the look of the bunkhouses and fields that the Mexicans had been driven out in trucks just before dawn.

My grandmother aired her anger all the way home, and then a heaviness settled in her face.

My grandfather and I went to the eleven o'clock service at church. My grandmother stayed home. She said she simply couldn't face it.

The outhouse was sitting in the middle of the street in the intersection by the Mercantile and the bank. A few people were walking around it, some were laughing, and some kids were pinching their noses at each other and saying in nasal voices: "Peu. Peu." Then when we crossed the street I could see the sign on the front that I had not realized was so important until it was seen where it now was.

> Property of the Coldwater Gazette
> Reserved for the use of Employees only.
> —C. J. Rankin

And below that, painted on the door of the outhouse itself was:

WHITE ONLY

Throughout the church service, while I sat beside my grandfather, who still thought that he was in terrible trouble, I thought about the outhouse. Also about Ezekiel and my grandmother and Mr. Rankin and Joel and me. It sure seemed that

I was going to sacrifice my grandmother. For I didn't have any plans to do anything but just keep quiet and let her go on bearing the brunt of the joke. And when I thought of how Ezekiel had come to our house and gotten control over where that outhouse would go, where he would secretly put it, and had gotten paid for doing it, too, I got so tickled, I felt even. It seemed then that my anger toward my grandmother's pushing and poking me into ways that I didn't especially want passed on to me lay down, spread out and stayed quiet. Maybe all along she was only trying to give me what she thought would prepare me best for this world. But my world was never to be the one she wanted to prepare me for.

I guess, too, if I were really pushed to admit it, a lot of my anger toward her was just some of my anger toward my parents and The Bust-up. I might never stop being mad at the part of the world that I knew I could not fix; but for that day, it seemed that the biggest tongue in the world had just been set down and stuck out at what neither Ezekiel nor I could talk back to or do much about.

My grandfather and I walked up the sun porch steps for the Sunday dinner that Louella had cooked. I was still half-afraid something awful would happen to me as punishment for all I'd done. But Joel wasn't worried, and his mood was catching. I figured if things got too hot for me, I could always join up with the Jews and become one. There didn't seem to be anything about that I'd mind.

The next Friday, my picture appeared on the front page of the *Coldwater Gazette*. Joel was holding my hand, his face turned toward mine, the word "Pool" poking out his lips like a disconnected kiss. My grandmother was embarrassed. I was a little embarrassed myself, but mostly proud, and tickled.

The sheriff hired Ezekiel to haul the outhouse out of the middle of Main Street, and Ezekiel took it out to Hersham's Farm. The article about my grandmother's annual Missionary Society luncheon didn't appear in the paper. Mr. Rankin wouldn't print it. But a lot of editorials and letters were written about the outhouse. In fact, there was a lot of community interest in it. Some people took my grandmother's side, and some took Mr. Rankin's side. A lot of people thought my grandmother was a heroine for showing up that fork-tongued liberal Rankin. But that worried her even more; for well-bred ladies never got in the middle of a controversy like that.

Since my grandmother's character was at stake, she said that she would wait until the next year when the Mexicans came again. Then she would find that Pedro and ask him, straight-out. Of course I knew that Pedro would say—quite truthfully —he didn't know a thing about it.

The medical licensing inspector came sooner than we expected. He arrived a few days after Halloween. My grandfather had discovered the broken window and the stolen medicine with the surprised relief of one of his patients learning his heart attack had been gas pains. Ezekiel was hired to fix the window, and my grandfather told no one anything.

Without my grandmother even knowing that the inspector was there, my grandfather set out his account books. And I stood, mum, proud, and pleased while the inspector looked around in the office, bent over the mixing tubs, put his hands on the tubes and stuff, which only my grandfather and I knew the use for.

Then after my grandfather showed him the storeroom and the empty shelves except for a handful of bottles, which my grandfather said were "all I have left now," my grandfather and I walked to the Rexall's for root beer floats.

The inspector even drove around town to stop on different streets and talk to people. He asked if anyone had bought any of Dr. Maulden's medicines lately. When he walked down Louella's street and knocked on her door as well as on her neighbors', no one said anything. Apparently a lot of medicine had been handed about in that section of town on the night the outhouse had been moved. I learned about that one day from Louella when I found her in the kitchen rubbing the Outside Medicine on her bursitis. She said that Ezekiel had given her the bottle. I knew then that Ezekiel and his helpers had passed my grandfather's medicines on to whomever wanted it. But no one was going to say anything about what they'd come upon, free. So when the inspector found out that someone had a bottle, or even a whole supply, whoever owned it could honestly say he hadn't paid a thing for it. My grandfather never reported the theft, never even mentioned it, despite the fact that, in his opinion, a lot of valuables were missing.

The inspector spent the night at Mrs. Harris's rooming house and in the morning came to our house, causing a stir because my grandmother was still in her dressing gown. She was worn out by the Missionary Society luncheon and the outhouse. But graciously she invited him in and had Louella pour him coffee and then went to get my grandfather who was shaving with Toulouse in the bathroom.

I could hear Toulouse screaming, "Up yours," as my grandmother opened the bathroom door and said, sort of loud: "There's a man here who says he's with the State Medical Licensing Board. What in Sam Hill is going on, Horace?"

My grandfather dried his face, put up his razor, and went into the living room. I pulled out a chair in the kitchen and sat down to pour Wheaties.

The inspector sipped his coffee and looked at my grandfather. "Well, I didn't find any evidence of medicine—or rather, homemade medicine—in your office. And your books are clean."

Putting her hand on her heart, my grandmother breathed shallow. My grandfather called for Louella to bring sausage and biscuits.

"Nothing wrong?" My grandmother barely whispered it.

The inspector looked at my grandfather. "I don't see any reason why you can't continue your practice as long as your own medicine is not prescribed. And there's no evidence that it is. I didn't see anything out of order. There are big mixing tubs and equipment. But they don't look recently used."

My grandfather passed the biscuits.

"There was only one thing I saw that was troublesome. But it's not my jurisdiction."

My grandmother put her hand across the top button of her robe and quickly asked, "What was that?"

He reached to catch the butter and jelly dripping out of his biscuit. "There's a toilet hole for an outhouse exposed near the back door—a public health problem—but, as I said, that's not my jurisdiction."

My grandfather laughed. My grandmother turned her head and pshawed.

The inspector left after a second cup of coffee and a few more of Louella's biscuits. It was no more than a matter of a few hours before my grandmother had contacted the sheriff and had him issue an order to Mr. Rankin to fill in the dangerous outhouse hole, since it was obvious Mr. Rankin was leaving it open for spite. And Ezekiel knocked on the sun porch door, holding a shovel. Mr. Rankin had hired him to fill in the hole.

He leaned on his shovel and looked at my grandmother. "Just how you want them lilies on it, Miz Maulden? In a circle?"

The air grew colder, and the leaves fell. The cotton fields were plowed under for the winter to rest.

Sometime after the outhouse was moved into the fields at Hersham's Farm, just before the cotton crop was ready to be picked, the old sign on the front was covered over. And then on the front, a new one was painted: Mexicans Only.

26.

New Times

I sat on the bed, watching Toulouse on the footboard. He tucked one foot up under him and dozed.

It was the beginning of the Christmas holidays, and I was leaving Coldwater for good. I was giving Toulouse to Gill. He would be here in a few minutes to get him.

I heard my mother's car in the drive as she pulled up beside the sun porch. Her voice was high and familiar and excited. "I'm here. Lord-a-mercy! I nearly had a wreck on the Mississippi River Bridge. I guess I was just rushing so. Where's my girl?"

I sat on the Man-from-Shiloh's bed, listening to my mother. She was going to travel to promote her record. Most of the year, I would stay with her. When she was away, I would live with my father. I would be split like a banana under ice cream. It wouldn't be fun. But I could stand it.

Before I could even put Toulouse in his cage and walk out with him into the living room, she had come to find me. She busted into my room, calling my name. We hugged, squashing Toulouse between us; and he squawked out a word that made my mother blush. "Shoot!" she said. "I haven't heard that in a month of Sundays!" We looked at each other and giggled. I guess Toulouse was the first dirty joke we'd shared.

"Sally!" My grandmother's voice came from the living room. "Mr. Williams is here for that bird."

I wasn't used to thinking of Gill as Mr. Williams. And then my grandmother added: "Praise the Lord!"

I walked out, carrying Toulouse's cage.

"I'll take real good care of him." Gill looked at me and grinned. He winked. At times like this, I usually hated winks. But this one wasn't as if for a little kid, or tacky or anything like that. It was Gill's way of hugging me.

"I know you will," I said. I passed the cage over to him.

"You take care of yourself now, you hear?"

"I will."

My mother and I drove out of Coldwater with me turned to the car window, looking out at my grandparents and Louella and Gill, waving, and then at Main Street. In the reflection of the store windows, it seemed that I could see people I knew. On the sidewalk some farmers stood, talking, leaning against the storefronts. Early that November I had run into Sam like that—passing him on the street when he had his hands full with a bag of groceries—Julie and Ellen with him.

He'd stopped and looked at me. "Hey, girl."

I'd said back: "Hi."

"How's things?"

"Fine."

He reached in his bag and pulled out sacks of lemon drops and packages of gum, offering them.

"Thanks," I said, taking one.

He looked at me, smiling. One side of his mouth slid upward into a half-grin, and it seemed that in the steadiness of the way he looked at me, I could see all the love, real and now understood, still there as I knew it always would be.

They walked off—he and Julie and Ellen. I stood on the

sidewalk watching them. In my mind, lots of times I pictured them, and when I did, I saw Sam as part of a family who had fun every damn minute of the day.

My mother's car bumped up over the railroad tracks with dust flowing out behind us. I had Joel's address in my suitcase; I'd probably write him almost every day. He was planning to come to Memphis, and we were going to go up on the Peabody's roof and dance and stay out half the night, and who knew what else.

After the holidays, I was going to a high school in Memphis. I would have to begin in the middle of the year, which wouldn't be easy. But I was like those butterflies that came in the fall to flit over the field in Coldwater, to light on turnip greens, and move on—their final destination Mexico, I learned—getting passed on to me real well, I guess, my grandmother's belief in fascinating facts. Because I found out that the butterflies were stopping over for a rest, would gather their strength in sun-warmed fields before moving on. And they were like the strength that sat in me, new and unexpected, silent but felt.

The water tower was tall and silver in the distance. I watched it grow smaller where it seemed to straddle the end of the alley. And then I joined my mother on a song with a chorus that would last all the way there, or until one of us went nuts and cried, "Kings."

On the notes of our voices, that long and crazy year played through my mind. And as it did, I laughed, thinking of how much—in one way or another—could be passed on. Including love.

P.S. Please don't write me for any of the Inside Medicine. I can't remember the recipe.